Feral Doves

A Novel

Pippa Stroud

Published in 2009 by New Generation Publishing

A CIP catalogue record for this title is available from the British Library.

Prologue

I see you.
When I look at the city I see it as if from above, as if I'm riding on the thermal gusts of foul air from its vents and subways; an effortless birds-eye view of the grid of the streets pinned out beneath me.
I see you and I know you, your routine and your rhythm. Office, gym, friends. Coffee shops and locations, feverish dots on a cold map.
I see you and I know the time is ripe.

Chapter One

Harriet Morgan

Stepping out of the gym and into the women's locker room, Harriet has the usual debate with herself about whether to shower at the gym or not. Much simpler, she thinks, to just pull on her sweats and then go home to lounge in the bathtub before joining the Saturday night phone tree, with its perennial, comfortable, where-shall-we-go what-shall-we-do; but getting onto the subway still insulated with a fresh sheen of perspiration is too disgusting, so as always she gives in to her own argument, strips off, and finds an empty shower cubicle.

Turns her face up to the warmish stream of water. Shower gel, shampoo, rinse, condition, rinse. The shower clicks off and she reaches behind herself to wring out her hair in a way that would make her Manhattan hairdresser wince. She has the sort of hair that makes people, mostly gay men, stop her in the street so that they can pet it, tentatively, as if it were a beautiful but potentially ill-tempered pedigree dog. The product of benign neglect, her hair is, its dark weight and length the result of spending too much time in countries with hair salons whose décor leans to the grubby pink and where hygiene is largely viewed as an American imperialist frippery. Thankfully you can almost always get a good bikini wax in any country, though. Not, she thinks, that there's been much air traffic on the landing strip of late; having Thomas tracking her round the city like a sort of crazed human spy satellite hasn't done much for her romantic life. Although he's gone strangely quiet just recently, which might just mean that either he's given up on being a stalker and gone home, or that he's found some other poor woman to fixate on.

Towels off, dresses; little t-shirt with an advert on the back for a long defunct strip club in Seoul, boy's sweatpants. Prefers the boys' sports stuff to the slightly saccharine girls', and age fourteen fits her perfectly; Harriet maintains a fictional, perennially fourteen year old nephew for salesclerks. Thirty one years old, five feet two, she doesn't know what she weighs but an old boyfriend used to tell her that she was a hundred pounds, of which at least ten was attributable to her long hair.

She takes a seat at the wide mirror to blast her hair dry, vaguely watching the parade of semi-clad and naked women pass behind her. The skinny, the plump, the nipple-ringed, the pendulous and the neat. Strange how nipple size doesn't seem to concur with breast size the way you think it would. The scarred and the tattooed. She herself has both, the scar a neat furrow tracking between two ribs, the tattoo a vertical line of Chinese good luck symbols inked below where the bullet had entered on its fortunately abortive trip.

Protection.

She hoists her backpack onto one shoulder and makes for the back door, tying her hair up into a knot on itself as she goes. Ever since Thomas started lurking outside the front doors they've let her go out the back to the service alley which, dominated by the subterranean rumble of the Queens Midtown, doglegs back to East 39th past dumpsters and a couple of long abandoned office buildings. As usual, the black security guard is at his station in the back hallway, huge, his magnificent braids held back by a startlingly feminine diamante clip. As usual, he rumbles 'Good night, little ponytail,' as she passes. 'Good night.' She returns, adding silently, 'Big braids' and hoping she doesn't actually say it out loud one day. Maybe they should date, she thinks, they have compatible hair.

Out through the fire exit and she pauses on the steps to listen for the door to click locked behind her and take her habitual deep breath of fresh air. Smells the heavy carbon smell of traffic competing with the sharp clean scent of ice blown down from the Canadian snowfields and something else. A male cologne, terribly green and pungent, that she knows very well indeed. And she's off the step and running away full tilt before she registers she's doing it. Hears a shout of 'Harriet!' and a car engine choke into life. Headlights in the alley behind her.

Shit.

Her thighs register their surprise at being asked to run again so soon but then the dizzying sickness of adrenaline surges into her blood and she's running as fast as she ever has in her life.

Needs to make the corner then there's just a short stretch of alley leading onto the main street. People. Cars. Streetlights.

There's a man on the corner, dark-suited, one shoulder hunched against the cell phone he's holding against his cheek. He looks at her, gives her a toothy, movie star smile, shakes his head slightly, and pushes back the flap of his jacket to show her the gun tucked in his waistband.

Simple message – No, you're not going down there.

She stops dead, turning back towards Thomas' big silver Audi which is cruising up the alley toward her, headlights blazing, both doors slightly open to block an escape to either side. Okay then, if that's the way you want it. Balls her fists and breaks into a flat run straight towards the advancing car.

Shem Jephson

Sitting on this third floor fire escape feels pretty much like the old days. The ones before they retired me out of the Army and I joined civilian life with only mild surprise that there weren't that many civilian jobs for an Army sniper. Which is why I drifted from South Carolina up to New York on the promise of a job in hotel security and lasted about two weeks before the boredom nearly killed me. They don't tell you that hotel security means sitting in a glass box watching so much TV. The programmes on the TV were the same night after night; drunken guests lurching to their rooms, pretending not to be drunk. Or that the woman on their arm is really their legal wife, and not a lady who charges by the hour. Fortunately that's where I met Art, the big Brooklyn Jew who put me on his payroll a couple of years ago; not that I've ever found out what my job title is. Or even asked. Fixer. Negotiator. Problem solver. We're about the same age, but I think that Art mostly keeps me around because I'm the total opposite to him. Art is loud, expansive, a hugger, a gesticulator while I'm quiet. I bide my time, think things through. No need to get excited or wave a gun around when all you need to sort things out is a gentle tap on the shoulder, a quiet conversation about how some things could be if other things don't change.

Tonight's problem to solve is for Art's friend, Thomas Birnbeck, who is having problems with a girl. Thomas is a slick Wall-Street lawyer, big bogus smile, firm handshake. All hat and no cattle, as they say in Texas. This girl apparently has become fixated on him and has been following him, standing outside his apartment at all hours, makes threats towards his family. Thomas told me, in a gentle and concerned voice, that he met her at a bar somewhere and she came on strong to him and although he tried to let her down gently, on account of his being happily married and all, she wasn't having it. Me, I know Thomas is lying, and that probably he had relations with the girl before throwing her over, but all the same making threats about the wife and kids just isn't right. The plan is to pick her up, take her to an apartment downtown that Thomas has borrowed from a client, and scare her just enough to turn her into a Christian. But what's troubling me now is that she started running before she could have even seen Thomas, before he yelled at her.

It just doesn't feel right.

There are four of us on this job. Art, who wanted to come along anyway and we needed a man to secure the alley onto the main street, me on the fire escape, Thomas himself, and a skinny kid, Will, who's in the car with him. Not sure I rate the kid but he works for Art and seems smart enough to do what he's told at least. I came up earlier to reconnaissance the take-down, just in case the office block wasn't was as abandoned as it seemed, but it was empty. Like it had been left in a real hurry, there were papers all over the floor and even some skeletal houseplants still on the window ledge. I wondered about the people who left their plants behind. Dust everywhere, the water cooler gone green like a swamp with algae.

And now I'm back up here with the dead plants in the window behind me, looking down at that fool Thomas with his big German car and the girl is running. Not panicking, just running all out. When she sees Art she stops in half a stride, the way a good horse can, and turns. 'Stay there.' I whisper, and I don't know if I'm talking to the girl or to Thomas but he drives toward her anyway, even though I'd told him not to. And the girl stands a moment and clenches her fists at her sides.

I know what she's going to do about a half second before she knows it herself.

She runs dead straight at the car and I see her lengthen her stride and kick off from the back foot, hair flying like a banner. She runs straight over the top of the car and I can see Thomas and the kid Will staring up through the windshield and she goes right up the hood, over the roof then half jumps, half falls down the trunk and I'm hurling myself down the fire escape ladder because this is about to go all to heck.

I grip the sides of the ladder and slide down because it's quicker that way, feeling the old paint flake and catch against my palms. I hear the transmission crunch as Thomas throws the car into reverse gear and as I hit the ground I see the girl launch herself at the high wall at the end of the alley. She nearly makes it to the top, too. Scrabbles for a moment, fingers fighting for purchase and then she drops back to the floor.

There's a moment of silence and then Thomas is out of the car and he grabs her, slams his forearm against her throat and starts to strangle her. She snatches at his arm and twists frantically but just as I get to them she relaxes, head dropping forward. As I'm thinking that maybe she's fainted she throws her head back, hard, and breaks Thomas' nose with a sound that goes right through me.

'That's gotta hurt.' Art grins, jogging up.

I take the girl by the arm, gently, and say 'good girl' to her because the fool deserved getting his nose broken for doing that. And then Art and I crowd her into the back of the car so she's sat between us, the kid Will scoots over into the driver's seat and Thomas hurls himself into the passenger seat, cursing, clutching one hand over his face, blood streaming between his fingers. 'Look what she did to my fuggin car.' He screams, and the kid throws the car into Drive and we take off out of the alley.

She's very quiet, sat there between us. She's a cute girl and I can feel her ribs working to catch her breath but she doesn't make a sound. She's sat half sideways because of the backpack over her shoulder so I ask her maybe she'd like to take it off. She gives me a wide-eyed look. I tell her its okay and I take the backpack, put it on the floor by my feet. The kid Will is driving nice and calmly now, just like we're a group of friends going for a little drive on a Saturday night. Except Thomas, who's cursing and throwing himself around in his seat and carrying on like a crazy person.

I tell him, 'We'll take her to the apartment now and then Will can drive you to the Emergency Room.'

Art is looking amused. 'You really should get that looked at, I think.' He adds.

Thomas twists himself around in the seat and makes like he's going to punch the girl but I catch his wrist and put just enough backward pressure on the joint to remind him to act like a gentleman.

'What she did.' I tell him, 'Was a fair shot.'

He takes his bloodied hand away from his face and smiles nastily at her. There's blood on his teeth.

'These men,' he says to her, 'Are taking you to the apartment and they're going to play all night with you. I even left some nasty toys there for you all to play with. And in the morning I'll come see you and we're going to have a conversation, you and me.'

The girl says nothing. Art leans back in his seat and gives me a long serious look and just as I thought this has gone all to heck.

Harriet Morgan

She knows now that when it comes, it's not how you expect. When the worst moment comes that you've always dreaded but simultaneously haven't because it can't even be thought about, only showing itself in scraps of nightmare or the tiny fragment of animal terror which occurs in between hearing the running footsteps, the laboured breathing behind you and the realisation that it's a only a late jogger, insulated from the night by his little white headphones. When the worst moment actually comes you think you'll kick and scream and go crazy but she knows now that they show you a gun and what you do is go quiet and wait for it all to happen to you.

The apartment is somewhere in a Soho backstreet, or maybe Tribeca. Iron-fronted buildings, heavy as lead. Not yet swept clean by the inevitable southward tide of gentrification but tired and grimy, windows thick with carbon deposits, tangles of graffiti on the frontages. The car tyres clack over missing cobblestones. The building they pull up outside of is in darkness aside from a dirty glimmer of light at a window somewhere high above, and once again they crowd her out of the car, three of them, the big dark-haired guy in front, the older one and the younger one to either side. Up the steps and in at the front door, a glimpse of silent elevator, dusty wooden stairs. A cork notice board with yellowing flyers. Up two flights of stairs and they're moving close together and quickly and quietly, like this was something they'd agreed. A greyish door in the dusty light, and the big one fumbles with keys and then puts his shoulder to the swollen door to open it.

He steps inside and then turns, stopping so abruptly that the rest of them nearly walk into him. He's handsome, large-featured, heavy-jawed. Dark hair, needs a shave, but she registers that he's probably the sort who looks like he needs to shave again by mid-morning. He drops two large hands on her shoulders and regards her seriously.

'I want to say to you that I never made love to a woman unless she also was a hundred percent enthusiastic about it. So you can put that stuff out of your mind.'

A note of disgust in his voice, as if she had answered an ad from the personals and deliberately come to the apartment looking for some rough group sex. He turns to the darkened apartment and spreads his arms, announces, 'I have *daughters*.' As if settling an argument.

Someone finds a switch and the lights click on. Industrial style strip-lighting on chains from an impossibly high ceiling and she can see that this is, in fact, probably one of the last genuine artist's lofts left on Manhattan. Huge. A moisture-warped wood floor, gritty underfoot, some white kitchen units ranged against the far wall and, at the back, two sheetrock cubes presumably concealing bathroom and bedroom. A dead Schwinn leaning against the wall beside the door, defeated on its flattened tyres. Tottering stacks of books, some big abstract canvases on the walls, orange with red streaks. By the windows stands a white

Formica table with four ridiculously camp chairs, heavy with gilt and curlicues: West Village Louis XIV.

The older guy pulls out a chair for her like a waiter. A grey man; grey hair and eyes. Buzz-cut military hair, precisely squared off on top as if it had been cut by laser-wielding men in lab coats rather than by any more conventional means. Not a big man but hard, all bone and sinew. A hint of a Southern accent with a slowing cadence to it. Dressed in black pants, grey stripe shirt, black down jacket, heavy boots.

'Why don't you take a seat here and I'll try and find some coffee.' He says.

'I better take Mister Birnbeck to the hospital.' The young one says. He has a face like a Korean, at once flat and angular. Trendy hair gelled into complicated peaks.

'Okay.' The military guy says. 'Come back here once you're done but make sure Thomas doesn't get here until morning. Call me, if it's anything different.'

The kid gives him a sloppy salute and leaves, dragging the swollen door closed behind him.

Military guy is opening and closing doors in the kitchen area; takes an opened pack of coffee from the refrigerator, finds a coffee maker, fills it from the faucet and plugs it in.

He says, 'You want coffee?' To the big guy who has wandered off into the bedroom.

'Jesus fucking Christ!'

The military guy winces. 'Its only coffee.' He says.

Shem Jephson

Art has found something in the bedroom and I go to take a look. When Thomas was talking about nasty toys I guess this is what he meant. A sports bag holding rope, duct tape and some other things. The sort of things people buy in Triple-X shops in the Meat Packing district. We both take a long look.

'This is really fucked up.' Art says.

When I walk back into the main room the girl is eying the distance between where she's sitting and the door, calculating that she won't make it before I get to her, which would be correct. I give her a mug of coffee and sit down at the table across from her.

'Tell me.' I say to her. She looks at me. Nice green eyes and all that dark hair falling over her shoulders.

'Tell me your side of it.'

'The whole story?' She asks.

I nod.

She takes a slow sip of her coffee and begins.

'My name is Harriet Morgan. I work for the United Nations; I've worked for them for about eight years, mostly on the Development Programme in various places around the world. Technically I've lived in New York for years but it's only since June this year that I've spent much time here.'

'Why since June?'

'I decided it was time to settle in one place for a while, so I took a job at UN Plaza. There's a bar near there that some of us go to for a drink after work, which is where I met Thomas. We got talking one night, I guess. Next time I went there, there he was again, and we talked some more. Same again next time. And then one day he invited me out for dinner so I said yes.' She narrows her eyes at me, defending herself.

'I liked him, okay? He was clever and charming, the real life and soul. And at that time I didn't really know anyone in New York apart from my co-workers so I thought it might be fun. So, we made a date and he picked me up from my apartment and we went to this really nice restaurant just across the river. And then just as the entrees were arriving he leant forward to hold my hand and I saw that he was wearing his wedding ring on a gold chain around his neck.'

'You didn't know?'

'Of course I didn't know! I wouldn't have gone out with him if I'd known he was married.'

Art has walked up behind her. He strokes her hair, gathering it into a ponytail at the nape of her neck. I see her shoulders tense.

'Leave her alone.' I say to him.

'Sorry.' He backs off, takes a seat at the table.

To her, 'What did you do?'

A ghost of a smile. 'I threw forty dollars on the table to pay for my food and walked out. He came out after me but I got lucky with a cab and just went back home. I thought that was the end of the story.'

'It wasn't?'

'It wasn't. I had the flowers, the constant phone calls, the e-mails, the text messages. He waited for me outside of my work, outside my apartment, outside the gym. Anywhere he thought I might be.'

Art says, 'Why didn't you go to the police?'

'I did. Spoke to two detectives at the 9th. But they said they were sorry, there was nothing they could do. Because he wasn't actually making threats, you know? Just saying that I was playing hard to get, being a naughty girl, all that kind of crap. So I changed my phone number, changed my e-mail address, got his calls blocked at work. Started going out the back door at the gym.' She looks me straight in the eye as she says this. 'As you know. But about two weeks ago it all stopped so I thought he'd finally given up. Until tonight.'

Art says, 'He told us that you were threatening his family.'

'Of course not!' Outraged. 'I just wanted him to go away and leave me alone.'

'I mean, he told us you were stalking *him*.'

'That's crazy. I mean, why would I? He's just some guy.'

She's telling the truth. Straight and simple and we have been completely suckered by Thomas, drawn into his nasty sick little game.

'One more question.' I say to her. 'When you came out of the gym you started running before you could have even seen Thomas. Why?'

A slight smile. 'I *smelt* him. He wears this really horrible cologne.'

Art laughs at this and then drops a little blister pack of white pills onto the table.

'What are these, do you think?'

She picks them up. 'I think they might be roofies.'

'I'm going to kill that motherfucker.' Art says.

I go to make more coffee. This is going to be a long night.

Harriet Morgan

Reeling from the abrupt change in her fortunes, the numbness of terror leaching away to leave only fatigue like the flat taste of black coffee on her tongue. The big one leans over the table to shake her hand, introducing himself as Art Silverman. His accent pure Brooklyn but something about the syntax of his words makes her think that American isn't his first language. Hebrew maybe? Military guy follows suit with the introdcutions. Shem Jephson. She finds herself almost smiling at the biblical tag; wanting to ask if his middle name is Ham.

Time passes, the streets outside starting to quieten down. Art has switched on the old TV, flipping through channels of bad reception until he finds what could possibly be a football game, tiny figures struggling through lurid fuzz. He settles down on the ancient sagging couch with a grunt of satisfaction. Strange to think that right now she should be elbow to elbow with her friends in some bar, shouting conversations above the hubbub, bottle of beer in one hand. Pushing her way outside for a cigarette, shivering in the sudden cold air, pretending she doesn't have a light to see whose hand holds out matches, a Zippo.

She finds a dog-eared old Philip K Dick novel amongst the piles of books and starts to read it. The concept of spying on yourself; odd how prophetic that turned out to be, long before this world of webcams and the internet. She wonders if Thomas ever took pictures of her walking down the street, buying coffee, groceries, standing at her window. Thinks it entirely possible.

Footsteps on the hollow stairs, and then the younger one shoves his way back into the apartment, one arm hugging a brown grocery bag.

'Where's Thomas?' Shem asks him.

'Safely back at home with the wife, wearing a big Band-Aid on his nose and sporting two lovely black eyes. Boy, is he pissed. He told the wife that two big black guys jumped him, then jumped all over his car.'

Art eyes Harriet. 'Two big black guys, huh?'

'Brought you some sandwiches.' The younger one dumps the grocery bag on the table and looks from the two men to Harriet and back again. 'What's happening?'

'What is happening.' Says Art. 'Is that Thomas Birnbeck is full of shit and we have all been fucking suckered by him.' He stops himself. 'Oh, please excuse my manners. Harriet Morgan, may I introduce you to William Vale.'

Will grins at her, says Hi, and she can't help feeling like the reluctant VIP guest at the strangest cocktail party on earth.

'Brought you some food.' Will repeats, pulling foil wrapped subs out of the bag, a bouquet of paper napkins. 'Uh, American cheese and tomato, salami or egg mayo. The chicken Mexican style is mine.'

'You're welcome to it.' Shem says. 'When's Thomas coming back?'

'Not until around nine a.m. He'll be telling the wife he's going to work.'

'He *is* a fucking piece of work.' Art says. 'Harriet, may I offer you the cheese, salami or the egg?'

'Um. The cheese, please.'

'Probably the safest choice. Which gives Shem the salami, I think.' Tearing into the egg mayo with very white teeth. 'What are we going to do with the motherfucker when he comes back? Put him out at the kerb with the fucking garbage?'

Shem unwraps his salami sub, looks at it for a moment, wraps it up again.

'Harriet, I think we need to get you out of here.' He says. Leans back, stretches, rubs one hand over the bristles of his hair. 'What I want you guys to do tomorrow morning is tell Thomas I've gone crazy and taken her off somewhere. But make like she didn't go of her own free will and that we all still think that Thomas is the good guy. Tell him I fed her the roofies, if you must. Will, I need you to stick close with Thomas because we need to know what he's going to do next.'

Will says, 'Okay. But could I, ah, go home tonight and come back early tomorrow? Its. You know. My wife. She's expecting our first and doesn't like to be alone nights.'

Art flaps a hand at him. 'You go. But be back at, what, six in the morning?' He looks at Shem who nods. 'Six a.m.'

Will waves at Harriet and leaves, taking his chicken Mexican style with him.

'Since when.' Art asks, getting up. 'Did they allow twelve year olds to marry? And have children also?'

Shem tidies up the food wrappers, crumpling tinfoil. Outside the distant bass rumble of Manhattan on a Saturday night out, car stereos dopplering past on the cross streets.

'You don't want your sandwich?' He says to Harriet.

'I'm not hungry, thank you. Maybe later.'

'We must have scared you pretty badly out there, for which I apologise.' Art says. He walks up behind her chair and leans two heavy hands on her shoulders. 'But I think you have a plan for us, Shem, yes?'

'Yes. I'd like to take Harriet up to my place to get her out of the way of this. We'll need to engage Thomas but we'll do it in a time and place of our choosing, and once we know what he's planning to do. I think there must be some other people involved here because…' He stops and looks at Harriet, reluctant to continue.

She says it because he can't. 'Because you think I wasn't meant to leave here still breathing, right? Because I don't see how I could have, if he was intending what I think.' She picks up the packet of roofies, turning it over in her hand but watching Shem. He looks away first.

'Yes. I'm sorry. But I think he might have had some more people lined up because it isn't easy to dispose of a...' He pauses, corrects himself. 'Of someone around here. Even a small someone.' He offers her a slight smile as consolation. 'So either he's crazier than even we think or he had some sort of a plan for afterwards.'

'That motherfucker is crazy but not stupid, I'm thinking.' Art says 'So I'll ask around and see if anyone's been hiring any clean-up specialists recently.'

'Good.' Shem says. 'In the meantime, Harriet, will you come to my place until this is done?'

'Where is your place?' She asks him.

'Poughkeepsie.'

'Poughkeepsie?' She can't keep the amusement out of her voice. 'Really?'

'Very good fishing in Poughkeepsie.'

Art says, 'He means that Jew Art Silverman doesn't pay him enough for him to live in Manhattan.'

'I mean that I couldn't stand to live in Manhattan and Poughkeepsie is the furthest away I can get whilst still working for Art Silverman.'

She looks from one to the other. 'So you work for Art and I think Will works for you too, Art. So what do you do?'

Art leans over her shoulder to give her his big movie-star smile in profile. 'Whatever needs to be done. A little import, a little export. A little helping of people to fulfil their contractual obligations. A little accountancy and maybe some banking services.'

'Oh, okay.' She knows enough about New York to understand what he means. 'And Thomas is a friend of yours?'

'Fuck, no. We played racquetball on a Sunday morning. Except next time he's going to be wearing the fucking racquet up his ass. And the ball. And possibly the court also.'

Shem Jephson

She asks when we're going and I check my watch. After midnight already, and I need to sleep. We all need to sleep. Art is on his cell phone to his wife, speaking his susurrating mother tongue in a coaxing voice. He ends the call looking chagrined.

'Looks like I'll have to go home via the diamond district tomorrow. Once more. Shem, my friend, tell me again why you are not married.' He says, yawns hugely, stomps off to check the kitchen for liquor.

In fact, I have been married. Twice. Both my wives had long hair right up until they decided to divorce me, when both had their hair cropped off. No coincidence, I suppose. Still, I can't help liking long hair on a girl, nothing is more feminine. Harriet is sitting sideways on an old couch, hugging her knees to her chest, reading – or pretending to read – a paperback book. Her hair is long enough to touch the couch at her back. She senses me staring at her and looks up, just as Art returns holding a whiskey bottle with about four inches of oily liquid left in the bottom.

'No glasses.' He says. 'So you'll just have to use your coffee cups.' He offers the bottle to the girl, who shakes her head.

'I'll pass, thank you.'

'Shem?' I take the bottle from him and spill some into my cup. Art drains the rest into his, yawns again.

'Let's get some sleep.' I tell him. 'And then we can leave early in the morning.'

'The lady can have the bedroom.' Art says

She looks alarmed. 'No! God, no. I'm not going in there.'

'Understandable.' I say to her. 'Art, why don't you take the bedroom? Harriet can sleep on the couch and I'll take the floor. As long as there's some bedding. Have you seen any?'

'In the closets at back, I expect.' Art says. 'Where are the roofies?'

'Why?'

'Because I want to put one in my own fucking drink. Might get a decent night's sleep that way. I'm used to sleeping next to my beautiful wife, not listening to you snore outside my door.'

'I never snore.' I tell him.

Harriet Morgan

She thinks she won't sleep but does, dropping like a stone into a blank unconsciousness until she wakes with a start, heart racing. Still dark outside.

Can't breathe.

Got to get out of here.

She sits up, fumbling for her running shoes by the smear of street light leaking in from the broken window blinds. Her skin feeling grimy from having slept in her clothes; thank god, she thinks, she showered at the gym at least. Art is snoring, a series of rippling grunts, a long, long pause, more grunts. Apnoeic. Shem is lying by the kitchen area, rolled up tidily in the sort of patchwork comforter that would probably be worth a fortune in an uptown antique shop. He sits up as she finishes lacing her shoes.

'Bathroom.' She explains as she passes him.

In the clinical, bluish light of the bathroom she checks her watch. Nearly five a.m. She washes her face, combs fingers through her hair and knots it up against her neck. The back of her head is still sore from its sudden contact with Thomas' nose, and there's something disgusting and crispy in the strands of her hair there. A lacy chain of bruises around her neck that look strangely fashionable, like those fake tattoo necklaces all the kids were wearing a few years ago. She drinks from the faucet, spits, does it again. Got to get out of here. Squares her shoulders and goes out to speak to Shem.

The lights are on and he's awake and up, shirt sleeves rolled, filling the coffee maker. He looks strangely like a suburban husband, fixing coffee on a Sunday morning.

'I'll go to Poughkeepsie with you.' She says, 'But I want to go back to my place first. I need to shower and change and pick up some stuff.' Fiddling with the coffee maker, he doesn't respond. He probably can't force her to go anywhere, not now, but she doesn't really want to put it to the test.

'I still have Thomas' blood in my hair.' She tells him, hearing the petulance in her own voice.

He looks up. 'I'll come with you.' He says.

They drink the coffee, and Shem goes into the bedroom to wake Art. She can hear the bass growl of their conversation but not make out the words. She zips up her hooded sweatshirt, walks to the window. No hint of light in the late October sky yet. Shem returns, pulling on his black down jacket.

'Let's go.' He says.

Outside, the wind is raw enough to make her eyes tear. She wraps her arms around herself.

'God, its cold.'

Shem casts a look skywards. 'Going to snow, I think. Here, take this.' Shrugging off his jacket.

'No, its okay.'

'Take it.'

So she does. It smells of nothing but a faint hint of laundry soap, making her suspect he might be a man who possesses no fingerprints or DNA. Nothing for a bloodhound or a forensic investigator to follow.

'Have you got a car here?' She asks him.

'No. Let's walk until we find a cab.'

They cut across to a deserted Bowery and start walking uptown. Not even the bums are around this early, but then looking at the stores they pass it seems there's no reason for a bum to be on the Bowery anymore, unless they suddenly wanted to buy designer light fittings.

'You were very quiet.' Shem says to her. 'When we picked you up, I mean. Most people would have panicked.' He seems to be paying her some sort of strange compliment. She looks across at him striding along, face forwards.

'Art showed me he had a gun.' She says. 'I've been shot once in my life and I wasn't willing for it to happen again.' Acknowledging to herself that it's a little cheap, to use that excuse, as the circumstances of her shooting were ridiculous and almost entirely non-life threatening. All the same, she wants him to think of her as quietly brave and not as the person reduced to a compliant silence by the sight of that gun. The memory gives her a flash of shame which curdles quickly into anger directed at the man beside her.

'How could you?' She swings around in front of him, forcing him to stop and look at her. 'How could you get involved with that?'

'Remember.' He says calmly, 'We believed at the time that you were threatening Thomas' family.'

'But how could you? Even so. How could you put me or anyone into that situation with Thomas, no matter what the reason?'

'The idea was to scare you a little, just enough to make you back off. No-one knew that Thomas had his own nasty plans. Look, I could tell you that I work for Art and he asked me to do this, but that wouldn't be right because he couldn't make me do something I didn't want to. But what I can tell you is that from time to time I go along with Art's plans just so I can make sure that nothing gets out of control, you understand? Art is a smart guy but he can be impulsive, sometimes.' He wants to walk on but she won't let him.

'So how does this all work out?' She asks.

'You know.' He says to her. 'What happens to Thomas now is really in your hands. He lied to Art, which is something he'll have to account for, but I told Art that it's up to you what happens next and Art agrees. You're the one that has been harmed by this.'

'Not harmed.' Her anger just as suddenly dissipates. 'Just pissed, I guess. And a little scared. Very scared.' She turns and they resume walking.

'Yes. Well, we need to see what Thomas is going to do next and then we can decide what to do about it.'

They get a cab near Chinatown and she gives the brown-eyed cabdriver her address on East 53rd. Wonderfully warm in the cab, a quiet radio speaking something that sounds like Punjabi. She wonders how foreign-born cab drivers always seem to be able to receive radio stations that white Americans can't find on the dial.

They accelerate northwards, little granules of snow pattering against the windshield, and she thinks - I need to speak to Chris.

She and Chris met on her very first day working for the UN. Technically her boss, back then, but they'd liked each other instantly and managed to carry on working together more or less ever since. A strange friendship; the twenty-five year age gap between them, Chris a man who lives for his hunting and shooting while she won't even touch dead meat or fish. But he's a discriminating hunter and eats everything he kills, which means that even in the middle of Manhattan his freezer is likely to be full of elk steaks, or partridge. Or unicorn, as she teases him. They share a sense of humour and a cynical pragmatism which means that they made for a good team in the ridiculous situations that the job often placed them, and she'd quickly picked up from Chris his normal response of 'Anyone likely to die from this?' to any panic, from the photocopy machine going wrong to anti-aircraft fire being heard over staff quarters. It was Chris who had held a spurious – and very drunken – awards ceremony for her after the shooting, solemnly presenting her with a trophy, which she still has on her desk at work, for nobly acting as a target for Serbia's most incompetent sharpshooter. And then wangled her two weeks extra vacation time by telling their bosses that she had been 'deeply traumatised' by being shot.

It's less than twenty-four hours since she was last in her apartment, but it feels like weeks. The sparse, mismatched furniture, the pale walls, the Afghani rug silently reproaching her for her absence. It's warm in there at least, and she snatches some clothes from the bedroom before dashing for the bathroom, stopping to point out the kitchen area to Shem on the way.

'Coffee.' Pointing to the coffee maker. 'Food.' At the refrigerator. What else do men need? 'TV.' At the screen on the wall opposite the couch. 'Help yourself.'

'You'll need to put some warm clothes on.' Shem tells her.

'Why? Are we kayaking to Poughkeepsie?'

'No. We're going on my motorcycle.'

'On your motorcycle.' She backtracks to the bedroom to unearth her skiing underwear. Dear god, she thinks, why couldn't the man have a big, comfortable, planet-killing SUV?

She sets the shower running and sits on the toilet lid to call Chris. Five thirty, but she knows he'll be awake and he answers on the second ring.

'Chris? It's Harry. Um, I've got a bit of a problem.' Predicting what his response will be.

'Anyone likely to die from it?'

'I sort of nearly did.' Feeling, for the first time since last night, like crying. It's only the effect of a friendly voice, she tells herself. Pull yourself together. He hears it, though.

'Do you want to come over here?' He asks.

'Give me twenty minutes.' She tells him.

'I'll make you some of that disgusting tea you love so much.' Chris, the only person she knows who always keeps Earl Grey tea in stock, even though he says it tastes like dishwater. Earl Grey with whiskey in it, for the real emergencies.

She showers, finally washing the disgusting crust of Thomas' blood out of her hair. Thinking, going to wash that man right out of my hair.

If only it were that simple.

Dries her hair and roughly braids it, pulls on layers of long underwear, jeans, t-shirt, shirt. That should do it. Collects her big leather backpack from the bedroom, walks back into the main room to pick up the little Toshiba laptop from the kitchen counter and slot it into the bag, just in case, spooling its cables around her fingers and adding them, too.

Shem is standing looking at the bug-eyed Indonesian mask that grins insanely over the couch, a cigarette wedged between its yellow wooden teeth.

'That's Ashley.' She tells him.

'Ashley?'

'Well, that's probably not his real name, but when I bought him someone pointed out that he looks exactly like a guy, Ashley, that we had on the team over there. Which he does, actually.'

Shem peers. 'Why does he have a cigarette?'

'Apparently they're supposed to, but I don't recall why. Probably an offering or something.' She reaches for her boots.

'You're ready?' A note of mild surprise in his voice.

'My bag is always packed. A bad habit.' She zips her boots; sheepskin lined, high heeled but should be clumpy enough to pass inspection. Gloves, tasselled Arabian scarf, sheepskin jacket.

'Will I do?'

Shem looks at her for about half a second too long.

'We should get going.' He says eventually.

Locking up, she tells him, 'I need to make a stop on the way.'

'Okay.'

'It's only a couple of blocks from here.'

'Okay.'

Why, when he doesn't ask, does she feel so compelled to explain? 'I thought it would be a good idea if someone knew where I was going. And who with. So I'm going to see a friend.'

'Boyfriend?'

'A friend friend. We work together.'

Two blocks down, one across. Some scattered traffic now and the snow has stopped, but still no sign of daylight. Chris' apartment block is an ageing brownstone above a pet store. No doggies in the window, this morning.

'You can't come in.' She tells Shem, feeling slightly cruel.

He sticks his hands in his pockets. 'Okay.'

'I shan't be long.'

'Fine.' He leans back against the wall and closes his eyes as she presses the bell for Chris' place. The door buzzes open and she sprints up the stairs, two at a time, the stairwell as familiar as her own. His apartment door is slightly ajar; she smells coffee and cigarette smoke as she gets to it.

'Harry!' Chris draws her into a hug against his plaid shirt and then sets her down again to inspect her for damage. Almost completely bald these days, Chris is only a few inches taller than her but radiates the sort of restless energy that always makes people assume he's bigger than he is. Up until today, he's been the only person she's told the whole story about Thomas to. He lights a cigarette and passes it to her.

'Thank you.'

'You ok?'

'I think so.'

He makes tea while she gives him the edited highlights of the last twelve hours of her life. Being Chris, he doesn't pass comment until she's finished, just passes her a mug of tea and then offers the whisky bottle which she waves away.

'I'd love to, but I better not in case I fall off the back of Shem's motorcycle, or something.'

'Do you trust this Shem person?'

'I think so, in so far as it goes. I mean, I'm highly aware that he appears to be the lieutenant for some sort of a gangster, but there's something kind of honourable about him, in an old-fashioned sort of a way. I don't think he'd lie to me. Does that make sense?'

'Sort of. I do think it makes sense that you're out of the firing line while they deal with Thomas. But all the same, I want you to call me, okay? At least every twenty-four hours. I want to know where you are and who you're with, and if you go quiet I'm going to get the police in on this. Deal?'

'Deal. Uh, Chris, there's one more thing I need to ask you.'

'What's that?'

'Can you lend me a gun?' A phrase she's never spoken before, not even close. Chris gives her a long look and then disappears into his bedroom. She drinks her tea, hearing him moving around, opening closet doors. The click of metal against metal.

He emerges with something lying flat on the palm of his hand. A gun. A noun you hear all the time on TV, in movies but the reality is different, somehow. It's surprisingly small; snub-nosed, black rubber grips.

'This,' says Chris, 'Is a .38. It can certainly kill someone, but not from a great distance. It has a swing-out cylinder – see? – and takes five rounds. I've loaded it for you. The safety is here, yes?' Showing her.

'Yes.'

He passes it to her, closing her fingers around the grip.

'I know you're a smart person.' Chris says, 'So I'll only give you one piece of advice about the gun.'

'Which is?'

'Which is that you must only show it if you're in a really bad situation and are fully intending to use it. There's nothing worse than having your own gun taken off you and used against you.'

She turns the weapon over in her hands, looking. It's surprisingly heavy, the metal parts slick to the touch.

'Is it registered to you?' She asks.

A smile. 'It's registered to no-one. If you have to lose it, then lose it, but try to do it safely. We don't want some kid picking it up and then playing Cowboys and Indians. Deep water is usually a good option for safe disposal if you need to get rid of it, for whatever reason.'

'I'll remember that. Look, I'd better go before my bodyguard gives up on me.' She wraps the gun in a t-shirt, stuffs it deep into the backpack, and then turns back to Chris, hugging him hard. He holds her for a moment, dropping a kiss onto her hair.

At the door, she says 'One more thing?'

'What? If you're after a ballistic missile, I'm afraid I'm fresh out.'

'I think I may need some time off work.'

'I'll tell them you're sick.'

'That.' She tells him, 'May be truer than we both think.' As she leaves, he calls out after her; 'Remember; if in doubt, keep moving.' Another of his phrases. 'A moving target is harder to hit.' She recites this in unison with him, and then she's running back down the stairs, the backpack heavy with its terrible new potential.

Outside, Shem has a cab waiting. As she slides into the back seat, she sees that the meter has only just started running, meaning that Shem is either psychic or extraordinarily lucky with timing. Thinks, probably the former. She hopes that he doesn't have X-Ray vision listed with the rest of his super powers.

Back downtown to last night's apartment, which reveals itself, in the first of the pre-dawn light, to be in a perfectly normal back street. A copy shop and a computer repairer's hide behind metal shutters at ground floor level and the apartment building lobby has the usual quota of take-out menus scattered on the floor and the usual terse messages pinned on the cork message board.

In the apartment, Art is standing with his back to the door, talking into his cell phone. For a second she thinks that he's wearing a black mohair sweater, possibly created by someone who had only just taken up knitting as a craft, then she realises that what he is in fact wearing is a luxuriant pelt of his own body hair; one with a thin line of knife scar tracing diagonally from right shoulder to spine. Art ends his call and turns to look at them, revealing that the hair thins a little over his belly before regrouping just above the waistband of his pants. Even Shem looks faintly shocked.

'Please excuse me.' Art says, whipping, with a flourish, a white shirt off the back of one of the gilded chairs like a magician revealing a smallish giraffe to a Vegas audience. Pulls the shirt on and starts to button up.

'There seem,' He says. 'To be a couple of new boys in the area.'

'Clean-up specialists?' Shem asks.

'Muscle only, it seems. But they have arrived by bus from whichever institute it is that grows such people, along with a ticket for a rental car and some directions to this part of town. This is rumour only, you understand, but I think maybe we need to assume that they have something to do with our friend Thomas.'

'I think we do.' Shem says. 'And we could also assume that they'll be turning up here sometime this morning. I think we should let them. You might like to talk to them, Art.' Art gives a sabre-toothed smile, to which Shem says, 'I do mean talk only. Let them stay with Thomas for the moment; we'll need to know if they've got any connections anywhere else. We can separate him from them easily enough when the time comes.'

Tucking his shirttails in, Art says, 'And in the meantime you have taken our guest here off to an unknown destination.'

'Exactly.' Shem says.

A knock at the door and its Will, once again hauling brown grocery bags.

'Breakfast!' He sings out, unpacking fruit, coffee, and finally a stack of Styrofoam boxes. Harriet takes a banana and Shem leans to look into the bag.

'Burgers?' He asks. 'At this time of the morning?'

'Perfect.' Says Art.

Walking down the street to the parking garage where Shem's motorcycle has apparently been left overnight, she feels jittery again. Waiting for Thomas and his muscle boys to pounce from behind a parked car or a mailbox with a silent movie villain flourish. Feeling the extra weight in her backpack she wonders whether Shem is carrying a gun himself; it wasn't in his jacket when she wore it or she'd have felt it in there. He's striding out, face forward, hands in his pockets while she clicks along beside him on her boot heels.

'What kind of motorcycle is it?' She asks him.

'You'll see.'

'Harley Davidson.'

'Nope.'

'Honda Goldwing?'

'No.'

'Ducati.'

'Like I said, you'll see.'

'You really don't give much away, do you?' She asks him.

He doesn't answer.

The parking garage is subterranean, dank. The usual cluster of slim, dark-skinned young men at the office; Shem goes in to speak to one of them while the rest eye her up dispassionately, like people carrying out an insurance appraisal on something they're not sure they want to buy. Shem emerges a moment later carrying a black leather saddlebag in one hand and a crash helmet in the other.

'Only one helmet.' He says. 'So you're having it.'

She obeys, cramming it over her hair and trying to look like she's done this every day of her life. The helmet is weighty and slightly claustrophobic. But warm, she tells herself, pulling her braid over her shoulder and tucking it into the front of her shirt. While she's doing this she notices Shem slip something from the small of his back and into the bag. So you do have a gun, she thinks.

Behind the office is a rank of motorcycles in various states of repair and cleanliness; some cherished, others workaday. The one Shem wheels out falls firmly into the cherished category; a perfectly preserved vintage Indian. Chrome gleaming, long leather seat buffed to a coy shine. The Big Chief logo with its dangling feather crisply painted. Something about the rake of it, the deep mudguards, suggesting it was made sometime in the Fifties. Shem bends to hitch the bag to the back side of the saddle & looks up at her.

'You ever ridden pillion before?'

'Not since a very long time ago.' Remembering one late night, an ill-advised lift home, jumping red lights, laughing and hanging on for dear life somewhere in Sri Lanka.

'You'll be okay. Just relax and let me do the work.' He slings a leg over the seat; kick starts the thing into a detonating roar that echoes off the concrete walls. She climbs on behind, suddenly wondering what to do with her hands.

'You might need to hold on.' He shouts over his shoulder, so she does; starts with her hands chastely above his hips but by the time they've rolled up the ramp to the street she's unashamedly wrapped her arms around his waist. The seat, she finds, is shaped like a horse saddle, narrower in front, broader and rising upwards at the back, which puts a passenger in unavoidably intimate contact with the rider. She can feel his back muscles shifting as he manoeuvres the motorcycle out of the exit.

'Okay?'

'Yes.' She says, thinking, No, but as they gather speed up the street the combination of mass, speed and acceleration start to make for some sort of algebraic logic and she tells herself, this is easy. Like riding a horse. She starts to sing to herself, an age-old trick to regulate her own breathing and prevent a panic attack grabbing her by the throat.

She can't see over his shoulder in front so instead looks at the cars they pass, at Shem's boot descending to balance the bike when they stop for a red light at Canal. Without much surprise she notes that there's a knife strapped to his leg just above the ankle.

'Still okay?' He asks.

'This is great!' And abruptly it is; an endorphin rush, the inbuilt superiority at being on two wheels while the rest of the world is parcelled neatly up into moving fish tanks of aluminium and glass. Shem unleashes the biggest smile that she's yet seen him display.

'Okay to go faster?' He asks, so she shouts a yes in his ear and they take off, changing lanes neatly and fast, heading west for the highway and then northwards up out of the dark gravitational pull of New York City.

Chapter 2

Shem Jephson

I knew that she didn't really want to go on the motorcycle and that I should of rented a car instead, but it's a vanity on my part that it's been a long time since I rode with a girl on the back of my bike. Plus, I knew she wouldn't be scared by it, not someone like her, and she isn't. Her arms tightly around my waist and I can feel the warmth of her body against my back. By the time we get to the Bronx tollbooth the sky is clearing, first light seeping in, and I don't want to stop at Poughkeepsie at all but take her off up into the Adirondacks somewhere, find a cabin, hunker down against the coming snow. Like I said, a vanity. I admit it, it feels good having her there and I don't want it to stop just yet.

We hit 9A and I open it up, the Hudson blurring below, the bike running sweet as honey. I can feel a vibration against my back and I'm worried that she's shouting, or maybe screaming, but then I realise that there's a rhythm to it, and what she's doing is she's singing. So that's the way we go, me enjoying the envious upturned looks of the motorists we pass, the girl singing to herself behind me.

By the time we get to the edge of Poughkeepsie she's quiet again. Probably cold. My own face feels rigid with it, my hands starting to cramp. There's a diner I know around here so I make a turn off the highway into the side streets. Hot coffee. Breakfast. I pull into the half-empty parking lot of the Wild Goose diner and stop. She doesn't move.

'You can get off now.' I suggest.

'Shem.' A whisper. 'I don't think I can. I think I may have frozen here permanently.' There's a laugh in her voice but I can see through the visor that she's deathly pale. Wonderful; I try to impress a girl and end up half killing her with hypothermia.

'Hang on.' I kick the stand down and dismount by swinging a leg forward over the handlebars, grab her by the waist, lift her bodily off the bike and set her down. She lands with her knees still slightly bent; I take off her gloves and rub her hands between mine.

'I'm sorry.' I say to her, and she pulls her hands away from mine and bends her head to remove the motorcycle helmet. Shakes back her hair.

'I'll live.' She says.

Inside the diner I tell her she should go to the restroom and run hot water over her wrists, and while she does that I get a table by the window and order coffee for the both of us. A standard-issue diner, block built, long breakfast counter at the back with a couple of truckers and a hunter or two occupying the stools. At the table opposite, an early family breaking a journey with home fries and milkshakes for the kids. Harriet comes back, shrugging off her jacket; there's a little more colour in her face now. She takes a seat opposite me and regards the menu on the table, wrapping her hands around her coffee cup.

Her fingernails are painted pale pink like the inside of a seashell. She looks up at me.

'You don't say much, do you?' She says.

This isn't the first time this comment has been made to me.

'What would you like me to talk about?' I ask her.

'Tell me about yourself.'

'Like what?'

'Like. I don't know. Are you married?'

'Used to be. Not anymore.'

'Any children?'

'One son. He's twenty four now. A Marine.'

'Were you in the Marines?'

'Army.'

'Did you see active service?'

'Desert Storm.'

'What was that like?'

'Like all wars. Lots of boredom with occasional excitement.' The waitress barrels up and we make our orders.

Harriet says, 'I didn't think Desert Storm was technically a war.'

'It looked like a war to me.' I tell her.

I've always been better at asking questions than answering them.

We eat and I notice that, outside, the sky is clouding over again. Snow for sure. I tell her that we're only ten minutes from my house.

'Okay.' She says. I think that maybe she's given up on the conversation thing, so it's my turn to make the effort.

'What about you?' I ask her.

'What about me what?'

'You married?'

She smiles, looks down at her coffee cup. 'No. The marital state is a little incompatible with the job I've had for the last few years. I mean, some people have patient spouses that trail around the world with them, but for most people it doesn't work out like that. Plus, it was never really my thing. I wasn't one of those little girls who played at make-believe weddings.'

'Why not?'

'Too busy falling off horses and out of trees, I guess.'

'Do you have a boyfriend?' I ask recklessly.

'No.' She looks me straight in the eye. 'Having a psychotic stalker seemed to put men off. Can't imagine why.'

'Some men are cowards.' I tell her.

It's snowing again by the time we get to my house, and already I can feel her starting to shiver behind me. As we approach the front door I hear my dog rushing up the hall to greet us. I unlock the front door and start to warn Harriet but I needn't; already she's holding out her hand for the dog to sniff, asking me, 'Who's this?'

'This is Rosey.'

'What sort of dog is she?'

'A Chessy. Chesapeake Bay Retriever.'

'Hey, Rosey.' Scratching up behind the dog's ears, then crouching to rub her hands over the dog's coat which sends Rosey into an ecstasy of happiness, tail wagging.

I like that she likes my dog.

Harriet Morgan

Singing most of her way out of New York in an ecstasy of acceleration, the thin adrenaline high of an escape from anywhere. Until the cold started to seep in, exhilarating to start with, then just cold. Really cold, a numbing pain in body and then brain.

She somehow manages to note that Shem's house is an average house on an average suburban street; one and a half storey, basement, tidy strip of grass out front, yard in back. Grey siding, white trim. More or less identical to its neighbours; not a place you could easily pick out in a line-up. She's pleased to see the big red dog, though, an uncomplicated canine welcome. She rubs her hands over its coat to embrace doggy warmth.

The house is as tidy and anonymous as she'd expected; cream-coloured walls, a faint residual smell of fresh paint. Hallway, a door off to either side – dining room and living room, she guesses, stairs up ahead, kitchen in back. She looks up at Shem from petting the dog. He looks down at her, and then walks to the foot of the stairs to point out where the bathroom is.

'On the left at the top.' He says. 'Why don't you get into the tub?'

Not a bad idea, she decides, anticipating hot water, steam, a return to life of her fingers and toes.

Shem goes back outside and the dog follows him, claws clicking on the tile floor of the hallway. Harriet climbs the stairs thinking that maybe its not a bad thing to have the dog there, another mammal to help fill the spaces between her and Shem which seem to be rapidly filling with sexual tension. Maybe I need to change my perfume, she thinks, I seem to be attracting the strangest people just recently. Not that it would be so awful with him, really; he's well built, clean, very polite. But she can't see much if a future in it, tries to picture them in an uptown restaurant, struggling to make conversation, Shem with a knife in his boot and a gun in the back of his pants. Perhaps he could be persuaded to leave the weaponry at home on really special occasions, say a birthday or anniversary. She'd have to put one of those Old West signs on her bedroom door: Please Surrender All Weapons Upon Entry.

As she'd told Chris though, he seems at least honourable, and she doesn't have many fears about waking in the middle of the night with his knife at her throat or – possibly worse – his tongue in her ear. But she feels anxious to avoid any sort of a misunderstanding all the same.

His bathroom is predictably clean and tidy. Sparse, no metrosexual is Shem; razor, shower gel, generic shampoo. Tylenol in the mirrored cabinet above the sink. She sets the hot water running into the big, old-fashioned tub and sits cross-legged on the bathmat to unfold the Toshiba, setting it to search for a WiFi connection. It finds nothing locally, but picks up a neighbour's, by the look of it, asks her opinion and then piggybacks it. Her desktop tells her that its cloudy and plus two degrees Celsius in New York, sunny and thirty one in Phnom Penn, and that the dollar is weakening on the international money markets. She opens up her e-mail. The usual spam, miss-spelt offers of pornography, grey-market pharmaceuticals, and an ad apparently seeking women with small breasts. At least they got that one right, she thinks.

An e-mail from her best friend, Kaye, which manages to strike a tone somewhere between irritated and concerned.

What happened to you Saturday night? Called your cell but it was switched off. You been abducted by aliens?

Carl somehow got us into B Bar where he drank too much vodka and talked crap all night. Well, more crap than the usual crap he normally talks, anyway.
I landed myself a cute blonde personal trainer from Clearwater who is apparently going to take me to the River Café as soon as our schedules allow. Problem is, when I'm not at work he's on the Upper East, toning the thighs of surgically enhanced society matrons. We'll see.

Kaye is plump, Mediterranean-skinned, huge brown eyes. Wherever she goes she gets followed by a trail of men offering dinner, diamond rings, flights on their personal jets or helicopters. Harriet e-mails back.

Sorry, spent the night either flat out asleep or in the bathroom, throwing my guts up. Still can't keep anything down so don't think I'll be at work for a couple of days.
Good luck with the Clearwater guy, tell him to buy the matrons a Thigh Master so he can free up some time to take you to dinner.

She feels bad about lying, but she'll tell Kaye all once this is over. Sees them giggling about Shem over a bottle of red wine somewhere. She opens a new e-mail, sending Chris Shem's address:

The ride up was exhilarating and freezing cold. Shem has a hunting dog that you'd love. Not sure what's happening yet but no doubt all will be revealed.
I've told Kaye I have stomach flu so probably best if you tell work that as well.
See you soon.

The tub full now, she turns off the water and there's a polite little knock at the bathroom door. Shem's voice calls, 'Cup of coffee out here for you.' She waits for his footsteps to disappear back downstairs before opening the door. Coffee mug and an airline miniature of Courvoisier. Smiling, she twists off the cap and dumps the cognac into the coffee.

There's no need for her to worry about any roofies because they're tucked safely away in her own bag.

She strips off in front of the mirror, regarding herself. Bruises on her neck, shadows under her green eyes, but not too bad, all things considered. Probably be a good idea to eat something other than breakfast one of these days. And drink something other than coffee.

The roofies aren't the only thing she's stolen from last night's apartment. She unearths the Philip K Dick, pins her hair on top of her head and sinks down into the hot water. Fingers and toes prickling as the feeling returns, skin going red. She lounges and drinks the alcoholic coffee, one hand above the water as she reads about the junkies and their terrible confusion with the gears on their bicycle.

Dried and dressed, she goes back down to the kitchen, the combination of the hot bath and the cognac making her feel like she does when she's come back from a day's mountain biking; languid and muscle tired. The kitchen cupboards are a slightly whimsical periwinkle blue; not a Shem choice of décor, she guesses, wondering if he's lived here long. He's feeding the dog, pouring dried kibble into a large bowl. The dog wags her pleasure at this and then plunges in, crunching noisily.

'Who looks after her when you're away?' Harriet asks him.

'My neighbour, Mrs Kowalski. In return I do some of her yard work.' Shem looks tired himself, she notes, the buzz cut not quite so precise this morning.

'What time is it?' She asks him.

He checks his watch. 'Around ten.'

'Is that all?' She yawns. 'Feels like it should be midnight tomorrow, or something.' Like having jet lag, everything happening at the wrong time.

'Why don't you get some sleep?' Shem suggests. 'I'm waiting for Art to call me back, but nothing's going to happen for a while. Go on, I've made up the guest bed.'

She doesn't want to sleep, really, but it seems like it might be a good idea to put some distance between her and Shem's careful regard.

'Okay.' She says. Waves to the dog, who's paused in her eating to look round, and then she trails back up the stairs feeling strangely like a child who's been sent up to bed just when the adults are starting to party downstairs. Retrieves her backpack from the landing, and then pauses to sneak a look in at Shem's open bedroom door as she passes. Perfectly tidy and normal, dark wood furniture, book on the nightstand. She can't make out the title but the cover looks military, men in combat gear and a helicopter with dangling winch cable hovering above them.

The guest bedroom is small, neutral. Dumps her bag, undresses again. Her sleep t-shirt has translucent patches of what can only be gun oil on it, so she puts her shirt back on. The sheets are cool and clean and she sinks immediately into a deep-water sleep, loose-limbed.

Shem Jephson

When she's finished her bath she looks better, some colour in her face and she's taken her hair out of its braid so it curls around her face and down her back. She looks pretty but tired and I suggest she gets some sleep just in case anything happens tonight. Not that I think it will, I think tomorrow will be the day I get to meet Thomas again and my fingers clench at the thought of getting my hands around his neck. Harriet has bruises on hers, like an obscene necklace, so it's only right. An eye for an eye; just like it says in the bible.

Art calls later, amusement in his voice. Tells me Thomas is a very worried man now that his little bird has flown the nest. I tell him that we'll need a nice remote place for us all to meet, and we agree to get together in a little place I know in the mountains. Art will tell Thomas that I'm considering ransoming the little bird back to him; no doubt he'll bring his muscle boys and a bag of cash with him as no doubt he's seen far too many bad movies.

He won't have seen the end of this one.

I walk the dog around the block and then settle down to sleep on the couch for a while. Sleep longer than I intend; it's dark when I'm woken by the phone ringing. My son, calling from Virginia to tell me his girlfriend has walked out on him. I carry the phone through to the kitchen and put coffee on while he talks. It's a shame, I tell him, but sometimes that's just the way things are. It is, especially when you're in the military. It's a hard life for a woman to commit to. Before he hangs up he reminds me to send him his Mudcats baseball shirt, which he left here last time he visited. I tell him I'll send it tomorrow.

Harriet walks back into the kitchen while I'm talking, so I end the call and offer her some coffee.

Harriet Morgan

Woken by the telephone ringing downstairs, she experiences a few moments of terrible displacement. The window in the wrong place, the bed too narrow. Not her apartment. Then it all comes back to her in a rush, and then all she really feels is slightly disorientated and very hungry. Pulls on her jeans, changes her shirt, drags a brush through her hair, feeling like she's slept for days. Puts on socks but no boots. Pads back downstairs, just in time to catch Shem talking on the phone.

'Well.' He's saying in tone of light regret. 'It's a real shame about her, but that's just the way it has to be sometimes.' A pause. 'Yes, I'll do it tomorrow'

She goes cold, scalp prickling, the little hairs at the back of her neck standing up like a frightened cat's. Don't panic, she tells herself, he doesn't have to be talking about you. It could be his mother, his dog. Don't men call treasured possessions 'She?' His car. His motorcycle. Mind racing, feeling sure now that coming here was the biggest, stupidest mistake she ever made in her whole life, walked straight into it like the bimbo in a horror film.

The one who just has to accept a dare to go into the graveyard at midnight, even though you're screaming at the screen for her not to.

Shem ends the call, offers coffee and she accepts, leaning over to pet the dog so she can hide her face from him for a moment. Thinks, play it nice, wait for an opportunity to get out.

'You hungry?' He asks.

'Yes, I am.' Trying for a social smile.

'There's a pretty good place down the street. You like Italian? It's walking distance, no need to get back on the motorcycle.' He smiles back at her.

'Sounds great.'

Wine me, dine me, hang me from a meat hook in your kitchen.

'I'll just go sort myself out.' She says, and runs back upstairs, digs around in her bag for some make-up which will give her the excuse to spend a few minutes alone, trying to get her heart out of her mouth. A train howls past in the distance. A train. Isn't Poughkeepsie famous for being the last stop on the MTA line out of New York? She thumbs the button to start up the Toshiba again. *Think.* Wants to grab the gun but doesn't believe for a moment that she'd be able to kill him in cold blood, she'd hesitate and he'd take it off her, just like Chris warned. Or else he'd draw his own, doubtless superior, weapon and they'd have either a Mexican standoff or a shootout, which either way would end very badly for her.

Blindly searching the bag's contents for mascara, her fingers find the little white pack of roofies. Interesting idea. Have a nice meal, maybe a glass of wine, come back here for a nightcap, drop a few roofies in his drink and get out while he's sleeping.

Drop the whole damn pack in; with any luck it might kill him.

Kneeling by the Toshiba, she Googles Poughkeepsie station, searching for the times of the early morning trains back to New York.

The station website proudly announces that it's also a stop on the Adirondack route to Montréal.

Canada.

Over the border.

She checks the timetable. The Montréal train departs Poughkeepsie at 9:10am. Get to the station, she tells herself, and hide out there for the train. Flips to a map of the town; the station is less than a mile from here. Easy. Flips to the booking page, which tells her that Coach is fully booked, adding helpfully that there's still availability in Business class. Harriet grabs her credit card. If she's going to flee the country, she's going to do it in style.

They walk down the street to the restaurant. The snow has stopped, leaving a sprinkling on the suburban lawns and sidewalk but none on the pavement. They seem to know Shem at the place, and all the fussing and how-are-yas and flapping of green, white and red striped napkins gives her the opportunity to focus long enough on the menu to choose some harmless-looking sort of pasta with a tomato sauce.

The waiter eventually drifts off and Shem regards her with a look of concern. 'Are you okay?' He asks.

'Yeah. Sure.' Forcing a smile. *Waiter? Waiter! I think tomorrow this man is going to try and kill me.* 'It's just, you know. It's been a strange few days.'

'Of course. It'll soon be over.' A gentle smile. 'I'm going to take you up into the wilderness tomorrow.'

Good thing she's not eating yet, or she'd choke. She hadn't expected him to be quite so explicit quite so soon.

'I spoke to Art earlier.' He continues. Yeah, she thinks, I know you did. 'He's set up a meet between us and Thomas. Thomas thinks I'm going to hand you over to him in return for cash.'

'You are? I mean, you can't do that at your place?'

He regards her seriously. 'We need to be somewhere quiet in case it gets noisy, you understand?'

'Okay.' *Yeah, I understand. Somewhere Mrs Thing, whose lawns you kindly mow, can't hear me scream. Bet you clear snow from her front path as well, don't you, you bastard.*

'We do need to teach him a lesson, you know.' *And what kind of a lesson are you going to teach me, Shem? Or is this likely to be more of a Show and Tell?*

He reads her expression, says, 'There's no need to be afraid.' *No, of course not, pal. Not at all.*

He leans forward, says quietly, 'I'll be there to look after you.' *I think you're advertising in the wrong newspaper, buddy.*

Trying again, he adds, 'We'll take my truck. So you can be warm this time.' *You bet I will be, nice and warm, right up until I go cold permanently.*

Play it nice, she reminds herself, forcing herself to look at him.

'I'm sorry,' She tells him. 'I think I'm just nervous at seeing Thomas again.'

'Don't be. Everything will be okay.'

Another forced smile. 'I'm sure it will be.'

They eat, and she manages to steer the conversation onto the places he travelled to in the Army, which gives her the opportunity to eat some of the pasta twists in their red sauce. Little rings of black olive, flecks of herb. It's probably pretty good, but she's having trouble forcing it down. A bottle of red wine arrives and she sips at a half glass, hoping he'll drink the lion's share, drop his guard a little. Need to spin this out a bit so they don't get back too early. Desperately trying to remember a magazine article: The Art of Flirting. Aren't you supposed to do something with your hair? Twirl it, or something? Or maybe you're supposed to put it up in the first place so that you can let it cascade sensuously down later. Too late for that, anyway. Instead she flicks her hair back from her face, smiling at him, looking him deep in the eyes.

Bingo.

They walk back home in the cold air, shoulders nearly touching. The dog rushes to the front door to greet them and amongst the dog-petting and the taking off of coats she asks him if he has any more of that nice cognac.

'I'll get it.' He says.

'No, just tell me where it is and I'll fetch you some. You go get comfortable in the living room.' Trying for a seductive tone. She probably sounds more like she has a strep throat, but it seems to work.

She finds the cognac in a kitchen cupboard. Pours two glasses, takes the roofies out of her pocket, and, pushing them out of their little blister pack, drops a couple into the left-hand glass. Watches them dissolve, adds another. Thinks, that should do it nicely.

Shem Jephson

This really is nice. I was worried about her earlier, she was acting like something had spooked her but she relaxed during the meal and we had a nice evening. I swirl the cognac in my glass and drink some more. She's watching me intently, then catches my eye, smiles and stretches out in her chair, crossing her ankles in front of her. She looks really nice.

'You know.' I tell her. 'I knew as soon as I saw you that night that Thomas had lied to us.'

She laughs. She has a nice laugh.

'You mean, I didn't look like a bunny boiler?' She asks.

I laugh, too. 'You didn't look like a bunny boiler. I mean, I think that stalkers must be lonely people and you don't look like you'd ever be lonely.' I seem to be slurring, feel far more drunk than I should be. Never mind. I lift my glass and drink some more. I really, really do feel drunk. The room is starting to soften at the edges.

And then the realisation of what she's done hits me with a terrible clarity.

The roofies. The damn, damn roofies. How many has she given me?

'What have you…?' I start to say, and at that moment she makes a run for it.

She would have made it, too, if she'd been a second quicker, or if I'd remembered to oil the bolt on the back door. As it is, I reach her just as she's struggling with it; wrap my arms around her waist to drag her away. She's stronger than she looks, all lean muscle and animal panic.

Strands of her hair crunch between my teeth. She kicks out backwards, a boot heel connecting with my shin hard enough that the pain of it arcs through my spine and I feel it in my back teeth. I grab her wrist; twist her arm up behind her back. She grunts and then cries out, so I clamp my hand over her mouth, keeping my palm arched away from her teeth so she can't bite.

She's bent over at the waist to try and avoid the pressure I'm putting on her shoulder, and I run her across the kitchen like that, slam her sideways against the basement door hard enough to knock the breath out of her while I take my hand away from her mouth to unlock the door. It crashes inwards and I shove her through, see her grab at the rail to stop herself falling down the stairs. I slam the door closed and twist the key in the lock.

I'm panting hard and my knees are going; I find myself kneeling with my forehead rested up against the door.

'Shem, please.' Her voice a whisper on the other side. 'Please don't do this to me.'

'I have to.' I tell her. 'I have to keep you safe.' Right now I can't remember who from, or why, but I do recall that it's very, very important.

'I heard you talking on the phone.' She says, but I can't reply because I don't know what she's talking about but I do know that I'm going to lose consciousness very soon. I push myself upright and stumble across the hallway and into the living room. Weave my way across a buckling floor, fending off furniture as it rushes towards me. Find the couch and fall onto it.

Somewhere at the edges of my fading consciousness I can hear someone sobbing, but I don't know what it could have to do with me.

Harriet Morgan

She hears him stumble away and then she sits, her back to the basement door. Left shoulder aching from the arm lock, right hip and arm feeling bruised from their sudden impact on the door. Feels the tears starting to gather in the corner of her eyes. Come on, she tells herself. Hold it together; you've done worse damage to yourself falling off your mountain bike. And then had to carry the damn thing for the four miles back to town when she'd taco'd her front wheel in Mexico.

Its pitch black there in the basement, making no difference whether her eyes are open or closed. She gets up and feels for a light switch beside the door but there's nothing; the switch must be in the kitchen. Breathe deeply. Hold it together. And then she realises that there's no point and gives in and cries; like she hadn't cried in years, big, ugly howling sobs, gasping for breath in between. Cries for the whole damn thing, for Thomas, for being chased down the street, for being taken to the apartment, for how badly she's screwed up this latest one.

She comes back to herself eventually, sitting on the cold cement steps, arms hugging her knees. And then hears something.

A scratching sound.

There's something scratching at the other side of the basement door. She flings herself away from the door in horror, grasping the stair rail behind her, imagining zombies, the world's largest bubonic rat. And then hears a snuffle, a questioning whine at the base of the door.

Rosey.

'Oh dog.' She says, laughing and crying at the same time. 'Oh dog, if you were Lassie you'd be able to unlock the door for me.'

Rosey is no Lassie, though, and loses interest after a while, clicking away across the tile floor of the kitchen to investigate the metal food bowl with her nose.

But the dog has given Harriet an idea. She puts her hands flat against the wood of the door, feeling slowly like reading Braille. An old door, tongue and groove wood smoothed with decades of gloss paint. She feels sideways towards where the back of the lock should be, finding it higher up than she expected. Hoping for an open key hole: the gap under the door isn't large enough to fit the key under, but might be able to somehow manipulate it from this side. Disappointment; the reverse of the lock is a blank plate, flat and cool under her fingertips.

Think.

The door opens inwards, as she'd experienced. Which means the hinges should be on this side. She feels sideways back across the door and finds them, two old-fashioned strap hinges held in place by big, dome-headed screws. Eight screws on each hinge; a pair together near the frame, then two spaced down the length of the strap. Four screws on the hinge where it fits on the door frame. This is a basement, right? There's got to be tools; remembering the pristine motorcycle. Unless he keeps them in the garage. No, there has to be something down here.

She tries to visualise the basement in schematic. Door from the kitchen, the stairs running down alongside the wall on the left. Thinks, if you were Shem, you'd have a workbench. And it would probably be on the right-hand wall, opposite the stairs, which would be the longest.

Grasping the stair rail she feels her way painfully slowly down the steps, feeling with a boot heel for each one. No good breaking an ankle down here, she tells herself, take it nice and slow. Reaches the bottom before she expects, her heel jarring on the floor. Being in complete darkness is giving her retinal hallucinations; ghostly lights flaring and disappearing at the edges of her vision. Moving slowly, her hands held out in front of her, skin crawling at the idea of its suddenly impacting with something sharp. Her hip catches the edge of something; she reaches and feels smooth corners. Washer, or dryer. At least that means there's water down here, she thinks, and then tries not to dwell upon the implications of that thought.

Turning, she shuffles slowly across to the far wall. Touches something, feels something like a high, narrow table made of rough wood. Workbench. And then the back of her hand brushes against a jar which teeters for an agonising moment before rolling off the bench. She grabs blindly and misses, and it hits the ground and smashes, scattering something metallic all over the floor.

Holding her breath and listening, trying to hear over the sound of her own pounding heart. Nothing. No shout, no footsteps. Wishes she'd checked how long the roofies were likely to last.

My kingdom for my laptop.

Starts feeling slowly over the bench again. Please, let there be something. A claw hammer, an axe.

And then a click behind her that makes her flinch, followed by a gathering soft roar. The furnace. The pilot flame in its little window flares, the light just enough for her to see, for a moment, the line of screwdrivers hung neatly up above the workbench in every size from watchmaker to construction worker.

Thank god for a man with tidy habits.

Slowly back up the steps to the door, and she finds that undoing screws, blind, isn't as easy as it seems. Hard to keep the screwdriver at the right angle, almost impossible to keep the head in the screw's little slot. She ends up positioning a finger at either side of the screw head while she wrenches the screwdriver with the other hand, meaning that every time the screwdriver slips, which it does frequently, it chips painfully into one finger or the other.

Four eventually loosened on the top hinge, she starts on the lower hinge. Harder, these screws, must be the weight of the door bearing down on them all these years. No idea what the time is, the darkness throwing out the mechanism of her internal clock, but this is taking too long. Far too long. The screwdriver bites and then slips. She can feel by the little curl of sharp metal against her fingertip that it's starting to strip the slot out of the head.

Deep breath, start again.

It refuses to budge. Deep breath, try a different screw. The same happens and she wants to scream. Deep breath. Think. A lingering memory of her father calmly oiling a stuck bolt on a childhood bicycle. *Lube*. There must be some here, somewhere.

Back down the stairs, slowly, slowly. Across to the bench. Feels across, then reaches up to the shelf above where the screwdrivers are hanging. Finds a spray can of something, it feels like; it rattles as she picks it up. Holds it to her face and sniffs, smelling the unmistakable scent of unreliable cars on wet days. Spray oil. Perfect.

There's another growing urgency; she desperately needs to pee. Damned if she's going to go in the corner of the basement like some animal. Think about something else.

Back up the stairs again. Shakes the can, takes the top off, feeling for the little hole in the nozzle so she doesn't spray it straight into her own face. Positions it, sprays, forces herself to wait. Looking down, she can see a faint hint of greyish light showing under the door. Deep breath, try again with the screwdriver. It bites, and then turns. For one awful moment she thinks she's completely stripped the head from the screw but then feels it turning sweetly, levering itself out of the wood. Three more to go.

Two shift, eventually, the last solidly refusing to budge.

She goes back to the top hinge, removing the screws completely, feeling the door sag downwards and slightly outwards. It's definitely getting light outside, now. She tucks the screws carefully into her pocket of her jeans, just in case she should get enough warning of Shem's reappearance to put them back in, give her a chance at a second attempt at another time.

Back to the bottom hinge, the last screw still stubbornly refusing to move. Then it strikes her, and she almost laughs at her own stupidity. Slides the screwdriver under the hinge, twists it, and levers upwards. The screw gives way, pulling out of the wood with a terrible screech. Too late to care, now. She forces the door outwards and squashes her way through the tiny gap into the kitchen.

The dog scrambles up to greet her.

Still carrying the screwdriver, she tiptoes her way into the living room. Needn't have worried about waking Shem; nothing short of World War Three could have done that. He's asleep on his back, snoring gently, a fleck of dried saliva at the corner of his lip. One arm has dropped off the couch and rests on its knuckles on the floor, fingers slightly curled.

She runs for the bathroom and pees with a sense of tremendous luxury. Light, air, freedom and an empty bladder. Grabs her backpack, runs back down the stairs still carrying the screwdriver. Something occurs to her. She stands looking down at the unconscious Shem for a moment, thinking; it's time to leave you a message, friend.

She plunges the screwdriver downwards, hard, and then runs for the door.

Shem Jephson

I wake to the worst hangover I've ever had. Terrible; pounding headache, dry mouth. Risk opening my eyes and I'm confused for a moment because I'm looking straight at an upright steel bar like a single prison bar. Then the room shifts sickeningly into perspective, and I realise that I'm looking at the shaft of one of my own screwdrivers that has been driven into the cushion next to my head.

Despite the pain of the hangover I can't help smiling.

You just have to admire that girl.

It's about ten minutes of nine a.m., and I've no idea how long she's been gone, or where, but I need to look for her. The basement door is still locked at one end, but off its hinges at the other. Clever girl. The dark of the basement behind the broken door makes me realise that she was in complete darkness down there the whole time. I grab my cell phone and the truck keys from the counter, make for the door and then double back to the refrigerator for a plastic jug of orange juice. Rosey has spotted the truck keys in my hand and stands between me and the front door, her body all tense with yearning. That dog just loves to ride in my truck.

'Alright then.' I say to her, and she goes bounding up the hallway in front of me.

Outside, Mrs Kowalski is brushing the snow from her front steps. I call out to her that I'll do it for her later. A little plump woman, a widow, she must be in her eighties but she's all good humour and energy. She walks to the wood fence between our properties and stops, hands on her hips.

'You should be ashamed of yourself, Shem Jephson.'

'What?' Oh, no.

'And I always thought you were a gentleman.'

'Excuse me?' I ask her.

'You could have given your young lady friend a lift to the station, at least.' She's teasing me, I realise, something saucy in the sideways look she's giving me.

'You saw her?' I ask the old lady.

'Not half an hour ago. But she was running so I figured she was late for her train.'

Thank you, Mrs Kowalski.

'I overslept.' I tell her. 'I'm just going to the station to see if I can catch up with her.'

'Better you do. You should buy her some flowers or something.' There's a yearning in her voice, as if she's remembering a time when men used to buy her flowers. 'She was a cute little thing, too. Lovely hair. I sure hope we see her around here again.'

'Me, too.' I tell her.

Rosey is sitting up in the passenger seat looking serious the way dogs do in trucks and I drive the truck one handed, drinking the juice with the other, remembering last night. Her desperate fight to get out. You fool, I tell myself, you should have just let her go. I pretty much knew she had something in her backpack that she didn't want me to know about, but I hadn't thought of the roofies. But I can't figure out why she was so scared. What spooked you, Harriet? I heard you talking on the phone, she'd said. I backtrack; remember talking to Art earlier in the day, then to my son later. Had I said something then which she'd misinterpreted as a threat to her?

Remember hearing her crying. Must have hurt her, and then slung her into the darkness of the basement. Wonderful, Shem, I tell myself. If she wasn't convinced that you were dangerous to her then, she certainly would have been after that.

You have to admire her, though. Remembering at the restaurant and then afterwards. She'd decided I was a threat and used her tactical advantage, which was my own vanity at thinking she'd be attracted to me. I should have known; like having a wild animal in the house, it might act domesticated but the trust only goes so far and the whole time it's looking for an escape route.

I've no idea what to do if I do find her, how to persuade her that she's safer with me than anywhere else. No idea how to convince her not to have a screaming fit and call the police. Honestly, officer, by beating on her and then throwing her in my basement I was trying to keep her safe from the man who'd actually employed me to abduct her in the first place.

I drive past the station parking lot and across the tracks, just in case she's looking out for me coming from there, leaving the truck in a lot beyond the overpass. Rosey wants to come with me and I let her, thinking that Harriet liked the dog so somehow it might help. The orange juice feels like battery acid in my gut. We jog back across the overpass and I see that the long Montréal train has pulled into the station.

She's not there. I check the station building and then walk the length of the Canada train, looking in at the windows in case she's got on there, but I don't see her. Long gone to New York, no doubt. People always go back to what they know; if a soldier goes AWOL you only have to check his girlfriend's or his mom's house because he'll always show up there sooner or later.

I'll find her again in New York, try and explain.

I get back in the truck and call Art to tell him that Thomas' little bird has flown away.

'What happened?' Art asks.

'I don't know.' I tell him. 'Something frightened her, I don't know what, and she got away from me.'

'And how did she do that, Shem?'

'Remember those roofies?'

'Yes.'

'There you go.'

'She Mickey'd you?' Art starts laughing. 'Please tell me…' He has to stop to laugh some more, collects himself. 'Please tell me, my friend, that while you were unconscious she didn't interfere with your person?'

My head hurts like heck but his laughter is infectious.

'I only wish she had.' I tell him.

On the way home I stop to buy Mrs Kowalski some flowers.

Harriet Morgan

There's around fifty minutes until her train leaves and it's around a mile or so to the station. Plenty of time, technically, but she sets off at a run to put some distance in between her and the black hole of that basement; discovering that it's easy to run in heels if she keeps her weight back. She remembers the voice of the trainer at her gym; keep your pace steady, keep your heart rate under 150 and you can run forever. So she does just that, a measured pace that won't scare any passers-by, she's just a woman who's late for her train. Poughkeepsie is going to work on a Monday morning, lots of people and cars around now. She doesn't seriously think Shem will be able to drag her off the street in broad daylight, but she feels exposed all the same; the skin of her back itching like it's caught in the cross hairs.

She gets to the station sooner than she expects, find the ticket hall, feeds her credit card into the machine which obligingly spits out her tickets in return. Avoids the churchy waiting room and instead makes for the ladies bathroom to hide. Thirty minutes to go. To give her a reason for lurking there in the echoing bathroom she searches through the outer pockets of her backpack for make-up; she has always maintained a strategy of throwing any department store samples into her bag for use later, something which sometimes backfires when she finds herself on the wrong side of the world with Peppermint Foot Scrub but no shower gel.

Today she finds Eyelid Colour Corrector, and wonders if there are women who worry about the colour of their eyelids, and whether she should. The stuff is a disturbing lemon yellow colour, but she smears it on and regards herself in the mirror. Has to admit, it makes her look perkier around the eyes. Emboldened, she applies kohl and mascara as well, rummages around in the bag again, comes up with Instant Shine Glosser for Long Hair, which sort of works. Washing her hands, she reflects that at least now she looks less like a woman who has spent a night crying in a locked basement and more like someone who'd be travelling Business Class to Canada.

Ten minutes to go. Steeling herself, she leaves the bathroom and finds the track where the train is expected. Stays towards the back by the station building, shielded, she hopes, by the press of people milling there carrying luggage, talking on their cell phones, towing reluctant small children by the hand.

The train pulls in and she hangs back from the crowding people for a moment. No sign of Shem, unless he has some particularly Shem-like ability to conceal himself behind a trio of fat, laughing executives, which is certainly a possibility. She rolls back her shoulders to get a crick out of them and then jogs across the concourse, checking carefully to left and right, and hops up into the Business Class coach.

Weaving her way through the groups of people who are settling their luggage on the racks, finding seats, taking off coats and gloves, she watches the station out the window. Fewer people there now, some looking like they're getting ready to wave to relatives on the train, the rest turning away to retrieve cars, get on with their Monday mornings. Past the laughing executives again, who step back out of her way as they're stowing their luggage, readying themselves to settle into an empty group of seats.

Then she sees, out the window, Shem's big red dog trotting across the station towards the train, its ears perked.

Shit.

Reflexively, she dives straight beneath the table nearest her.

And comes eye to eyelet with the biggest pair of hiking boots she's ever seen. Tan nubuck, slightly worn but clean, thank god. A glimpse of brown wool sock and long dark pant legs suggesting a considerable length of shin beneath. Arranging herself in a crouch which seems less suggestive than kneeling at this stranger's feet, somehow, she tries to think of some reason, some excuse for her to be there.

I dropped my purse. My necklace fell off.

Then she hears the owner of the boots telling the train steward that she's lost her contact lens under the table. A quiet voice, but deep. Canadian accent; the sort that can flatten vowels whilst losing some consonants completely.

She breathes a silent thank you to the boots for his quick thinking; she doesn't want to get thrown off the train for strange behaviour and straight into Shem's waiting arms.

The owner of the boots leans down into the empty seat next to him to give her a description of someone looking in at the window; someone who can only be Shem.

Not a scary face, Big Boots; long boned, round eyed, nondescript blob of hair on top. He looks like the manager of a local coffee shop, the one that gives you extra sprinkles on your cappuccino just because you're wearing your new jeans and are feeling particularly fine that day.

'Wait a moment.' Big Boots says.

She feels the clunk shudder through the train as it closes its doors and then Big Boots flashes her an OK sign under the table. She backs out from under the table, dumps her backpack on the seat opposite him and bolts for the train's restroom, remembering to maintain the fiction of the recovered contact lens on the way for the benefit of any curious onlookers.

Locking herself in, she eyes herself in the mirror, feeling suddenly flushed and embarrassed. Unwinds her scarf, shrugs off her jacket. Now all the needs to do is find an excuse to change seat away from Big Boots, and then she can sleep all the way to Montréal, safe in the knowledge that she's drawing ever further from Shem, Thomas and the whole damned lot of them.

Chapter Three

Rusty Hanover

Don't ask me why, but when I take the Montréal train I always I think I'm going to meet women – or even one woman, in the singular. It sure is the triumph of hope over experience because not once in two years has this actually happened - unless you count a conversation with a French nun travelling to see the Cathedrale Marie-Reine-Du-Monde which, educational as it was, I personally don't.

Maybe all the woman are in Coach, which means I may have to travel economy on my next trip, or maybe women – who after all are the great pragmatists of our species - just cut to the chase and fly from La Guardia instead. One and a half hours instead of nearly twelve on the train, I mean, who wouldn't? But the honest truth is that flying scares the crap out of me and so I save it for essential business purposes. In fact, the real truth is that I'm not so much scared of flying as I am scared of the consequences should I freak out; someone my height losing it in the cabin would be no joke, believe it. So I only fly when I absolutely have to, and preferably along with someone who can keep feeding me Xanax and Canadian Club in the precise proportions required to prevent me flipping out in case of, say, violent turbulence, or the peanuts falling out of their little packet into the exact pattern of the Mark of the Beast. Otherwise I'm scared that one day I'll get to continue the flight plasticuffed to my seat with an Air Marshal's gun resting gently against my temple. And then get permanently banned by all reputable carriers, meaning that a trip to California would mean going via Murmansk.

So it's the train for me. I should travel overnight in one of their cute full-service cabins, but then they're only fun if you're travelling with a woman. Jerking off - alone – in one of those things is about the loneliest thing an adult male can experience; believe me, I've tried it. So I arm myself with all those things human beings need for long trips - the New York Times, MP4 player, book, and then ignore them for pretty much the whole trip while I gaze out the window and try not to have too many detailed sexual fantasies.

I know what you're thinking.

Rusty Hanover isn't getting a lot, is he? Well, no, mostly because I've pretty much spent the two years since my divorce drinking too much and acting like an asshole. Two girlfriends in that time; one of whom dumped me because, quote, I 'wasn't ambitious enough.' I'm told that this translates as 'not rich enough'. I'm actually doing pretty well, thanks to the endless repeat fees for a certain little sit-com I produced, but this is New York, baby, and mostly the girls seem to expect being flown off in private jets on dates, to which my German-built SUV isn't really any match. The other girlfriend dumped me because, apparently, I was 'just too tall', which was odd since at forty two years of age I hadn't actually grown any since I'd first met her.

So now I'm on the train, going to see my oldest friend Leon and his lovely wife, Carole. You might have guessed from the names that they're both French, which gives Leon and I the opportunity to deploy as many racial epithets against each other as we can fit into any conversation. Leon is smart and funny and also a very sweet man, in truth, and has hauled me out of many a drunken and maudlin situation, especially in the last couple years.

Leon and I met early in my career when I'd been hired to play a slasher / serial killer in a schlocky Canadian Gothic Horror called, if memory serves me right, 'Fatal Excursion'. Leon, at a few years older than me, – a fact which I never forget to remind him - was playing the wise but saturnine Gallic detective while I got to plunge my butcher knife into a succession of surprisingly willing teenage girls. The film tanked, of course, although references to it to turn up sometimes in the seedier backwaters of the Internet, but Leon and I went drinking on the first night of the shoot and agreed that there might be more fun ways to earn a living than sloshing around in the rain in Saskatchewan in February. Actually, that was one hell of a night and if you look closely at the graveyard scene in the film you can actually see how bad my hangover the next day was. We both nearly got fired, several times, but it sort of set the standard for our behaviour together ever since. The lovely Carole rolls her eyes but doesn't really seem to mind that we've been banned from a number of bars in the greater Montréal area. Leon says that when I'm in town, the police put out an automatic ABP on the short Franco freak with the tall Anglo freak.

I know what I look like, mostly on account of complete strangers feeling compelled to tell me. 'Long drink of water' being probably the kindest, 'long streak of piss' being my least favourite, and the most recent being from a drunk at a bar in lower Manhattan who looked up from his slumped position at me waiting politely behind him to get a beer. He did a long, sloooow double take and announced to the world, 'Yo, dude, you are one tall motherfucker.' Sequoia. Freak. Geek. Sasquatch. How's the weather up there? Which basketball team you escape from?

I am indeed one tall motherfucker but I comfort myself with the thought that I've made more money playing freaks, geeks and motherfuckers than most actual freaks, geeks and motherfuckers. In fact, I've probably made more money than the square-jawed, broad-shouldered all-American Wall Street assholes I watch streaming downtown every morning, clutching their briefcases and double decaff skinny lattes, but you wouldn't know it to look at them. Or me, probably.

Fortunately, in the last few years I've done what my mother calls 'grow into myself' - which always makes me sound like a sort of runty steer - partly due to hitting my forties and finally putting on a bit of weight, and also by finally making myself establish some sort of a gym routine. Not jogging, though. There are things that only a best friend can tell you, and it was Leon who told me that, jogging, I look like a moose on a treadmill. Up until then, I was wondering why there were more than the usual number of traffic accidents every time I ran up the edge of the West Side Highway.

The train slows for Poughkeepsie and I'm starting to think about breakfast. I've learnt that its best not to accept breakfast when the steward offers it, which is about ten seconds out of Penn, but delay for as long as possible, otherwise you're left with nothing to look forward to until lunchtime, which occurs at somewhere around Saratoga Springs. Likewise with the drinks. My advice? Avoid the cocktails until at least Ticonderoga otherwise – if you're me at least – you'll find yourself with non-functioning knees in the underground francophone chaos that is Gare Centrale Du Montréal.

The train clanks itself to a stop at Poughkeepsie and I amuse myself by watching the knot of people pushing toward the train. A lovely woman catches my eye; I'm an acknowledged fan of a woman in boots and these are a particularly fine example. Both the woman and the boots, I mean. She's standing back against the ticket office, watching everyone else. Early thirties, athletic little body, long, long dark hair. Small breasts, though. They say that more than a handful is just a waste and these would add up to less than one of my handfuls, but then again my hands are larger than most of the rest of humanity's so maybe that's not a fair test. She squares her shoulders and steps toward the train and that's when I see it. In my business we notice things like posture, ticks, and gestures – mostly so we can steal them and use them again elsewhere - and this woman is moving with a body language that any herbivore in the world would recognise. Head up, short strides, eyes checking left and right. It's the posture of a prey animal that has seen, or smelled, or somehow cleverly inferred that there's a tiger hiding somewhere in the long grass.

Who are you hiding from? I think. The law? No. The boots and jacket are expensive, and she has that polished, cared-for look that prosperous women have. Not the law. Who then?

Who are you hiding from, lovely woman?

She pauses by the train and I press my forehead against the glass so I can continue watching her. The startled deer metaphor is too much of a cliché, even for me, but in fact what she looks like is one of those tough little antelopes. The cute looking ones with the dewy eyes that actually have legs made of tensile steel and skip off over the veldt at a hundred miles an hour, leaving that old tiger behind, all panting and humiliated.

She checks up and down one last time, steps up into the train and just as I'm mourning the sudden departure of this fine woman from my life the door to my car slides back and here she comes. She checks us all out as she enters but clearly doesn't find anyone alarming among us – me, three businessmen, an old couple – and walks on up the car, watching out the windows as she comes. And just as she's almost level with my quad of seats I see her eyes widen, she gasps 'shit!' and without pausing she dives straight under my table.

Well, here's a turn up. Almost instantaneously there's a steward at my elbow, asking if he can get me a drink, sir, when what he really wants to ask is why there's a woman under my table, sir. There is one obvious explanation which occurs to me immediately, of course, but as it's one that would get us both thrown off the train, and probably earn me a painful slap in the process, I can't use that one.

'Two coffees, please.' I say smoothly. And then: 'Pardon us, but my girlfriend seems to have dropped her contact lens under the table.'

Brilliant, if I don't say so myself. Actually, not quite as brilliant as I would have liked; I was trying to sound like an urban sophisticate, and ended up sounding about as Canadian as I ever have in my whole life. I sound like the farmer's son that I in fact am. But at least the train staff is now happy with my explanation, and my brand-new, make-believe girlfriend might just be impressed with my reaction speed.

I check out the window and here he is, walking oh-so-casually up the train and glancing in at the windows. Grey eyes, grey hair, buzz cut in that squared off, ex-military guy style. His eyes meet mine briefly, and then he walks on. I lean down into the empty seat beside me to look under the table.

'Grey military buzz-cut?'

Eyes all pupils, she nods.

'Stay there a moment.'

Then the train doors slide shut and Military Buzz Cut is walking back up the station, foiled. Ha. I flash her an ok sign under the table and she backs out from under in about as elegant a way as a person can in that sort of a situation. On her index finger she has balanced an entirely non-existent contact lens. She flashes me a bogus smile, says, excuse me a moment, and walks off down the car to the restroom, still carrying the pretend lens on her finger.

Not a bad bit of acting.

When she comes back I can see her eyeing up the empty seats in the car but – thank god – the coffee arrives, complete with the little jug of cream and some of those high class brown sugar lumps that look more like tiny random geological formations. Now at least she'll have to drink the coffee with me, or look impolite. I pray she's not the not the type of person to be rude; or at least, not that particular sort of rude, if you know what I'm saying. She's taken her jacket and scarf off, and as she sits down opposite me I look at her and in that moment everything changes because around her neck is an unmistakable set of purplish bruises.

Someone, in the last day or two, has made a fairly serious attempt at strangling this woman.

I've never really had much of a temper, apart from an ability to throw detailed and imaginative curse words at drivers who infuriate me, but this sort of thing makes me seriously mad. I mean, look at her, she can't weigh more than about a hundred pounds, she's tiny. I remember Mr. Military Buzz Cut and wish for the first time in my life that I owned a gun. I'd run back down the track - moose impression or no moose impression– and shoot the bastard right between the eyes.

She interrupts my violent thoughts by saying a very quiet 'thank you', though I'm not sure if it's the coffee she's thanking me for, or my fast explanation to the steward. I lean forward across the table.

'Look, I think you're in some sort of trouble'. She looks up at me quickly, then down again. She doesn't want to discuss it, but I push onwards. 'You seemed pretty scared back there. And by the bruises on your neck, someone's tried to hurt you.' No reaction. 'Was it Military Buzz Cut man?'

Now she meets my eyes. 'No, it wasn't. Strangely enough it was the man who he was working for who did it.'

I lean back. 'Jesus.'

'Would it help if I told you that shortly afterwards I broke the nose of the guy who did this to me?'

'Not really. Buzz Cut was hunting for you, wasn't he?'

'He was, sort of.' She rubs a hand slowly over her face. Pale skin, green eyes. Tired-looking. 'It's a long story.'

I check my watch. 'I've got around eight hours.'

And then she tells me the story. The whole thing. And you know why I believe her? Because she doesn't give a damn whether I believe her or not. To her, I'm just some random, inquisitive guy she happened to meet on the train to Montréal and will probably never see again.

Obviously, I'm not about to let *that* happen.

Our coffees have gone cold by now so I ask for some more, and with it the breakfast menus arrive. She stares down at hers like it's written in Swahili. I check quickly that they haven't given her the Swahili version by mistake but no, it's the perfectly ordinary one, headlines in English, French subtitles. The steward is lurking, so I order a full-on Western breakfast with whole wheat toast, just to show what an organic sort of a guy I am, and as she's obviously staring at the menu without reading a word of it I tell the steward that my girlfriend will have the pancakes, thank you. For the benefit of the steward I add:

'You just love those pancakes, don't you honey?' And make a big kissy-face at her. On reflection, the kissy-face would probably be enough to make most women run screaming from the room, but she's clearly made of stronger stuff and it earns me an amused sideways look. Something about the tip-tilt at the corners of those lovely green eyes makes me think she has a sense of humour, which would possibly account for what I decide to do next. It's a high-risk strategy but, hell, it's the only one I have.

She's stirring cream into her coffee and I can see her hands are shaking slightly.

'You want some sugar in that?' I ask her.

'No, thank you.'

'I really think you should have some sugar.'

She shrugs, clearly deciding to appease this dangerous, sugar-obsessed lunatic sitting opposite her, and reaches for the sugar bowl. Instead I snatch it away from her, flip one of the little sugar rocks up high into the air beside me, turn, catch it on my tongue, turn, and spit it straight into her coffee with admirable speed and accuracy, if I don't say so myself.

For about half a second I think I'm about to be wearing the coffee but, no, it works and she starts laughing, showing me some very good North American dentistry before burying her face in her hands, shoulders heaving.

‘Oh my god.’ She says, recovering herself. ‘I can’t believe you did that. That’s amazing. You should do that for a living or something.’

‘What? Spit in people’s coffee? I don’t think Starbucks is about ready for that, do you?’

‘You could, I don’t know, you could work for the CIA, spitting polonium into dissident’s cocktails.’

‘Seeing as it would probably kill me too it’s an interesting career idea, but somewhat short-lived, I think.’ I tell her. ‘By the way, you don’t have to drink the coffee. I’ll get you some fresh.’

‘No, its fine.’ And drink it she does. Am I an over-optimistic fool to be pleased that she’s willing to drink something with at least a small percentage of my spit in it?

‘What do you do for a living?’ she asks me.

‘Guess.’ This is sort of a test I use on women, but then I’d probably forgive her even if she came up with a dumb answer like basketball player.

‘Guess? Oh, okay.’ She thinks a moment. ‘Veterinary surgeon?’

I’ve not had that one before. ‘Why so?’

‘You have long fingers. Someone once told me that the best veterinary surgeons have long fingers.’ She suddenly realises the full implications of what she’s just said and this sets her off laughing again. ‘Oh, I’m really sorry. Concert pianist, that’s what I meant to say.’

‘Interesting guesses, but wrong, I’m afraid. I’m an actor. Was an actor. Am-stroke-was an actor’

‘Theatre?’

‘Film, mostly. Romantic comedies, though not the romantic lead, you’ll be amazed to hear. Usually the slightly geeky best friend of the romantic lead, or the building super, or the mailman. The one who gets the fat girl at the end and everyone’s happy.’ I think it best not to mention mine and Leon’s slasher film at this point.

‘I’m sorry; I should probably have recognised you. I just haven’t spent much time on the American continent in the last few years.’

‘Even if you had, you probably wouldn’t. I was briefly famous in Canada, which pretty much adds up to not-at-all famous anywhere else in the world. I don’t do much of it anymore, anyway. Mostly now I produce programmes for TV, and do occasional voice acting.’

‘I always wondered what producers do.’

‘No-one knows, but it pays well, which fortunately means that I don’t have to work too hard at it. Meaning I get to watch a lot of daytime TV and can take time out to go to Montréal on the train to visit my lovely friend Leon and his lovely wife Carole, which is where I'm headed today. You should come with me.'

Damn. I'd been formulating a little plan to get her to go to Leon's with me, but hadn't meant to ask quite so soon, or in such a dumb way. Now I sound like a hopeless sophomore asking the pretty cheerleader for a date.

'Oh no, I couldn't, but thank you. I mean, I don't even know your name.'

'Rusty Hanover.'

'Harriet Morgan. My friends call me Harry.'

'Harry.' I take her narrow little hand in mine & we shake. 'Most people call me Rusty, although I'll let you into a little secret and tell you that my given name is actually Russell, but no-one's called me that in twenty years and I wouldn't answer if they did. Really, you should think about coming with me to Leon and Carole's place. They have a huge house, their kids are off at university, they'd be delighted.' Not to mention how delighted I would be, I think to myself, to turn up there with you.

'No, thank you, I couldn't.'

'Why not? I'm not a serial killer or anything, I'm a Canadian. Us Canadians don't really have the genetic make-up to be serial killers.'

'Oh no? What about the pig farmer guy?' That lovely amused little tip-tilt is back.

'I probably shouldn't tell you this.' I tell her, 'But my parents are dairy farmers. You can consider yourself to be safe, though, because you can't feed human beings to Guernseys, it would taint the milk.'

'I'm very reassured by that.' She tells me.

'I meant you to be. What were you planning to do in Montréal, anyway? Do you even speak French?'

'A bit of European French, yes. I was planning to find a nice old fashioned hotel, do some sleeping, do some thinking, have a look around the city.'

'Canadian French is very different, you know.' This is sort of a lie, but what the hell. 'No-one will understand a word you say & they'll go all Gallic and superior on you in your nice old fashioned hotel. Whilst on the other hand Leon and Carole are both completely bilingual and as a result the city of Montréal will be our *moules*. Or whatever oyster is in French.' I can see that she's totally busted me for lying, but I can also see her weakening. The honest truth is that I'm afraid that if she stays on her own she'll get seduced by some lonely, rich and attractive French businessman and I'll never see her again, and then I'd have to spend the rest of my life worrying whether she really did meet a

French businessman or whether her psycho stalker and his gang caught up with her and she was dead in a ditch somewhere, possibly with minute traces of my spit-based DNA somewhere in her system. At which point I'd probably spend the rest of my life in jail, although in that case at least I wouldn't have to worry about the businessman, I guess.

'I have a suggestion.' I tell her. 'I'll call my friends now and if they're both not totally overjoyed about you joining me we'll help you find a nice old fashioned hotel to stay in when we get to Montréal. Deal?'

She gives in. 'Okay, deal.' We shake hands again and I flip open my cell phone to call Leon, praying that he answers and she doesn't have time to have second thoughts.

Thank god, he answers on the third ring. 'Âllo?'

'Hey, Leon.'

'Rusty! You're on the train, right?'

'I'm on the train and hoping that breakfast arrives before I have to eat my own luggage. Leon, can I ask you something?'

'Anything, my friend, as long as it's not actually indictable. But Carole says a summary offence is acceptable, if that's any help.'

'Nothing like that. Would it be okay if someone joins me at your place?'

There's a pause. 'Would that be a female type of a person?'

'Yes, it is a female type of a person.'

'Wow. Excellent.' Then I can hear him take the phone way from his ear and shout, 'Carole? Carole! Rusty's got a woman with him.' I can't make out her answer, but when he comes back on the phone I tell him his surprise that I'm with a female is extremely unflattering, which makes Harriet laugh.

'Carole says to tell you that's great, and to tell your female friend that there's always too much testosterone in the house anyway when you and I get together.'

'Leon, just one thing.' I put a finger to my lips and make a face at Harriet. 'My friend is, um, one whole lot of woman, if you get my meaning, so I'm hoping your floor joists are up to it.'

Harriet flips me the finger, which makes me laugh, and Leon whoops 'Bullshit!'

'Oh, okay. She's actually very small and doesn't eat much. You'll hardly notice she's there.'

'Bring her, bring her. We'll see you at the station tonight, *mes amis*.'

I flip the phone shut and tell Harriet, 'There you are. Totally delighted. Carole said that you'll help rebalance the excess of testosterone that occurs when Leon and I are together, except I can't think what she means by that.'

'Won't they think it strange that you arrive with someone that you only met about an hour ago?'

'By the time we do arrive it'll be about eight hours but yeah, I get your point. We need some sort of a cover story.'

Breakfast arrives. I pack mine away while Harriet drizzles maple syrup and eats about a half of one pancake.

'Are your pancakes okay? You can get something else if you'd prefer.'

'No, they're very good, I guess I'm just not very hungry. I was just thinking about that cover story. You know, with my job its quite possible that we could have met somewhere, and then I went away to somewhere with my job, say, Cambodia, and just came back unexpectedly last night and decided to join you.'

'Brilliant.' I tell her. 'Where did we meet?'

'At a gallery?'

'No. I'd never be able to remember what gallery, and what I was looking at and why I was even there in the first place.'

'Oh, okay. At a bar?'

'My neighbourhood bar in Tribeca. In Reed Street. You were there with some friends, you caught my eye, I spat a cocktail cherry into your drink to impress you and your heart was mine.' I clutch both hands to my chest and flutter my eyelashes at her like a Victorian maiden. She grins at me.

'While I was in Cambodia we communicated by e-mail.' She suggests.

'We did.' I tell her. 'I wrote you poetry.'

'You didn't!'

'I totally did.' I tell her. 'I wrote you poetry which was sort of funny and romantic at the same time.'

'As long as Leon and Carole don't ask me to actually quote any of it.'

'If they do I'll have to make something up.' I tell her. 'Hey, why did you come back from Cambodia so unexpectedly?'

'That's easy. I'm classified as 'non-essential staff' so if the security threat level goes up to a certain point they ship people like me back home pretty fast.'

'Okay. I guess I should probably know some more about your job. What do you do for the mighty UN?'

She pushes the pancakes away and settles herself down in her seat. 'Its development programme stuff. You know, where a country's infrastructure has been shattered by war or just hasn't developed because of poverty and having a crap government the programme sweeps in and makes everything perfect. In actual fact it just makes a few things slightly better but you get the drift. My area of speciality is land use, which means I get to argue a lot with multinational corporations trying to land grab in this week's sexy new developing country.'

'Wow, I'm impressed.' I am impressed. I have a sudden – probably completely erroneous - mental image of her wearing a hardhat and arguing with ranks of swarthy foreign backhoe drivers. 'Best thing about working for the UN?' I ask her.

'Going to Cambodia, probably. Beautiful country, consistently lovely people even though they've been consistently beaten down for generations.'

'Worst thing?'

'Ummm. Probably when I got shot in Serbia.'

'You got shot?' I yelp, making the old couple sitting across the train from us actually jump. She covers her face and groans. 'Actually it was not at all dramatic but it was completely embarrassing. Mostly because I was drunk at the time and didn't even realise I'd been shot.'

'How did you manage that?'

'Well, back then – and this was a few years ago – there were still a few streets it was best to run down because of snipers. I don't think they were even real snipers, just bored teenage boys but there were still a lot of firearms around because of the war. Anyway, me and my girlfriend Kaye had been out drinking some really good local wine and we were running back to the hotel, but possibly not running quite as fast as we should have been. I actually heard the shot but I thought I'd hit by a stone or something, but when we got back into the hotel I could feel something weird, so I lifted up my shirt and there was this bullet sticking up between my ribs. And that was the point at which I fainted, I'm embarrassed to say.'

'The bullet went right through you?' The old couple are desperately trying to listen whilst desperately trying to look like they're not listening.

'No. Apparently what happened was that the sniper was technically out of range so the round hit me in the side, and sort of skidded round one of my ribs to the front. The problem was that everyone thought I was dying from a bullet wound, rather than fainting at the sight of my own blood, and not even very much of it. But there was a big panic and I got rushed to hospital and the UN immediately evacuated everyone out of the hotel because it was supposed to be in a safe area and no-one knew what had happened.'

'And then?'

'Well, nothing really. A lot of people made a lot of jokes at my expense for a while. And I learnt that being shot really doesn't feel the way you expect it to.' The old couple opposite smile and relax. A happy ending. Harriet reaches inside the neck of her shirt and pulls out a leather thong with the actual bullet on it, brassy and slightly flattened. 'There you go. They gave it to me at the hospital. I figured it had my name on it, so best to keep it close, right?' I reach and take it in my hand; it's surprisingly hot to the touch from being against her skin and I find myself trying to think about something else for a few moments. She has those little hollows above her collar bones that I suddenly want to lick raindrops out of. Or maybe snowflakes. Stop it, Rusty. Concentrate.

'Right.' I say. My voice comes out about two octaves lower than it normally does. I cough and change the subject.

'What's that I'm hearing in your accent?'

She smiles. 'You got me. I'm half English. On my mother's side. My father was American which I think makes me not one thing or the other.'

I tell her, 'I think that makes you an honorary Canadian.'

I excuse myself to go to the washroom and when I get back she's talking on the phone, turned in her seat to face the window. I pretend to politely read my newspaper but of course I actually listen in to everything she says. There's a warm, slightly teasing tone in her voice which suggests that she likes whoever she's talking to very much, but I can't tell if the person on the other end of the line is male or female.

'No.' She's saying. 'The Canadian border. I figured it was closer to Poughkeepsie than Mexico, but I did decide to take your advice and keep moving.' A pause. 'He didn't. We had a disagreement about that and I got to spend some quality time in his basement.' Another pause. 'Well, obviously I did, on account of the fact I'm talking to you now. No, I'm fine. Yeah, Montréal.' She cuts her eyes across to me and, too late, I pretend to read an article in the paper about industrial espionage in the insurance industry. 'I've got some friends there I can stay with. I'll be back Wednesday night, okay if I come straight to your place? Great. I'll email you tomorrow. Okay.'

I'll have to change my ticket, I think to myself. Mine's for Thursday. Perhaps we could get one of those cabins.

She hangs up and turns back towards me.

'Boyfriend?' I ask her.

'No, a friend friend.' She tells me. 'I don't have a boyfriend. You?'

'A boyfriend? Actually, I prefer women.'

'You know what I mean.' That tip-tilt again.

'No; I'm divorced. No girlfriend.'

Harriet Morgan

It should be disgusting. It is disgusting, in fact, having that sugar cube spat into her coffee, but simultaneously very funny indeed. Not so much the action itself, but the fact that this reasonably normal-looking middle-aged man should look so very smug about having done it. She feels an emotional gear-shift take place; from flat panic to amused, and the fact that he's clearly done it in an attempt to cheer her up is touching, somehow.

Regarding him sitting across from her, she sees that her initial assessment of his looks has been a little unfair, and what saves his face from terminal geekdom is a back-slash, forward-slash pair of impressive, almost Slavic, high cheekbones and a long hard jaw line. Early forties, she guesses, but when he smiles he shows that he has a badly chipped incisor, which makes him look slightly boyish. He's incredibly tall, even sitting down, must be a touch over six and a half feet and whichever way she sits his knees brush against hers under the table. She can't imagine what his ancestors would have looked like, whereas her own are fairly obvious: a small, pale skinned people built for deprivation, for subsistence farming in the rain. His lot were probably the long-distance runners, the accomplished spear-throwers.

When he asks he to guess what he does for a living she can hardly say coffee shop manager, and anyway there's a quiet confidence in him that suggests a certain income bracket. Subtly expensive watch, a heavy, dull silver chain worn on the other wrist, fleece lined Schott jacket on the seat next to him. Plus the mention of living in the Tribeca district of Manhattan which should probably tell her even more about his income bracket except that she can't remember if Tribeca is now officially fashionable, or now officially over.

His offer for her to stay at his friends' place was rash, and her acceptance possibly even more rash, but it makes sense to her in terms of staying concealed. Impossible, these days, to check into any hotel in North America without them taking a credit card imprint, and she knows that these imprints rapidly become electronic footprints, revealing time and location to anyone with a modem and the know-how. Not sure that Thomas would have the know-how, himself, but he would undoubtedly be able to recruit someone who did. Although Shem didn't strike her as a techie, either. She has a creeping, slightly shameful feeling that she might have got it all wrong about Shem's terrible intentions for her, but she decides to shelve that thought for consideration later.

Tired, anyway, of being told what to do and where to go by anyone who has anything to do with Thomas.

She lies to Chris on the phone a little, pretending that Leon and Carole are established friends that she can stay with. Was tempted to come out with a trite, greeting-card explanation along the lines of a friend being a stranger you haven't met yet, but it would take too long and anyway Chris would think she'd gone nuts. Or suffered a serious blow to the head. Anyway, they just sound like perfectly normal, cheerful middle-class Canadians, and if it doesn't work out she can always revert to plan A. Or at least try and find the sort of hotel that will accept anonymous cash in return for a room. Probably the rates would be by the hour, though. She's stayed in a few of those before, in various countries, the sort of place where you only realise what their principal business is when you notice that all the other guests are couples made up of pretty, giggling young women accompanied by heavily built older men.

Getting up to go to the bathroom, she wonders if the Canadians even have those sorts of hotels in their cities.

Rusty Hanover

I watch her returning from the washroom; she has the long stride, the slightly arrogant hip and shoulder counterpoint which marks the way that very fit people move. Something about her lean thighs suggesting a woman who knows how to ride a horse.

We return to our getting-to-know-you questions; I introduce the sport round.

'I can ride a horse.' I tell her.

'You can?'

'I grew up on a farm.' I tell her. 'Of course I can. You?'

'Yes. Well, not for a few years now, but I assume I still know how.'

'I guessed as much. What else?'

'I have a mountain bike.' She tells me. 'But it hasn't seen much action of late. Oh, and I fence.'

'Post and rail or barb wire?'

She laughs. 'Foil.'

'Is that the stabbing one or the slashing one?'

'The stabbing one. I only really took it up when I was working for the UN abroad because the airlines don't mind you taking your foil in the hold and anywhere the British Army is, there'll be someone to have a fencing bout with. In fact, what's really great is that the Brits call a bout an 'assault', which means that British officers were always coming up to me in a bar somewhere and asking if I fancied an assault sometime.'

I'll bet they did, I think. Instead, I say 'I liked watching the Olympic fencing on TV.'

'I can't watch sport on TV at all. Even the ones I love, I just find it too dull.'

'I'll watch hockey anyhow. Any place, any time, live or on TV.'

'You play?' She asks me.

'Badly. Too tall, I think my centre of gravity's wrong. Used to play football, but not anymore. Oh, and I can ski, but that's a given, being Canadian. I do play tennis sometimes.'

'I'm the worst tennis player in the world.' She tells me. 'Seriously. I have a very good backhand which never actually connects with the ball and I don't know why. So if there's any tennis matches I tend to get to be the ball girl. So to speak.' She giggles at her own accidental double entendre and I grin back. 'It's a shame because some of the UN teams used to have great no-rules tennis matches. Where the ball was in play anywhere, over the fence, on the highway outside. Strip tennis, on occasion.' I raise an eyebrow at her. 'No, I didn't take part else I would have lost immediately and very badly. I always volunteered to umpire on those occasions.'

What a shame, I think. Otherwise there might have been some photos somewhere on the internet.

'The UN,' I tell her, 'Sounds like an unexpectedly fun place to work.'

'It was ok. I mean, what happens when you're in the nastier parts of the world is that the team gels very quickly and you all tend to have a lot of fun whenever you can. Lots of drinking, lots of parties. But I've pretty much stopped the travelling bit now. I had to when I realised that I was thirty-one years old and had never actually owned any furniture.'

'You don't?' I think of all the possessions that have passed through my hands over the years. Houses, furniture, electronics, white goods, cars.

'Well I do now – since June – but I'm very much an amateur. I confess, I understand why people need to own stuff but I'm still confused about why we're supposed to own quite so much of it.'

'We have to, as good citizens. So we can throw it away when we're bored with it, buy new stuff and so keep the economy going.' The train is slowing on its approach to another station. 'Oh, hey, look, its Ticonderoga.' I point out.

She looks up. 'It is?'

'It is. Ticonderoga means its cocktail hour.'

'It does?'

'Absolutely. It's a train rule. If you don't have a cocktail somewhere around Ticonderoga they throw you off before the border.'

'I'd better have one, then.' That tip-tilt at the corner of her eye which always precedes a smile. Nice teeth, generous lips.

'I'll buy you a drink.' I challenge her. 'If you can name me three famous Canadians.'

She thinks a moment. 'Easy. Douglas Coupland, Margaret Attwood, William Gibson.'

'Nuh uh, cheating, they're all authors.'

'Still famous, though.' She insists.

'Maybe, but I don't think they get photographed falling out of clubs drunk.'

'I always thought that Douglas Coupland probably does.'

'Possibly. Oh, okay, I'll accept your first answer, but for a bonus drink, name me one Canadian who's famous in the electronic media, not the printed.'

She thinks longer this time. 'Dan Ackroyd?'

'Correct answer, if a little dated. What are you drinking?'

'Gin and tonic, please.' I order it for her, a double Canadian and soda for me. She stirs hers with the little swizzle stick and sips.

'Okay', I tell her. 'Character round. What do you consider to be your worst fault?'

'Impatience, probably. I've never really been able to understand why everything can't happen exactly when I want it to. I'm not really impatient with people, though. Except maybe really big people who walk too slowly and block the sidewalk.'

'Oh, me too. Always end up walking in the traffic for that reason, which is a pretty dangerous thing to do in New York. More of an extreme sport, really. Any other faults you're prepared to admit to?'

'I'll tell you a fault I've been told I have.' She answers. 'Although I personally don't regard it as a fault.'

'Go on.'

'I've been told I'm unnecessarily independent. To the point of it being infuriating, apparently. I don't like asking for things and I can't stand being told what to do, even if it's done subtly. Perhaps especially if it's done subtly.' She swirls the drink in her hand, sips some more, regarding me over the rim. 'How about you?'

'Me? I don't consider myself to actually have any faults. But I'll tell you the faults I've been told I have.'

'Such as?'

I count them off on my fingers. 'I've been told that I can be a cynical bastard. And that I have a crude sense of humour, which is possibly true.' I pause a moment, tell her, 'There is a third one but you'll just have to find out about that one yourself.' The third one is, of course, that I'm obsessed with sex; an accusation levelled at me by the woman who was shortly to become my ex-wife. I recall that my response at the time was that it was easy to become obsessed with something I wasn't getting, which on reflection may not have helped the situation very much.

'Okay.' I say. 'Leading on from faults, let's do bad habits.'

'You first.' She says.

'The ones I'm prepared to admit to? Well, I'm afraid to say that I smoke cigarettes when I'm drunk.'

'Me, too.' She says. 'And then I wake up the next morning feeling horrible and wondering why I did.'

'I take cocaine occasionally.' Best to get that one out the way.

'I'm not very good with stimulants. But I do smoke weed sometimes. It helps me sleep.'

'I never have problems sleeping.' I tell her.

'I often do. But I come from a family of insomniacs; you could always tell which our house was on any street because it'd be the one with all the lights on at three a.m.'

'You have any brothers or sisters?' I ask.

'Only child. You?'

'Two brothers, one sister. In order of birth: Robert, me, Ricky, Rachel.'

'All Rs.' She notes.

I deliberately pretend to mishear her. 'All arses? That's not very nice. You shouldn't judge the rest of my family just by meeting me, you know.'

'Rs, I said. As in, R for Romeo.' Laughing.

'Oh. Well, my mother said it was a shame but once she'd started she couldn't stop.'

'Couldn't stop having children or couldn't stop giving them names beginning with the letter R?' She asks.

'Both, probably. Be grateful that the fourth one was a girl, else they'd be more of us around.'

Lunch menus arrive, which moves us into the food round and she asks me what my least favourite foodstuffs are.

'Salad dressing.' I tell her. 'Doesn't matter which type, Thousand Island, Blue Cheese, Ranch, they're all disgusting. It's a texture thing. Can't stand mayonnaise, either, for the same reason. Sour cream I can just about cope with, especially in relation to Mexican food. You?'

'Well, I don't eat meat or fish, so that rules out most horrible things. Celery, I think, because it's so stringy and pointless. I mean, a food that actually causes you to expend more energy eating it than you get from it, what's that all about?'

'I can tell from that statement that you've never dieted in your life.' I tell her. 'You haven't, have you?'

'Well, no, I haven't, I'm just lucky, I guess. And I've also probably spent too much time in countries where maximising calorie intake is pretty important for some people, in terms of continued survival.'

'Living in America must really drive you nuts.'

She laughs. 'No, I love it really. But sometimes I do think that America doesn't know how lucky it is.'

I tell her that New York sometimes feels more like a third world country to me.

'It does to me, too.' She says. 'In fact, what New York feels like is a third world country where a quarter of the residents won the lottery and the rest didn't. It's strange, isn't it? Walk two blocks and the whole thing can change completely. I guess that's why I like it so much, it's pretty hard to get tired of.'

'Wait until you see Leon and Carole's place.' I tell her. 'It's gorgeous. Big, sprawling place up on the hill. Great views. Every time I go there I think, this is it, I'm giving up on Manhattan and moving out here. And then after two days I realise that I couldn't because I'd go crazy with boredom.'

'Didn't you grow up on a farm?'

'I did.' I tell her. 'And I went crazy with boredom.'

We eat a fortunately celery and salad dressing free lunch, talk some more, have another drink, talk some more. By my calculation, by the time we arrive we would have spent roughly the amount of two date's worth of time together, except sadly without that tantalising doorstep am-I-going-to-get-asked-in-for-coffee moment at the end. Enough, anyway, that we should be able to pass as enough of a couple not to freak Leon and Carole out.

Twilight now, and the towns along the way have thinned out and been replaced by trees, scattered houses, more trees. A farmhouse in the distance has its outside lights shining on an empty yard in a way that makes it look weirdly exposed, like a brightly lit target in the darkness surrounding it. I spy on Harriet's reflection in the window, she's looking down at the table, lost in her own thoughts, and I wonder if she's thinking about me or her stalker. Me, hopefully. Then the guard interrupts my little reverie by shouting an announcement, first in French, then in English, along the lines that we're stopping at Rouses Point for a half hour for a crew change, and that any passengers wishing to sneak a smoke on the station should avail themselves of the opportunity.

'This is my favourite stop on the whole journey.' I tell Harriet. 'Care to join me?'

'Sure.'

We hop off the train into the cold air outside. It's the first time we've been stood up together and the difference in height is extremely obvious; she doesn't even come up to pocket height on my shirt. Praying that the height thing isn't too much of a turn off for her, I light a cigarette and pass it to her.

'Thank you.'

'You know.' I tell her. 'My mom was wrong about one thing.'

'Which was?'

'Smoking didn't stunt my growth.' She laughs. I say, 'Six feet seven, in case you were wondering.'

'Five feet two, in case you were. I always thought that being tall would be to feel really conspicuous. Does it feel that way?'

'Sometimes, because it makes it difficult to sneak into places unnoticed, but it is really great if you want to show off. Which is what an actor essentially does, so it works for me. What's it like to be short?'

'I always forget I am. I mean, a while ago I was walking down the street with a guy who's around six feet tall, I guess, and he was pointing out this bird perched on the side of a roof across the street. And I couldn't see it, and he was saying, no, it's up there, and I still couldn't see it. And then he crouched down to my height and said, oh no, you can't see it from here, can you? Which was sort of a shock for me, don't ask me why.'

We're interrupted by the engine driver who joins us for a smoke. He tells us that there's some snow fallen up ahead, and that it's early in the year for snow, and we chat awhile about the weather. He can't keep his eyes of Harriet but I can't help noticing, with a little surge of optimism, that she keeps her body turned toward me while we're talking. Eventually he grinds his cigarette out under one boot heel, announces, 'Better get home for my dinner,' and walks off the station, pausing to greet the new crew members walking up the long train to the locomotive and we climb back up into the warmth and light of the car.

Full dark outside now; the train stops at Cantic for the border check. Always a creepy, strangely World War Two movie moment that, actual crossing guards boarding the train to check actual paper documents. Anachronistic in this age of retinal scans and electronic fingerprints. Even though I'm a genuine Canadian citizen it always makes me feel like I might suddenly find that my papers aren't in order, after all, and that I'm about to get dragged off the train to stand shivering and surrounded by guards holding back large salivating Doberman dogs.

The Customs guard who approaches our seats is one big Canuck, belly straining at his uniform belt with all that macho paraphernalia hanging off it. The passport Harriet holds out to him isn't an American one at all, but a tired, faded blue like jeans that have gone through the wash too many times. He examines it closely, and just as I think she's maybe about to have her own Second World War movie experience, he straightens up and gives her a very smart salute. She salutes back.

'United Nations?' He rumbles. 'Welcome to Canada.' I can't help noticing that he's looking her deep in the eyes, and as he gives her back her passport he makes sure to brush his fingers against hers. Back off, buddy, I saw her first. My own passport he gives a cursory examination to and then drops dismissively back onto the table. I don't, I notice, get welcomed to Canada by him.

'Seems you have a fan there.' I tell her as he walks away.

'No, it's just my UN passport. People always assume it means I'm in the Peacekeeping Forces, so they imagine I'm out there fighting for freedom and democracy, or whatever.'

And then it hits me. I'm surprised that I hadn't noticed it before, but then there aren't that many women around like her. Almost all of the terrible things that have happened to her in the last few days are, just possibly, attributable to that one thing.

She has absolutely no idea of how attractive she is.

The train draws into Montréal, and we join the shuffling line of people collecting their luggage from the racks at the end of the coach. Her packsack is her only luggage, it seems, which makes me slightly embarrassed about the amount I have. Big bag, garment carrier, hat box. I sling the bag and carrier over my shoulder and carry the box.

Looking at it, she asks; 'Are you Jewish?'

'Not Jewish.' I tell her. The line shuffles forwards, we're next to disembark. 'There's nothing about me which is. I could prove that to you, but I'd get totally and utterly arrested if I did it here, you know what I'm saying?' For some reason I sound like a farmer again and she hears it.

Skipping down from the train she says; 'They really don't have the letter 'T' in the Canadian alphabet, do they?'

If I knew her better I'd swat her on the bum for that. Instead, I take a long stride forwards and catch hold of her little hand. 'Just remember.' I tell her. 'That I'm a lot bigger than you and can hold you upside down by the ankles anytime I choose.'

I get a look from under her eyelashes.

'You could *try*.' She suggests, and, striding out with her skittering beside me, I'm feeling all full of vim and lust and thinking that it might, in fact, be kind of fun to try.

Chapter Four

Harriet Morgan

She knows that it's Leon and Carole they're walking towards because of the way their eyes find Rusty in the crowd, then look sideways to her. What she sees most on their faces is relief, though whether that's because of the way Rusty looks, or her, its hard to tell. They aren't what she'd expected, anyway, Leon is a tidy, round-faced and quietly handsome man in his fifties while Carole is a little younger, mixed race, maybe African and European; gorgeous. Hourglass figure, spirals of magnificent black hair, latte skin. An animated, lovely face. Already Harriet feels small, pale and somehow desiccated next to her. They sweep her up into the round of hugs and cheek kissing, greetings and, on Harriet's part, apologies for crashing the party.

Carole takes her arm as they walk across the concourse. 'No, no. Like I said, I find I'm overwhelmed by the guyness of it when these two get together so it's a pleasure to have you here.'

Outside, Leon leads them to an enormous blue Jeep and opens the back. 'Your costume?' He asks Rusty as they load his bags into the trunk.

'Costume?' Harriet repeats.

Rusty lets out a loud, fake, horror film type of a gasp, and the two men goggle at each other for a moment.

'She doesn't have a costume.' Announces Leon. 'I'm sorry, Rusty, but you'll have to send her back.'

Leon and Rusty turn to regard her for a moment.

'She won't do.'

'No, she really won't do.'

Carole punches her husband lightly on the shoulder. 'Leave it out, you two. I'm sorry, Harriet, they're treating you just like they treat me, but they forget that I'm used to it. If you don't have a costume then that just gives us ladies the perfect excuse to go shopping together tomorrow. While you guys stay home and pick fleas off each other, or whatever it is you do when you two get together.'

Carole drives, Leon turned round in the passenger seat to talk to Harriet and Rusty in the back.

'I'm sorry.' He tells Harriet. 'It sounds like maybe you weren't aware that we're going to a Halloween party tomorrow.'

'It's a 'P' party.' Carole adds.

'Excuse me?' Harriet says politely.

Rusty laughs. 'No, not that sort of a party. All costumes to start with the letter 'P'. You know, pirates, priests, prostitutes.'

'Proctologists, palm-readers, politicians.' Leon adds.

'Police officers, pineapple growers, pea-pickers.' The two men are trying to outdo each other now, so she tunes them out a while, watching the old city gliding by outside. A weird hybrid of European and American, it looks; old European architecture on a scale that would give a European architect vertigo. The effect is faintly gothic and slightly disturbing so she turns her attention back to the inhabitants of the car. Rusty still has hold of her hand and is rubbing her wrist gently, and probably unconsciously, with one long finger. Her wrist, she notices, is unexpectedly reinventing itself as a previously undiscovered erogenous zone and beginning communications with her other, more traditional erogenous zones. She turns to regard Rusty, that lovely jaw line. And Carole, stopped at a red light, looks round and catches her at it, giving Harriet a wonderfully saucy wink which surprises her until she remembers that this is, after all, exactly how she should be looking at her pretend boyfriend. If he wasn't actually pretend, that is.

She rejoins the conversation, adding; 'Princesses, pilots, pornographers.'

'Pornographer!' Leon slaps himself on the forehead. 'Why didn't I think of that?'

'What would a pornographer wear?' Rusty asks.

'Who cares?' Leon answers. 'It would mean that I could spend my time at the party persuading people to take their clothes off.'

Without taking her eyes off the road, Carole reaches over and lightly pinches his ear lobe between two long scarlet finger nails.

Rusty was right, their house is gorgeous. Large and sprawling, set on a hill above the city but just far enough away that the lights twinkle promisingly; woods behind, a broad sweep of snowy lawn running down at the front to the road. The big trees growing to the front and side with the house lights showing through their branches make her feel strangely Christmassy, two months early. There's even a big marmalade coloured cat waiting for them on the wraparound porch. Leon picks the cat up and sets it on his shoulder where rides looking backward at Harriet, regarding her seriously before issuing a series of odd, one-syllable quacking noises.

Rusty whispers loudly to her. 'The cat is actually animatronic, but don't tell Leon, he thinks it's real.'

'My cat.' Says Leon, 'Is not animatronic. Although I have had reason to believe on occasion that you might be, Rus.'

The ground floor of the house is open plan, spacious, decorated in glowing jewel colours. Bookshelves, paintings, cushions. It's clean, but just untidy enough, Harriet thinks, so that you don't feel like you're messing the place up just by being there. A family house, warm.

Safe.

Rusty Hanover

Carole shows us up to our bedroom which is, of course, the one room. With one adjoining bathroom. And one large bed. I'd obviously anticipated this, but hadn't really liked to say anything. Harriet drops her bag on the bed. She has her back to me, but something about her stance suggests amusement.

'I could tell Carole I'm Catholic.' She suggests.

'She might make you recite the creed to prove it.' I tell her. 'Could you do that?'

She laughs and turns to look at me. 'No. Oh, look, we're both adults, aren't we? We can do this.'

'Sure we can.' I tell her. 'I can sleep on the floor.' Please, god, don't let her make me sleep on the floor.

'This may sound weird, but it wouldn't be the first time I've shared a bed with someone I'm not, you know, with. In fact, several people on occasion.'

I smirk. 'Really?'

'No, I mean, it's sort of a work thing.' She's really digging a hole for herself here, realises it, and starts giggling. 'No! If the UN crew were staying in a place and some fighting broke out then we'd all cram into whoever's room seemed to be the safest. So sometimes we would end up several to a bed. Except we'd normally all be wearing flak jackets.'

Thank you, god.

'I can ask Leon if he has one to lend me.' I tell her, 'If it makes you feel more comfortable.'

She goes to take a shower and I go downstairs to talk to Leon; mostly because I haven't seen him in a while, partly because I don't want to be sat in the bedroom thinking about her naked in the bathroom next door. Leon is sprawled on the couch watching a news channel. I pick the cat up off the armchair opposite Leon and place it gently on the carpet, whereupon it lets out of noise of pure feline disgust and marches off, tail in the air. I've never really got on with cats; for some reason they all hate me.

I take a seat. 'How's the kids?' I ask.

Leon smiles. 'Great. At least I think so. Since they've both been away at university its like they're in the hands of some benign kidnapper. We get phone calls demanding money and hinting at dire consequences if we don't come up with it, so we send cash, and then it all goes quiet again for a while.'

'Doesn't Karine graduate next year?'

'Yes, so maybe some of the extortion will stop then. A high achiever, our Karine, I think she already has plans to take over the Canadian Bio-Chemistry industry.'

I remember Karine, a pretty, scarily intelligent girl. 'Well, with Carole's looks, and Carole's brains, she's bound to go far. And Felix?'

Leon laughs. 'Felix is the sensitive one of the family. In fact.' He pauses, looking suddenly uncomfortable. 'I shouldn't really say this because I haven't discussed it with him. It's awkward, you know? But you remember Felix; he always feels things very deeply. And a bit of a drama queen. But I've had my suspicions about him for a while. I think he might turn out to be...' Leon pauses again.

'What?'

'I think he might turn out to be…'

'You can tell me, Leon.'

'An actor.' Leon whispers, in horror.

'Oh, Leon. I'm so terribly sorry.'

'I know.' Leon is miming wiping the tears from his eyes. 'I told him, please don't do it, just look how your uncle Rusty turned out, but he's determined.'

I laugh. 'Thanks.'

'You're welcome. How about you?'

'How about me what?'

'You and your new lady. You look happy, my friend.'

'I do?'

'Happier than you have in a long time.'

'Well, its early days yet.' I tell him. Something of an understatement, but what the hell. 'But I like her, she's pretty and smart and funny.'

'And a total hard body.'

'And a total hard body. Thank you, I had noticed. But, Leon, you probably know me better than anyone. And I think you'd probably agree that I'm not exactly known for being subtle.'

'Rusty, you have many fine attributes but subtlety isn't one of them.'

'Well, I'm trying to be. I think this one may require a subtle approach and basically I'm trying desperately not to fuck it up. On the grounds that if I do, next thing I know I'll be getting a postcard from her from Basra or some damn place. She works for the UN, in case I didn't already tell you that.'

'You didn't. But I shouldn't worry too much, I've noticed the way she looks at you, boy.'

'She does?' Really?

'Sure. But I can't imagine what she sees in you.'

'Thanks, pal.'

'You're welcome.'

Harriet Morgan

The bathroom has some sort of limestone tiles on the walls and floor that feel warm, almost sandy to the touch. She showers for a long time, enjoying the hot water needling down from the huge chrome rose of a showerhead and thinking about Shem. Is it really possible that she got it so terribly wrong about him, about his plans for her? She tilts her head forward out of the stream of water and applies conditioner, combing it through her hair with her fingers. The bruise on her hip, peach sized and plumb coloured, is still aching from its impact on his basement door. She throws her head back to rinse the conditioner out, deciding that she needs to check something she seems to remember reading about roofies.

She dries her hair and dresses in the bathroom. Watching the steam clearing itself from the mirror she sees that the marks on her neck are still visible, so she goes for a high-necked, modest-women-type-country-approved white shirt and long grey skirt combination. Not sexy, but it would do. Adds some silver jewellery, make-up. Unearths the Toshiba and thumbs the button to start it up, but it signals desperately to her that its batteries are running low, so she carries it out to the bedroom to plug it in to the socket there. The Toshiba finds the household LAN, hooks in, and she Googles Rohypnol.

The contents of her backpack are generally enough to keep her in clean clothes for two days, maybe three, more if laundry facilities are available. She wonders if Leon and Carole will let her use the household washer and gathers up her dirty clothes to go and find out.

Carole isn't around, but Leon and Rusty are sprawled in the living room watching what sounds, from the excited French of the commentator, to be a hockey game. Rusty looks up, smiles.

'Hey.' He says. 'You look great.'

'Thank you. I seem to be running out of clean clothes, though. Leon, may I use your washer?'

'Of course. It's in the basement.' Of course it is, she thinks, how inevitable. The older man starts to get up, but Rusty stops him.

'I'll show her where.' He says.

The door to the basement is, of course, in the kitchen. Rusty gives her a sideways look and opens it for her, finding the light switch.

'You don't need to come down.' She tells him. 'I'll be okay.'

'I know you will. Actually, I just wanted an excuse to sneak a look at Leon's wine collection. Perhaps we should take a corkscrew with us, knock back a bottle of his hundred dollar Chateau Neuf while we're down there.'

The basement is huge, brightly lit, and taken up with a mixture of wall-mounted wine racks and family junk. Piles of skis and poles, two matching pairs of well-used snowshoes, what looks like a tennis net with footballs wrapped up in it. A stack of garden furniture brought in from the cold. She notes, without meaning to, that there's a large door to the outside world on the far wall next to the washer and dryer.

'Look at this.' Rusty reaches up to one of the wine racks, selects a bottle and offers it to her over his arm, displaying the label like a wine waiter. 'Champagne? Proper European stuff, too.'

'I'd love to, but if I start drinking now I'll probably fall over before dinner.'

'You're probably right.' With a look of exaggerated regret, he returns the bottle to its resting place. Rusty in his cheer-up-Harriet mode, but there's something different about him, tonight. Gentler.

She opens the front of the machine, stuffs in underwear, shirts, the t-shirt with the gun oil on it; the little gun still in her bag, now wrapped safely up in a blue bandanna that she found at the bottom of her backpack and can't recall ever wearing. She starts the usual going through the pockets routine with her jeans, turns up her outward train ticket, loose change, and a handful of large, dome-headed screws. Seven dome-headed screws, to be precise. Rusty walks up to offer her a carton of laundry soap and peers over her shoulder.

'Thinking of doing some home improvements?' He asks.

'No. These are Shem's.' Watches him while he remembers.

'Oh. Yeah, of course.' He picks the screws up from where she'd dumped them on top of the washer and lines them up in a neat little row, head to tail. 'I wanted to talk to you about that. What are we going to do about it?'

She stoops to fiddle with the controls of the machine, ostensibly looking for a short wash, letting her hair fall over her face. 'Don't feel you have to do anything. This is my problem, Rusty. You're not a part of this.'

'I am a part of this. Of course I'm a part of this. What do you expect me to do, huh? Say, oh, hey, look me up back in New York, if you're still alive. You really think that little of me?' Not a voice she's heard him use before; he sounds genuinely irritated. Great, she thinks. Well done Harriet, you've managed to piss off another one of them.

'I didn't really mean it that way.' She says, feeling the pinched feeling in the corners of her eyes that means she's going to cry. Thinks, deep breath. Keep it under control. Pours soap powder, finds the button for short wash and presses it.

'Oh, look.' His voice softens, his hands on her shoulders. 'I'm sorry; I didn't mean to upset you.'

'You didn't.' She tries a smile over her shoulder. 'Please don't be all sympathetic and nice because I'm trying to hold it together here.'

He picks her hair up from her shoulders, starts smoothing it back into a ponytail at the nape of her neck which makes her remember Art doing that, and Shem telling him to stop. Seems like a million years ago.

'You ever wear your hair up?' He asks her.

'Sometimes. Generally more for practical reasons, though.'

'I can do you a lovely French braid, if you're interested.'

'You can?'

'I'm a man of many unusual and interesting talents, most of which I hope you'll find out about in time. This particular one comes from having a sister who is ten years younger than me, was born assertive and decided when she was a little girl that I was absolutely the only person in the world who was going to do her hair. Don't ask me why. But let's see if I can still do this.' He drops the nascent ponytail, goes and lifts a wooden garden chair from the stack and sets it down, drops the green plaid cushion from another on the floor in front of it. 'Come on.' He pats the cushion. 'Sit.'

So she sits as instructed, between his knees facing away from him while he starts to gather strands of her hair from above her ears. Strangely soothing; she resists a desire to rest her cheek against his leg. Somehow it's easier to talk to him while not looking at him, too.

‘The thing is.’ She starts. ‘I think I may have got it badly wrong about Shem when I thought that he had some terrible plan for me. I was checking on the effects of roofies earlier, and one of the things I’ve found is that they tend to make someone who has ingested them, quote, exhibit uninhibited behaviour. End quote. And the last thing he said to me before he went and presumably passed out was that he had to keep me safe. I’m not sure if he’d had plans to do otherwise, he’d have been able to say that to me at that particular point.’

Long fingers, smoothing and twining.

‘Okay.’ Rusty says. ‘But I’d have to say that throwing you into his basement wasn’t exactly the best reaction in the circumstances.’

‘Maybe not. But he had just realised that I’d drugged his drink, so maybe it wasn’t so disproportionate.’

‘I don’t think so, but we may have to just agree to disagree on that one. So what next?’

‘Really I need to speak to him. But I don’t have a way of contacting him, so I guess I’ll have to go back to New York and see if he contacts me.’ And hope to god I’m right about him this time, she adds silently. Because if I’m wrong then he’ll be extremely angry and this is likely to end very badly for me.

‘Your ticket’s for Wednesday, isn’t it?’ He asks. ‘Mine’s for the day after but I’ll change it and come back with you. You can hide out at my place for as long as you like, if you want to. And before you say anything, Leon and Carole won’t mind us leaving early, they’re used to me coming and going.’

‘Okay, thank you.’ Thinking that it might come in useful to have another place to hide; Shem knows where Chris lives and if it goes bad she doesn’t want to drag her friend Kaye into it.

‘For the record.’ He adds, ‘My place is on the eighth floor, so I absolutely don’t have a basement.’ His hands have reached the nape of her neck.

‘I haven’t developed a basement phobia, you know.’ She tells him.

‘I’d think it entirely reasonable if you had. I didn’t tell you about my phobia, did I?’

‘You have a phobia?’

‘Everyone does. Except that the more I know about you, the more embarrassing mine is. Alright, I’ll tell you: I’m scared of flying. You may now laugh at me, as I’m aware that you probably catch flights like other people catch buses. Or do you hail them, like cabs? Stick out your hand and a Boeing screeches to a halt on Fifth Avenue?’

'No, I tend to have to catch them from airports, like everyone else. And I'm not going to laugh at you because my phobia is actually more embarrassing than that. I'm terrified of thunderstorms. Hate them. Which is very childish, I know.' From the floor above she becomes aware of the sound of Leon and Carole chatting in French.

'I did used to know someone who was afraid of balloons.' Rusty says. 'A birthday party was his idea of hell. How sad is that?'

'Balloons!' He's succeeded in making her laugh.

The door from the kitchen above opens. Rusty leans forward and whispers in her ear, 'Its Carole, come to tell us off for laughing in her basement.' Which makes her laugh even harder.

It is Carole, but she just calls down to them to check if they'll be ready to go out to eat in a half hour.

'Coming right up.' Rusty calls back, then to Harriet. 'I think we're done here. Have you got a band or something to put on this?'

'Not on me, but I think I've got something in my bag.'

'Well.' He leans forward to pass her the end of her braid over her shoulder. 'You'll just have to hang on to it for the moment. But it's a pretty good effort, if I don't say so myself.'

She runs a hand over the back of her head, feeling the neat vertical line of the braid.

'Thank you.' She says, and yawns.

'Anytime. You tired?'

'A bit, I think.'

'I've got something in *my* bag that could help you with that, if you're interested. I'm just going to take a really fast shower, so if you want, come see me in a few minutes.'

She yawns again. 'I think I may have to.'

Up in the kitchen, Carole is looking fabulous in a scarlet knit dress and black leather boots, a twist of gold and rubies at her throat.

'Love your dress.' Harriet tells her.

'Thank you. Love your hair.' The simple call and return of two women who have decided to be friends.

Carole adds, 'I never did master doing one of those; I thought it was impossible to work behind your own head.'

'Me, too. Rusty did it.'

'He did?' The older woman gives her a flirty, pursed lip look. 'He really does have hidden talents, doesn't he?'

'So he tells me.'

'You need something to secure the end of that?'

'I think I have an elastic band or something in my bag.'

'That deserves something more glamorous than elastic. Hold on a moment.' Carole swirls out of the kitchen, returning with a jewelled clip, grey and jet. 'There you go.'

'Thanks.' Harriet snaps the little claws of the clip over the twisted ends of her hair. 'That's lovely.'

'Its just rhinestone. Keep it, looks better on you.' The two women smile at each other a moment, and Harriet fights a sudden desire to hug Carole, tell her all her problems, ask her advice.

Instead, she says, 'Thanks again, then. And thank you for letting me crash the party.'

Carole flaps a hand at her. 'Really, it's good to have you here; Rusty is certainly on his best behaviour and I think it can only be your influence.'

'Is he really that bad?'

Carole laughs a lovely deep laugh. 'The two of them together can be. I will tell you some stories, but I'll tell you over dinner so I can embarrass them both, it'll be more fun that way. But don't worry, its nothing terrible, just boyish misbehaviour, and mostly very funny. Except sometimes I have to act like I'm Mom, and pretend to be cross when really I'm dying to laugh.'

Rusty Hanover

I shower down and towel off, noticing in the mirror while I'm dressing that I need to get a haircut. I have the sort of curly hair that does nothing for ages and then overnight turns into something that looks like it'll need a large Australian wielding a pair of shears to control it. I rub a blob of gel into it in the vain optimism that it'll help. Hopefully the restaurant will be dark enough so that Harriet doesn't notice that her ersatz boyfriend has hair that looks like bad topiary.

When I open the bathroom door she's sitting on the bed, reading, wearing a high-necked long sleeved blouse and an ankle length skirt, both well enough cut to hint at the lithe body underneath. Barefoot, she looks like a woman from the sort of cult or sect that prefers its women attractive but insists on them being covered up, and the braid I've given her somehow echoes that while bringing out the lovely slant of her eyes and cheekbones. A genius move on my part, that; a nice, non-threatening physical contact even though I had to forcibly restrain myself at times from leaning forward and kissing the naked nape of her neck.

I casually ask her if she wants to indulge in some marching powder and she nods. 'Kindly step this way, if you will.' I say, waving her into the bathroom where I've set out a couple of lines on my travel mirror; the bigger one for me, a littler one for her on account of how she obviously doesn't do this often and I don't want her eyes to be spinning like pinwheels during dinner. I roll two twenties – U.S., of course, I'm not going to despoil the Queen with narcotics - and hand one to her.

When we're done having our noses in the trough I wipe the residue off the mirror with a finger tip and lick it, wishing I knew her well enough to offer to let her suck my finger instead.

'It would probably be better.' I suggest. 'If you don't mention this to Leon.'

'He's anti-drug?' She asks.

'Not especially, but there's a bit of history. Many, many years ago Leon and I did stand-up together, with a reasonable amount of success. Problem was, I graduated very quickly from enjoying a nice glass of red wine before going onstage, to needing the entire bottle plus industrial quantities of cocaine. Leon called a halt to it; I mean, both the stand-up and the cocaine. Which is probably a good thing, else I'd have ended up wearing my nose in my hand. But I think Leon would be a little unhappy with me if he knew I still used it occasionally.'

She smiles up at me. 'Okay.'

'That's very understanding of you.'

Something, possibly the coke, has brought a gleam to her eye and a flush to her cheek.

'Not at all.' She says. 'I just thought it might be useful to have something to threaten to blackmail you with, if needs be.'

I reflect that if she was from the sort of sect that likes to control its women, she'd certainly be trouble.

Leon shouts up the stairs that the taxi has arrived and I pause to wait for her to zip her boots up, which is always a fine thing to watch a woman do, and then we gallop down the stairs together. I manage to arrange getting into the cab so that I'm crammed in the back seat with Harriet next to me in the middle and Carole next to her; Leon gets the little jump seat opposite us.

On the way into to the city Harriet asks Leon if there's likely to be an ATM anywhere near the restaurant. 'I just realised I don't have any Canadian dollars.'

'We call it an ABM around here, sister.' I tell her. 'But its okay, I have cash.'

'Can you change me some US dollars for some Canadian?'

I take advantage of the taxi swinging around a tight turn to rest my thigh against hers. 'Who was it who described you as being infuriatingly independent?' I ask her. 'No, you'll just have to buy me dinner in return when we're back in New York.'

'Watch out, Harriet.' Leon says. 'Or he'll have you buying him dinner in Nobu.'

'That'll be fine.' She says. 'As long as he doesn't mind dining on a glass of water and a bread roll.'

'Unlike you.' I tell Leon. 'Harriet isn't impressed with places like Nobu.' This is a wild guess on my part, but something tells me I'm right.

'No, I'm not really.' She says. 'For a start, I never know what to wear, but really I'm just not that much of a foodie. I always think that eating out is more about who you're eating with, rather than what you're eating or where you're eating.'

'I take your point.' Carole says. 'But ideally, shouldn't it be a combination of the two things; good food and good people?'

'I'm sure you're right.' Harriet responds. 'Maybe I'm just biased, because the best restaurant that I ever went to in New York was with someone who turned out to be the worst person. I didn't last beyond the appetisers.'

I'm sure she's talking about Thomas.

Leon says, 'Well, I hope you get to the entrees tonight, at least.'

The taxi ride takes us through downtown and along a couple of Montréal's more notorious streets, lined with neon-lit clubs promising girls, girls, girls. Or rather, *filles, filles, filles*. The type you pay for, I mean, and some particularly French legal quirk means that around here you can actually get to touch the dancers; a fact made explicitly obvious by the signs outside some of the clubs. It's the sort of thing which makes me feel vaguely ashamed of being male; in fact, in Harriet's company it's the sort of thing which makes me want to find a lawyer and swear out a deposition, signed and sealed, along the lines that I'd rather shoot myself in the head than have to pay money to touch a woman, especially an exotic *danseuse* already sticky with other men's fingerprints.

The restaurant is one I've been to before with Leon and Carole; French, of course, but a nicely laid back version of French, along with a decent wine list. Dark, raw brick walls and almost entirely lit by candles set in front of mirrors which are set next to other mirrors, so that to casually glance at your own reflection is to see infinity, which is horribly confusing when you're drunk. Not that I'm drinking much, tonight, because if I'm going to be sharing a bed with this luminous creature sat opposite me I need to be able to do it without committing any major crimes. Preferably not any minor ones, either.

Harriet Morgan

The drug has lent her a pleasant caffeine buzz, rather than any major high, and she decides to relax and enjoy the evening as a break from reality; time enough to start worrying about Thomas and his accompanying cast of characters once she's on the way back to New York. A strangely intimate thing, though, taking the drug with Rusty; standing next to him in the bathroom made her suddenly aware of the tremendous difference in their respective heights. Tonight he's wearing a burgundy stripe shirt, black pants, black shoes, looking very tall and handsome. Of all the times for her dormant libido, long scared away by Thomas, to return and start scratching and meowing at the door she wonders why it has to choose now.

What the heck, she tells herself. Relax and enjoy.

Despite being in a sleazy part of town, the restaurant is lovely, brilliant stars of candle light all around the walls. Once they're seated and done with the menus and wine lists, Carole asks her about the UN.

'What places have you travelled to?'

Harriet dreads this question, because to list them sounds like a boast and then to say that some of them were very much like the others sounds arrogant. She partially avoids the question.

'Some of South America, Eastern Europe, some Asian countries.' She responds. 'I tell you what, though. Before today I've never been to Canada.'

As predicted, this produces mock-horrified gasps around the table.

'Well.' She explains, 'Almost all of my travel has been for work and for some reason Canada has never required the assistance of the UN development programme.'

'Well, it should.' Rusty says. 'Because you won't get shot in Canada. At least, you won't get shot unless you should happen to go up into the woods, dressed as a caribou.'

'You've been shot?' Carole asks, concern on her face.

Harriet gently kicks Rusty under the table, which he responds to by letting out an exaggerated howl of pain.

'Only once. And it was only a scratch, not at all dramatic. Or interesting.' She pulls a face at Rusty who responds by blowing her a kiss. Time to deflect the conversation away from herself. She reaches for her wine glass and asks, 'What do you do, Carole?'

'I work for Leon.' She says. 'But don't ask me what my salary is, because I don't have one.'

'Ouch.' Says Leon. 'These days I direct films, in case you were wondering, Harriet.'

'Leon.' Says Rusty, 'Directs very clever, intellectual films which tend to have a lot of sex in them. But the sex always takes place in almost complete darkness, which makes them artfully erotic rather than pornography, apparently. Interestingly, Leon has never ever given me a part in one of his films.'

'They're French language films.' Leon defends himself. 'You don't speak French.'

'Of course I do.' Rusty says, and quotes in a polished French accent: 'Je ne regrette rien.'

Leon laughs. 'That's a line from a song.'

'Your point being?'

'My point being that just because you can sing, say, a Youssou NDour song, doesn't mean you actually speak Senegalese.'

'As a matter of fact, I can sing a number of Youssou NDour songs. And as a result I'd get by fine in Senegal; just as long as anything I wanted there was seven seconds away.'

'He actually sang that one in French.' Says Leon. 'Which sort of proves my point.'

Carole leans over to Harriet. 'Now do you see why I'm so glad you're here?' She says. 'Otherwise I'd have to put up with this on my own. Which reminds me.' Carole drains her wine glass and a waiter spins by to refill it. 'Harriet was asking me about your escapades, you two.'

Rusty groans. 'Oh no. Please, Carole, don't. In case you haven't noticed, I've been trying to impress this woman. You know, telling her how rich and famous and classy I am.'

'Well, its time to undo all that. But I can't decide which one to start with. Possibly the most recent? Which would be the infamous statues incident, I believe.'

'Please, Carole.' Rusty says. 'I'll give you money. Honestly.' Getting out his billfold. 'How much do you want?'

Leon leans back in his chair and laughs, tells Harriet, 'Carole is referring to a little misunderstanding we had with the police the last time Rusty and I went out drinking.'

'You're no help at all, are you, Leon?' Rusty says. 'Alright, I'll tell the story. Well, it was a beautiful moonlit night in July and we were walking along, looking for a cab home. It was the sort of moonlight that makes everything look amazingly white, you know? And as we walked past the statues by the museum we thought…'

'You thought.' Interrupts Leon.

'As I was saying.' Rusty continues, 'We thought that it might be fun to be statutes ourselves, and then frighten passers-by when we suddenly moved. Unfortunately, we then thought…'

'You thought.'

'We then thought that it might be more authentic if we took our clothes off.'

'Oh no.' Harriet starts to giggle.

'We didn't take all our clothes off.' Leon reassures her. 'I definitely remember that we kept our underpants on.'

'And then the police turned up.' Rusty continues, 'And they didn't think it was funny, which was a real shame because we did.'

'You got arrested for indecent exposure?'

'Actually, for illegal solicitation. The police decided that we were doing it for the money, the way those human statue guys do in tourist places.'

'And then I.' Carole interjects, 'Get a three a.m. call from Leon asking me to find a lawyer and come downtown.'

'Did you?' Harriet asks her.

'Hell, no. I turned over and went back to sleep. I knew they were in a safe place.'

'In what way.' Rusty asks her, 'Did being in a jail cell in our underpants seem safe to you? We very nearly made some new friends that night.'

'I have to tell you.' Leon says to Harriet, 'That we were actually sharing a cell with each other and no-one else. Just in case you're worried.'

Rusty says, 'All the same, by morning I'd started to find you attractive, Leon, which is worrying in itself. But there was a happy ending, in that the police eventually dropped the charges and let us go home. And the lovely Carole relented, and came to pick us up.'

'Fortunately.' Carole says. 'The police had given them their clothes back by then.'

Rusty says, 'Harriet can't pretend to be too shocked by this. I've heard all about those UN strip tennis games.'

'We only ever held those where there was an enclosed court.' Harriet defends herself. 'Just in case anyone was concerned that we were upsetting people in the kind of country where a woman showing her bare arms counts as indecent exposure. And in my defence I never played; I only umpired on those occasions.'

Rusty smiles at her, looking her straight in the eyes. 'I think that actually makes it worse, saying that. It makes you sound like some sort of kinky voyeur.' He catches her feet between his two ankles and holds them a moment, just in case she decides to kick him again.

'Somebody had to keep score.' She tells him.

Rusty Hanover

The food arrives and we chow down, and I talk to Leon for a while about his latest project which sounds like another of his darkly sensual and tragic gothic romances, and likely to be just as phenomenally successful as all the rest. The two women are talking about Islam and I tune into their conversation for a moment, hearing Harriet say, 'I have actually worn one of those. What's horrible about them is that you totally lose your peripheral vision, which makes it impossible to cross the street. And if you're out with female friends you either have to stick very closely together or hope that you'll be able to recognise them by their shoes.' I wonder briefly what she's talking about, then realise she's talking about wearing a burkha. I'm not sure if it makes me racist or sexist that I find the concept of her wearing one of those quite sexy. Probably both. Leon then says something to me which I miss completely.

'Pardon me?'

He laughs at me. 'When you've finished drooling over your girlfriend, I was asking you if we should get another bottle of wine.'

'And some water.' I suggest. Leon raises an eyebrow. 'I don't want to be too drunk tonight.' I tell him. He smirks, and turns to wave at the waiter. While they're chatting away in French, presumably about which exact estate the water comes from, I tune back into the conversation beside me.

Harriet is saying, 'It's an advisory one for governments in terms of land use. Because as soon as a country starts to develop in economic terms, land values rise sharply, so we give them advice about putting policies in place to ensure that their vulnerable people don't miss out. Like demolishing shanty towns to make way for luxury hotels, we advise them on striking deals with the developing corporation to secure land or homes for the people who have been displaced.'

'Wouldn't it be better.' Carole asks, 'If if the people in the shanty towns just went back to their farms or whatever?'

'I don't think so. Because anywhere an economy starts to heat up it starts in the cities and you'll get urban drift of the population, no matter what. And farming isn't where it's at anymore, not if you want a decent chance of feeding your family and educating them and getting them some sort of healthcare.'

'Doesn't it worry you that you're just exporting a sort of imperialism to these countries? Like, 'you should do it this way because we have'?'

'I hope not. The stance I take is that I'll advise a government that this paradigm has worked here, this one hasn't worked, this one has partly worked. There are some really good examples coming out of Scandinavia on how to mix development, so you'll get some employment, some big houses for rich people, some subsidised houses for poor people. Unlike the U.S. policy model, which seems to be that you should build a big wall around your poor communities, at least metaphorically, and then leave them to it.'

Leon has started listening in by now, and mouths the word 'paradigm' at me. I wave him away; I'm listening here. But Harriet has seen him, and stops.

'I'm sorry.' She says. 'I'm talking too much.'

'No, you're not.' I tell her. This is a new Harriet, animated and passionate, and I'm fascinated. 'But I have to take issue with your farming comment, because that's my background and I have to say that none of us actually starved to death.'

'I don't know about Canada specifically, but I bet you.' She responds, 'That the income from your family farm is subsidised by the government.'

'Ok, you win, it is.'

She offers me a smile as consolation. 'Almost all first world farming is, otherwise it wouldn't survive.'

'There's an argument.' Carole says, 'That subsidising farming in the richer countries is unfair on the developing ones, because it stops them being able to compete.'

'And I'd agree with that in principle.' Harriet responds. 'But there's one really important reason why all countries need to maintain their capacity to produce basic foodstuffs. Rusty will know why that is.'

I will? She's looking at me very levelly and I know I'm being challenged here. I fish mentally for the answer and it comes back to me, thank god.

'Because a country that can't produce its own food is basically screwed if it ever goes to war with its neighbours; in this example, the States.' I say. I hope I get an 'A' grade for that one.

'So how do you do it?' Leon interrupts. 'I mean, persuade governments that they should be looking after their people. Wouldn't it be easier for them not to?'

'Pure economics.' She says. 'Really poor people are expensive. They get ugly diseases and put tourists off. They might riot and threaten your administration or discourage inward investment. So as a government either you try and kill them off, which has been tried in some places, or you support them to a point where they can at least become a low paid, but reasonably healthy and motivated workforce. I can't remember who it was said that most governments aren't very good at keeping their people alive; I think that's true. But all governments understand economics.' She reaches for her wine glass. 'And now I'm going to be quiet.'

Governments, wars, macro-economics. Unsurprisingly, my backhoe image of Harriet was completely wrong.

'I bet you're a killer in the boardroom.' I tell her.

'Me?' A half smile. 'No, I'm just a pussycat, really.'

'One with claws. And sharp little teeth.' I get out my pack of cigarettes. 'Lets take this outside.'

The restaurant has a nice patio out back, complete with seats and candles, but also fortunately cold enough to give me the excuse to put an arm around Harriet's shoulders and draw her in under the side of my coat. She doesn't object, and we stand and smoke in companiable silence like that for a while.

'I like your friends.' She tells me.

'Good. They like you too. Especially Carole, I think. She doesn't always take to, uh, people, immediately, so that's a compliment.' Thinking about my ex-wife, who Carole had hated on sight with a passion that was quite unlike her, and then the two of them maintained a relationship based on frosty politeness for the entire five year lifespan of my marriage.

'I never did find out what she does when she's working for Leon.' Harriet says.

'She was a make-up artist when they met. A good one, too. Now she mostly works as wardrobe mistress for his films.'

'I always think the title 'wardrobe mistress' sounds wonderfully sort of S&M.' She says.

'It does, doesn't? Along with 'weapons master'. But 'best boy grip' is even better as a film credit. Or even 'rigging grip'.' She laughs at this and I hug her to my side, briefly, and then let her go.

Back inside, Leon and Carole are leaning across the table talking to each other and they both stop and look up in a way that tells me that they've been talking about us.

'It's okay.' I tell them as I sit down. 'You can carry on talking about us. In fact, we were talking about you. Harriet thinks that the title 'wardrobe mistress' sounds kinky.'

'It can be.' Carole says. 'That depends entirely on the movie. In fact, I remember a movie some years ago, Rusty, when you…'

'Oh please don't.' I interrupt her. 'I haven't yet told Harriet about that particular film; I was saving it as a surprise. Please Carole, I'm begging you.'

'Oh, alright. It's so nice to see you crawl, Rusty. But I do know that Felix downloaded it from the internet, so if you don't behave yourself I'm going to mail the DVD to Harriet.'

'Why.' I ask the room in general. 'Do I seem to spend my whole time being blackmailed by women?'

The two women in question disappear to the washroom together to do whatever it is that women do in washrooms together. Which is an interesting thought, but possibly not one I should pursue considering one of the women is the wife of my best friend and I'm supposed to have reasonably honourable intentions toward the other.

Instead, I ask Leon if he thinks I should be concerned that my girlfriend appears to have a considerably higher IQ than me.

Leon shrugs and smiles. 'Welcome to my world.' He says. 'It's never done me any harm.'

The women return, and I can't resist asking Harriet what it is that they do in washrooms together.

Harriet turns to Carole. 'He doesn't know.'

'Leon doesn't know, either.' Carole responds.

'Wait a minute.' Harriet is looking perplexed. 'I thought it was law that, once you were married, you had to tell your husband exactly what it is that women do in restrooms together.'

Carole frowns a moment, and then her face clears. 'I see the misunderstanding here. You're confusing the American matrimonial restroom disclosure law with the Canadian washroom disclosure law. In fact, in Canada it's not law at all, but only voluntary disclosure. But of course Canada has always been at the forefront of women's rights.'

'Ahh.' Harriet says, regarding me over the top of her wineglass. 'I see. That's very interesting.'

Leon looks from woman one to the other. 'Harriet.' He says. 'If you don't mind me saying, I think you've been spending a little too much time with Rusty.'

Chapter Five

Harriet Morgan

Once they're back home at Leon's place the two guys settle themselves in the living room with a bottle of whiskey but Carole excuses herself to go to bed, so Harriet takes the opportunity to do the same. Which gets her neatly around the potentially awkward moment where she and Rusty would have had to work out how to undress and get into the same bed whilst physically avoiding each other, but she then remembers that the t-shirt she normally sleeps in is still sitting in a damp pile at the bottom of Leon and Carole's washer.

Damn. She really has nothing else which would count as decent enough to share a bed with a stranger in. If there is such a thing.

She walks to the head of the stairs and calls down.

'Rusty?'

'Yo!'

'Can I borrow one of your t-shirts?'

A short pause, then, 'Sure. Look in my big bag, should be something in there.'

'Thanks.' She delves into his bag, coming up with a Calgary Stampede t-shirt, size extra-huge, that hangs off her shoulders and comes down to her knees. Fine; perfectly respectable, perfectly unsexy. She does the bathroom thing, lets her hair down out of its braid and then gets into bed, making sure to roll over on her side to face away from the currently vacant side of the bed. No idea what side of the bed he normally sleeps on, but too late to worry about that now.

She dozes for a while, then is woken by Rusty moving around the room in that exaggeratedly careful way that the slightly drunk do when they're trying to be quiet. She lies there and listens to the man noises in the bathroom. Pee, flush, water running in the sink. The brushing of teeth. Rinse, spit. The lights in the bedroom go off and she feels the mattress shift and adjust to his weight on it. And then she sleeps a luxurious few hours before waking to find that, during the night, Rusty has wrapped his considerable length of body around her.

It's dark outside, but feels like early morning. She's still lying on her side, facing away from him, legs slightly bent. His knees tucked against the back of hers, his face in her hair, one arm slung over her waist with his hand flat against her stomach. And his erection nudging gently but persistently against her left buttock.

Ah.

What she should do is unwrap him gently from around her, and manoeuvre him, still safely asleep, back to his side of the bed.

And then his hand starts to move. Very slowly, over the fabric of the t-shirt, brushing across her stomach, down to her hip, back again.

Oh.

Oh, yes.

The hand, questioning, travels upwards, nearly to her breasts, pauses, travels back downwards.

Oh, yes.

Oh, yes, *please*.

And then his voice in her ear, gravely with early morning and last night's drinking. 'Are you okay with this?' He says.

'Oh, yes.' She says, and stretches her body down against him, arching her back, pointing her toes.

'I'd love to kiss you.' He says. 'But I think I have terrible breath. But I could…' He lifts her hair and kisses the nape of her neck and across to her shoulder and she can feel his stubble against her bare skin and has to clamp her back teeth together to stop herself from moaning out loud. Trying not to start the big give-away flexion of her hips.

She enjoys this for a while but aware that she's being selfish, she rolls over to face him.

'Would you like to..?' He asks quietly.

'Oh, yes.'

The difference in their respective heights makes it feel exotic, almost dirty; like two different species mating.

Rusty Hanover

Harriet has sprinted up to bed alone, which possibly isn't a good sign, and then calls back down to ask if she can borrow a t-shirt.

Oh god, as if this wasn't hard enough, she hasn't brought anything to sleep in.

So I have a couple more drinks with Leon, on the vague grounds that this will help me go to sleep, and then have to turn in before I get drunk enough to try anything stupid.

She's sound asleep when I get up there, so I tiptoe around so as not to disturb her and then sort of slide into bed and lie there on my back because I have to, basically, and pray for sleep to come.

And then I do sleep, and wake up, warm, comfortable, and with a woman in my arms.

I'm fairly sure there shouldn't be a woman in my arms.

I'm absolutely convinced there shouldn't be a woman in my arms.

During the night my body, without the express permission of my brain, has tucked itself cosily around her; my hand on her stomach, my face in the wild tangle of her hair which smells, I notice, of perfume and that faint, burnt popcorn tang of cigarette smoke. My legs bent against the back of hers and my morning erection, I'm afraid to say, resting against her ass.

What I'll do is ease myself slowly away to my side of the bed and go back to sleep.

What I'll do any moment now is ease myself slowly away to my legitimate side of the bed and go quietly back to sleep.

What I really will do right now is ease myself slowly away to my legitimate side of the bed and hope that I can go quietly back to sleep. Except that my hand, still acting without my brain's permission, finds something on the flat of her stomach.

It feels like a piercing, the kinky little thing.

This obviously needs to be explored, so my fingertips go on a little foray of their own and establish that what she has there is a navel piercing, the type with the little bar that goes through the skin above, with what feels like a jewel resting there on her belly button.

Well, well, well.

Just to check that there are no other interesting surprises, my hand moves itself down to the smooth ridge of her hip. She's wearing my Calgary t-shirt, and the fabric of it is definitely getting in the way of much further exploration.

What to do.

They say that a stiff penis has no conscience but most of the rest of me does, in fact, so I prop myself up on one elbow and look down at her. Her hair is over her face and her eyes are closed, but I swear I detect a faint smile there.

'Are you okay with this?' I ask her.

Definitely a smile. 'Oh, yes.' She says.

Oh yeah.

After all that garlic and wine and everything else consumed last night I know I have kryptonite breath which is a shame because I really want to kiss her. Instead, though, I realise a shortly but passionately held ambition, and lift her hair away from the nape of her neck so I can kiss here there and then down over one naked shoulder.

That t-shirt is definitely getting in the way here.

I start to ask her, 'Would you like to...' but struggle with finding the appropriate verb: 'fuck' being too brutal, but 'make love' being altogether too soft focus to describe all the things I want to do with her right now this minute.

Fortunately she saves me the trouble by saying yes anyway. And then she drops the bombshell.

'Do you have a condom?'

A condom.

I definitely do not have a condom. Why don't I have fifty of the damn things, in various colours, flavours and textures? In fact, and in purely technical, prevention of pregnancy terms, we don't actually need one, but if I say that I'll sound like a man trying to get out of wearing a condom, which is not exactly how I want to come across right now.

'I don't.' I say hopelessly. 'Do you?'

'No. Oh, hang on a minute...I might, just...stay right there.' She dives out of the bed, revealing on the way that she's not wearing any panties, a fact which I'm very grateful I didn't know a few hours ago.

She rummages in her bag and comes up with something plastic wrapped, which she throws to me and I sit up and catch. It is, the writing on the little heat-sealed bag tells me, a US Army Comfort Pack. Disposable razor, toothbrush, doll-sized tube of toothpaste, sachet of shower gel. And three condoms.

'God bless America.' I tell her, tearing into the bag with my teeth.

We end up kneeling on the bed, facing each other, and I pass her one of the condoms which she unwraps and puts on me with neat, rather nurse-like gestures. Once I'm safely shrink-wrapped she bends to plant a kiss on me, and then pauses to look up at me from possibly the best angle that a woman can ever look up at you.

'You'd better go easy on me, big guy.' She says. 'I'm not sure whether to be impressed or scared.'

I think that this may be one of the happiest moments of my life so far.

I really can't wait any longer, so I pull off my t-shirt, I mean the one of mine that she's wearing, and then the one that I'm wearing, and lose my underpants somewhere and wrap myself around her. She has a swimmer's shoulders, tapering down to a narrow waist and boyish hips, small breasts which are completely perfectly formed. I offer each one a greeting with my lips and she throws her head back and I totally can't wait anymore.

I bear down on top of her and we arrange our limbs in the traditional way. She's hard-thighed and tight muscled when I enter the velvet of her and I start to move, very slowly, very carefully, easing myself up over the topography of her hips, ribs, breasts. Her eyes are closed and she's biting her lip, which leads me to think she might be noisy, given the right situation. Nothing sexier than a woman who can vocalise her pleasure.

'You alright down there?' I ask her, and she opens her eyes wide, and looks at me for one terrible moment as if I wasn't who she was expecting to see there at all, and gasps, 'Oh, no.' And then she comes, hard; I can feel the shockwaves move through her body and she brings her knees right up against my ribs and clamps her heels against my ass, driving me on like I'm a horse.

I'm not normally lost for words but the most detailed explanation I can offer her for what's about to happen to me is; 'If you…I can't…'

And then it's all over for me, with a rush that feels so good it's almost painful.

If I collapse on top of her she'll probably suffocate so I roll off to one side and we lie there a while, panting. The little jewel in her belly button is an emerald, I note, and just above I can see a little puckered scar with a line of crinkled skin leading to it from between her ribs.

'Is that where you got shot?' I ask her. 'Looks more like a burn.'

'It is a burn, technically. Bullets are hot, as I found out.'

'I guess they are.' I say. I trace it with a finger. 'It's kind of sexy, actually.'

What isn't sexy at all is the fact that I'm still wearing the condom, upon which our fluids – so lovely in their place – are rapidly cooling and becoming rather disgusting. Nothing for it but the bathroom sprint. If this was Hollywood there'd be a convenient sheet I could wrap around myself at this point, but if I steal the quilt it'll leave her naked and cold, which isn't exactly gentlemanly, so there's nothing for it but for me to roll out of bed and make for the bathroom naked, hoping that my ass looks ok to her.

As I flush the condom I call out, 'Swim boys, swim for the ocean' to my departing seminal fluid. I wash and brush up, and when I jump back into bed beside her she's still giggling about this.

'They're going to be so disappointed when they find that they're in a Montréal sewer.' She says.

'Don't all sewers lead to the sea? I have a hope that they might make it through, and surprise an octopus. Did you know that octopuses have a sort of detachable penis which swims off after the female?'

'No, I didn't know that.' She says, amused.

'It's a good thing that us humans don't have that facility. Imagine, you go to a party and your penis detaches itself and starts following the hostess around. Or, worse, someone leaves a window open and it takes off after the pretty parking attendant outside.'

She gives this some consideration. 'Human evolution being what it is, I think the women would have come up with something to deal with it. Like, we'd all be wearing catcher's mitts the whole time.'

'Think how terrible that would be for us guys. Instead of 'no, I don't want you to call me' it'd be, 'here, have your penis back'.'

She laughs at this and I roll over and kiss her on the lips. She pulls away.

'Cheating.' She tells me. 'You've brushed your teeth.' She slips out of bed and I make a grab for her ankle and miss. As she crosses to the bathroom I notice that she has a tattoo next to her spine and one hell of a bruise on the back of her hip.

'My little antelope.' I say to her when she returns, smelling of toothpaste. I draw her back into my arms, her little feet cold against my shins. 'That's what you reminded me of, when I saw you at Poughkeepsie. One of the springy ones. You're lovely, do you know that?'

Possibly to shut me up, she kisses me and we spend some very pleasurable time at that, kissing, touching. Somehow her supple body has ended up on top of mine and I'm hard again; something that she can't have failed to notice.

'Care to go around again?' I ask her. She braces herself away from me, her hands flat on my chest.

'I'd love to.' She says. 'But on the grounds that I may actually have to be able to walk today, I can't. In fact – what time is it?'

I grope for my watch on the nightstand. 'Around eight thirty.'

She gets up. 'I'm going to go take a bath.'

'Mind if I join you?' My feet are sticking out of the bottom of the quilt and she grips my big toe between her fingers as she passes.

'Go back to sleep.' She tells me.

'In a minute. Just for the record, I was totally asleep when I intruded on your side of the bed; just so you know I hadn't intended to molest you without your consent. But I'm very glad that you didn't run away screaming.'

She pauses in the bathroom doorway. 'Oh, I couldn't have run away.' She says.

'What was it that stopped you? My animal magnetism? My raw male sexuality?'

'No.' Her eyes tilt with an incipient smile. 'I couldn't have moved at all, at the time. You were lying on my hair.'

Harriet Morgan

She lounges in the tub for a time, reading, enjoying that old feeling of deep tissue relaxation that, she has to admit to herself, she hasn't felt in a while; her body feeling simultaneously slightly tender and very pleased with itself. After a while she hears morning noises starting to come from the rest of the house; a toilet flushing, someone running down the stairs and then back up, so she gets out, dries off, dresses in last night's skirt and a clean long sleeve shirt, remembering her laundry still left in the machine downstairs. Her hair is still crinkled from last night's braid so she leaves it that way, pushing it back from her shoulders.

Out in the bedroom Rusty is asleep on his front, arms flung out to either side like a man who's been crucified. As she goes to collect her bag he wakes & rolls over. Smiles. White teeth against dark razor stubble; she resists a sudden desire to crawl straight back into bed with him.

'I'm going after some coffee.' She tells him.

'Great idea. I'll join you in a few minutes.'

She's putting the coffee on when Carole walks into the kitchen, barefoot and yawning, wearing a wonderful leopard spotted robe.

'Good morning.' Carole says. 'Sleep well, did you?' She's looking highly amused about something.

A terrible thought occurs to Harriet. 'You couldn't hear us, could you?'

The older woman laughs. 'Oh, no, honey. It was the singing gave it away.'

'Singing?'

Carole turns for the door, crooking a finger over her shoulder, and then starts to tiptoe up the stairs in exaggerated, cartoon-like fashion. Harriet follows her. At the top of the stairs they pause by the door of the guestroom, Carole holding a finger to her lips, eyes wide. Harriet listens; hears the sound of the shower running, and Rusty, singing lustily in a very fine baritone. Harriet should probably already know that he can sing, but all the same the lyrics are a dead giveaway; he's singing, slowly and caressingly, a song about love being like a train, the lyrics loaded with innuendo about travelling through the night and stopping at every station. The women exchange a grin, and then Carole whispers, 'Help yourself to anything you want. I'm going to get dressed.' She starts to walk away, then stops, turns, adds, 'If they offer to make you an omelette for breakfast, just say no, okay? Or at least make them sign something to say they'll clean up afterwards.'

'Okay.' Harriet agrees, mystified.

'Its best you don't know.' Carole assures her.

Harriet grabs the laptop from her bag and goes downstairs.

Down in the basement, she retrieves the wet ball of her clothes from the washer and puts them in the dryer, then e-mails Chris with Leon and Carole's address. Something about the house, its cosy family normality makes her wonder if she's got it right in her life. Wonders if she could settle somewhere like this, gather possessions and cars and friends and actually be happy to spend the rest of her life in one place. Then remembers what Rusty had said about going crazy with boredom, figuring that he might be right. It's just that this is a bolthole from the strangeness that your life has become recently, she tells herself, that makes it so attractive.

She becomes aware of someone moving around in the kitchen above, humming. Rusty.

Rusty Hanover

I glide down the stairs and into the empty kitchen, where the cat is sitting on the countertop, staring. So I pick it up and waltz with it awhile until it starts struggling violently and issuing multisyllabic feline swear words at me, so I let it go. And then Harriet appears from the basement with an armful of clean clothes so I embrace her, instead. Fortunately she seems to enjoy it more than the cat did, but just as I'm bending to give her a proper good morning kiss, I hear Leon's voice behind me.

'For God's sake get a room, you two.' He says.

'I'm just helping her with her laundry.' I tell him.

'Strange way of doing it.' He notes. 'Hello Harriet. Sleep well? Fancy some breakfast - an omelette, perhaps?'

'No, thank you.'

'Carole told you to say no, didn't she?' I ask her.

'She did. But I don't know why.'

'Ah, good.' Says Leon. 'This means that you will require a live demonstration of exactly what it is that we're not allowed to do. Rusty, Prepare the equipment!'

I get out a pan and pour a little oil, while Leon offers Harriet a seat at the far side of the table. I don't light the burner under the oil, though, having learnt the first time we did this that the combination of a fast moving egg with hot oil can produce a spatter that reaches an astonishing way across the kitchen, mostly in the direction of what is probably my most favourite part of my own anatomy.

'Harriet.' Leon says in a very serious tone of voice. 'What you are about to witness is being performed for you by complete idiots, and on no account should you attempt to replicate this without the proper safety equipment.'

He unbuttons his cuffs and rolls his sleeves up. 'Let's get started. Eggs!'

'Eggs.' I pass him the carton from the refrigerator.

'Dessert spoon!'

'Dessert spoon.' I rummage for one and hand it to him.

'Little rolly do-dad!'

'Little rolly do-dad.' This last is a non-specific piece of kitchen equipment like a tiny marble rolling pin; I've no idea what it's supposed to do, but it does make an excellent pivot for the spoon. I fetch it from the drawer and give it to him.

Leon sets an egg in the bowl of the spoon, which he then carefully balances on the rolly thing, shifting it backward and forward until the spoon is perfectly level and balanced with neither end touching the table.

I take a step backwards. Leon fusses for a moment, walking to Harriet's side of the table to take a sight line, waving me back toward the stove by half a pace. He then walks to the balanced spoon, pauses dramatically, and then hits the handle of the spoon with his fist, propelling the egg into the air.

Except that he doesn't hit it hard enough, meaning that the egg hardly gains any altitude at all before it falls back onto the table top, rolls, and then before anyone can stop it, falls and smashes itself to bits on the floor.

We all look at the egg for a moment. 'I'm sorry, Mrs Licken, but we couldn't save your son.' Leon says gravely. 'Never mind. Sometimes we have to sacrifice the one for the many. Let's go again.'

Harriet is giggling uncontrollably. I pass Leon another egg.

This time he hits it far too hard, propelling the egg at considerable velocity past my shoulder where it splatters on the tile wall behind.

'Oops.' Leon says, then, 'Again!'

I pass him an egg. 'This is the last one.' I warn.

'Fine, fine.' Leon says, pushing his sleeves up. 'A little pressure is good for a performer. Here we go.'

This time he gets it exactly right and the egg gains altitude perfectly, spinning end over end. I lunge forward and catch it in my mouth; the aim, of course, being that I then spit it into the awaiting pan. Except that Carole enters the kitchen at that precise moment, distracting me for a vital half second.

The egg breaks in my mouth.

'Aw, shit. Fuck. That's disgusting.' I'm hunched over the sink, spitting eggshell and uncooked yolk. Harriet is bent double with laughter, Leon and Carole creasing up.

'That's brilliant.' Carole says, tears in her eyes. 'That's actually funnier than what you were trying to do.'

'For you, maybe.' I tell her. 'I think I'm going to hurl.'

Harriet gets up and runs for the bathroom, still bent double, meaning that either she's going to hurl, too, or possibly that she fears she's going to wet herself. I follow her out and wait until she emerges to grin at her.

'Do you find me sexually attractive right now?' I have eggshell in my teeth.

'Can I think about it, and let you know?' She replies.

I dive past her for the mouthwash.

Back in the kitchen, Leon is cleaning up bits of egg and Carole is making toast while Harriet pours coffee into mugs on the table. I take the coffee jug from her and finish the pouring. Carole deals out the toast and we spend some minutes passing the butter and munching.

'Harriet and I are going shopping this morning for her costume.' Carole tells us. 'I think I have a good idea for something that will look good, won't take long to put together, and begins with a P.'

'What are the rest of you wearing?' Harriet asks.

'Secret.' I tell her. 'An old tradition. None of us know what the others are wearing. Then tonight we all get dressed, have a fashion parade and the one voted winner gets choose what we have to drink.'

‘I was thinking eggnog this year.’ Says Leon.

I tell him to go fuck himself. ‘Anyway, I’m definitely winning this year, and I have my eye on your champagne collection, Leon, so you’d better put some on ice.’

Leon ignores me and launches a stream of smoochy French at his wife. I don’t actually speak much French but I definitely catch the word for ‘eggs’ somewhere in there.

Carole turns to us, smiling. ‘In case you were wondering, my husband here was trying to convince me to buy some eggs this morning, as we seem to have run out. And I’m about to tell him that we don’t have time for grocery shopping, buddy, as we have far more important things to do. But you guys can have the car, as we’re going to be taking a cab into town in case we want to have a drink later.’

‘We’ll come with you.’ I tell her. ‘I need a haircut.’ Everyone looks at my hair.

‘You do, don’t you?’ Leon says.

‘Do you know a place?’ I ask him. ‘Preferably not the one you use.’ I lean back in my chair to regard the incipient bald spot at the back of his head.

‘I think I know of a place.’ He says.

Downtown, we make arrangements to meet up for lunch and go our separate ways, the women walking off in one direction, arm in arm, talking intently, while Leon and I go in another.

‘I know of a great place for your haircut.’ Leon tells me. ‘But it’s very traditional, very French. In fact, they don’t really like English speakers there, so best if you let me do the talking, okay? I know how you have your hair.’

‘Fine.’ I tell him. After the wonderful start to my day, I’m feeling far too relaxed to care.

He leads me down a couple of windy backstreets and in at the door of an old-fashioned barber shop. They exchange greetings and Leon chats away to them in French. Everyone nods and smiles, including me, and I’m ushered to a chair and shrouded up. Leon then starts talking to me about my latest project and we chat away and the barber snips away and I don’t notice the approach of the clippers at the back of my neck until its far, far too late.

‘What?’ I clamp my fingers to the suddenly cold back of my head.

‘Relax.’ Leon tells me. ‘Trust me. They know what they’re doing.’ It’s far too late to do anything, anyway, so I sit with my eyes closed until they're done, wondering if Harriet will still fancy me if I have to wear a toque 24/7 for the next few weeks.

When they've finally stopped, I open one eye cautiously, and then the other. What they've done is left my hair longer on top and then given me a buzz cut down the sides and back. It looks pretty good, actually. In fact, it looks really good. I perk up.

'Hey Leon.' I say. 'Do they still sell condoms in barber shops?'

The barber turns to me. 'What do you think this is?' He asks me in perfect, Canadian-accented English. 'The nineteen fifties? Try a drugstore, for Christ sakes.'

Leon is still laughing when we get outside.

'You bastard.' I tell him.

'I can't believe you fell for it.' He responds. 'But you owe me one, because I could have got them to do something really awful to your hair.'

'I'm amazed you didn't.'

'I was going to, but then I thought it would actually be poor Harriet who would have to look at you, so I relented. Speaking of whom, what's all this about condoms?'

'I need to get me some.' We start walking down the street. 'Wow. My head is really cold.'

Leon ignores my attempt to change the subject. 'Meaning you haven't told her.'

'Meaning.' I tell him. 'That my sperm count, or in fact the complete lack of anything to count, hasn't exactly come up in conversation.'

'You will have to tell her.'

'Really? I thought I'd wait, see how things turn out, and then tell her in ten years or so. Anyway, as responsible adults, isn't wearing condoms exactly what we're supposed to be doing? At least, that's what the advertisements tell us.'

Leon shrugs. 'It's your life.'

'I'm glad you think so. But I do need some because the one's we're currently using were generously donated by the American army – please don't even ask. But if they'd known they were going to be used by a Canadian they'd probably have added anthrax in the manufacturing process.'

At the drug store we stand and stare, amazed, at the variety of condoms on offer.

Leon reads down the row. 'Lubricated, ribbed, flavoured, extra safe.'

'If I get the lubricated she'll think I'm in too much of a hurry, the ribbed and she'll think I'm kinky, the flavoured will make her think I'm expecting her to blow me, and the extra safe will make her think I'm expecting something far worse.'

'Who knew this would be so difficult?' Leon says. We eventually locate the normal ones which have, for some reason, a rather tasteless picture on the pack of a soft-focus couple embracing on the hood of a red sports car.

'I'm loving the serving suggestion.' Leon says. 'Is that a Porsche?'

'No.' I take the packet from him and slap it down on the counter. 'It isn't.'

We wander down to the market, which is bustling despite the cold grey sky overhead, and Leon stops to look at the wares on offer on a jewellery stand; a big purchaser of jewellery for his wife, Leon is. The stand has chunky ethnic silver displayed on dark velvets, and I notice something. 'Oh, hey, look.' It's a silver hairclip, bowed, the type with a thick wooden pin that slots through either side. What's caught my eye, though, is the design carved in relief on it: a little antelope.

'Kudu.' The East Indian stall holder tells me.

'Pardon me?'

'Kudu.' He repeats, and then clearly realising he's speaking to someone who's a bit slow on the uptake, he puts his hands to either side of his head, making prongs of his fingers. 'Is antelope.'

I buy it, totally failing to bargain him down on price, but what the hell. He wraps it in some tissue paper and I thrust the package into my pocket with the condoms. There's something uneasily transactional about the proximity of the two things, but I decide not to think about it.

Leon gives me a sideways look. 'You have got it bad.' He tells me.

'Antelope.' I say to him. 'I was telling her, that's what she reminded me of when I first saw her.'

Leon smirks.

'What?' I ask him.

'Your last girlfriend reminded me of something more bovine, particularly in one department, if you don't mind me saying so.'

I think about this for a moment. 'Possibly true. But you can herd cattle, as I know. Try that with antelope and they probably just take the fuck off over the horizon.' My ears are cold and I feel suddenly depressed.

'Trouble in paradise?' Leon asks.

'Sort of. But not of either of our making.' I pretty much know that she wouldn't want me to tell Leon, but I want to tell him. I need his advice. 'She has a stalker. A very serious one who's extremely well resourced.'

'She needs to go to the police.' Leon suggests.

'She did. They were very sympathetic, apparently.'

'But wouldn't do anything?'

I nod. 'I'm scared for her.' I tell him. 'In fact, I'm about ninety-nine percent scared for her, and about one percent scared for me that she'll just decide it's easier to take off and leave New York permanently. Please don't tell her I told you, because she didn't even want to tell me at first. But when I said to you yesterday about getting a postcard from Basra, I wasn't really joking, because I know that she can do it.'

I'm expecting Leon to tell me to pull myself together, not to be so melodramatic. He stops and looks me straight in the eye, extremely serious.

'If someone was stalking Carole, or my daughter.' He says. 'I'd want to kill him.'

'Don't think that hasn't crossed my mind.' I tell him.

Harriet Morgan

Carole leads her down a cold backstreet in the old city to what looks like an Army Surplus store; grimy windows showing displays of uniforms, tarnished and menacing weaponry. Not a place that she'd normally dare go into, but Carole sweeps straight in, an old brass bell clanking tonelessly to announce their entrance. The man at the counter has his meaty forearms planted on the magazine he's reading; he looks up, slightly irritated at the interruption. Then he recognises Carole, smiles, and leans forward to grasp her hands and draw her in to plant a kiss on either of her cheeks.

'My best customer, eh?' He says. 'And what are you needing today, ma belle?'

Carole gestures to Harriet. 'A flight suit.' She says. 'Just the one.'

'Ah.' He regards Harriet for a moment. 'The smallest I have is a thirty four.'

'Then we'll need a belt. And dog tags. Do you have any aviator sunglasses?'

'P for pilot.' Harriet says, realisation dawning.

'Exactly.' Carole responds.

Together, Carole and the man organise her into a curtained-off changing room with a pile of military bits and pieces. She starts to strip off, listening to Carole and the man talking about reproduction Canadian Air Force uniforms outside. Of course they know each other, Harriet thinks. She's a wardrobe mistress.

Just as she's stepping into the flight suit, Carole joins her in the changing room, straightening the legs of the suit, zipping her up, tightening the belt, adding the dog tags and sunglasses. Carole stands back a moment to admire her handiwork, steps forward, lowers the long front zip a couple inches.

'You need.' Carole says to her. 'A padded bra. In a bright colour; cerise, maybe.'

'I don't got any of those here.' The man says from the other side of the curtain.

Carole gives Harriet a gentle shove in the back. 'Go admire yourself in the mirror outside.'

Doing what she's told, Harriet has to admit that she looks pretty good. Definitely needs to take Carole up on the bra suggestion, though. A thought strikes her.

'Rusty.' She says to Carole. 'He's afraid of flying, right?'

The man answers her. 'Seeing you like that might just change his mind, chérie.'

'Coffee.' Says Carole once they're outside, Harriet carrying the bag stuffed with her new possessions. 'That's the rule here; one purchase, one coffee.' Carole leads her to a tiny coffee shop around the corner, its windows running with condensation. Inside, the air is thick with the steam being issued in noisy gouts by a huge chromed espresso machine being attended by tiny moustached old man. 'Best coffee in town.' Carole assures her.

They get their coffees, poured with frowning concentration by the old man, and take a seat at a high round table by the window.

Carole blows across the top of her coffee. 'That's a doozy of a bruise you got on your hip, girl.' She says casually.

'Oh.' Harriet starts to mentally concoct a sporting injury story, and then stops. She doesn't want to lie to this woman, not any more than she has had to, anyway. 'I've got a bit of a situation.' She tells the older woman.

'Not Rusty?'

'No. God, no. Not Rusty.'

'I didn't think so.' Carole says. 'But I guess you never know. Bizarre, isn't it? We spend all our girlhood being warned about stranger danger, only to find out that the ones statistically likely to hurt us are actually the ones we know. But don't worry, I didn't really think it would be Rusty, I just had to check in case you needed me to go after his testicles with the vegetable knife.'

'If it had been, I'd have done that myself.' Harriet tells her. 'But this is stranger danger. Well, sort of. It's complicated, but I have a stalker who's a bit crazy. The bruise just came from something that I got myself into that I thought I needed to get out of fast, and I got bumped against a door. Nothing too terrible.' She looks down at her coffee. Steam rises.

'But Rusty knows about this?' Carole asks.

'It mostly happened before we met but yes, he does.'

'Honey, the feminist in me weeps to say this, but you might just have to let the guys sort this out between them. Sometimes a guy will listen to something another guy tells him where he wouldn't listen to a woman. You know what I'm saying?'

'Yes.' Harriet says, thinking of Shem.

'But in the meantime, if you need a bolthole, you just come to us. In fact, even if you don't need a bolthole, you'll come see us again, won't you? Either with or without Rusty.'

Harriet feels her eyes fill. Why is it that when people are being kind to her it makes her want to cry, when really it should be the other way around? 'Thank you. I will.'

'Now hurry up and drink that coffee. We need to go buy us some lingerie.' Carole says.

It's no surprise to Harriet that Carole turns out to be a champion shopper, and she finds herself swept down into a huge, subterranean department store. Very French, almost Parisian, she notes as they stride through its perfumed sales floors. Furs, designer dresses, underwear. Carole snags her a bright orange lacy brassiere combination.

'Perfect, with your colouring. Thong or bikini?'

'Bikini.'

'Let's try the thong. And this for me, I think.' Carole picks up a camisole in a rippling, metallic gold fabric and they cram together into a cubicle to get changed.

Carole's right, of course, the orange does look good. 'It's even a sort of appropriately Air Sea Rescue colour.' Harriet notes.

Carole shrugs the camisole over her head and straightens up, the gold fantastic against her dark skin.

'If only the guys could see us now, huh?' Carole says.

'I was just thinking that. Rusty would be asking for photographs, wouldn't he?'

'Leon, too. He'll probably try to get Felix to hack into the store's security cameras.'

Giggling, girlish, they get dressed and go back onto the sales floor.

'Hang on to those a moment.' Carole says. She gives Harriet a long look, top to toe. 'You need a miniskirt, girl.'

'I do?' Harriet looks down at herself.

'I look at you, I see a person who's spent too long in Muslim countries. Don't worry, I'll let you wear it with nice thick pantyhose, but you have great legs and the world deserves to see them. Come with me.'

The rest of the shopping trip takes them almost to lunchtime.

'Multiple purchases.' Carole declares, 'Deserve more than coffee. Let's go to the lunch place and see if we can't get a drink in before the guys arrive to spoil our fun.'

The cafe they've chosen is barn like, airy. The waiter shows them to a table for four, fetches drinks and a dish of peanuts, and lingers long enough to flirt with them both, Carole in French, Harriet in English. As he departs, Carole notes, 'That's a fine looking boy, but too young for me, I think. Now, Harriet, there's something I'm needing to ask you.' Carole is trying to keep a straight face but there's a wicked gleam in her eye.

'What?'

'I've known Rusty a long time. A very long time. But there's something I don't know about him.'

'And what's that?' Harriet can't keep from grinning, either, guessing at what's coming.

'He has big hands and very big feet. So, is it true what they say?'

'It is. Well, it is in his case, certainly. In fact, when I first saw it I told him I didn't know whether to be impressed or scared.'

Carole laughs her lovely laugh. 'Marvellous. I'm so glad.'

'But I'm thinking it may actually be a bit of a problem, in that there might be some positions that we just can't do.'

Carole considers this for a moment. 'From behind, you mean? Let me give you some advice. Try it on your side, with him behind you.

That way you can clamp your thighs together to control how deep he goes, and he'll be so happy he won't know the difference anyway.'

'Thank you, I'll remember that.' They laugh together, making the young waiter look over and smile at them.

'Carole, can I ask you something in return?'

'Leon? On the generous side of average, I'd say.'

'That's not what I meant, but thank you. I wanted to ask you about Rusty. I mean, its early days for us, but is he okay? I think what I'm trying to say is that a brief fling would be sort of alright, but I don't really want to be a notch on someone's belt.'

'Is he a dog, you're asking me?' Which makes Harriet think, obscurely, of Shem's big red retriever, Rosey. Beware of the Dog. 'I don't think so.' Carole continues. 'He can certainly be a bit vain and self-absorbed, but then all actors are and I don't think he's a particularly bad example of the type. Actually, I think he's a bit of a romantic, at heart. But then I think most men are.'

'You do?'

'You don't agree?'

'I'm not sure.' Harriet couldn't imagine someone like Shem as a romantic, couldn't picture him buying flowers.

'Consider the evidence.' Carole says. 'Us women are far more practical because we have to be. It's the men who go all sappy, give them half a chance. But some of them hide it well, certainly, and they're probably the worst in terms of being hopeless romantics.' Carole pauses, looks up. 'Speaking of hopeless romantics, here's two of them now. And I'll tell you something quickly, although you've probably already worked it out for yourself. Rusty is just like Leon, he'll try to cover up what he's really feeling by being funny. And he can be very funny indeed. But don't let him catch you out that way.'

'I won't. Thank you.' Harriet says.

The two men approach. Rusty, Harriet notices, has had a very good haircut that brings out his cheekbones.

'Oh, let me….' Harriet reaches out a hand so he obligingly drops into a crouch by her seat so she can rub the newly bristly back of his head. She works it with her nails a little bit and he responds with a low rumbling growl, deep in his chest. Dog like.

She looks down at him. 'You know,' she says, 'You're the only white guy I know can do that.'

'Harriet.' Leon says. 'I really don't want to hear what you're going to say next, but all the same I know I'll have to listen.'

She feels herself blush slightly. 'Nothing like that. I mean the way he can crouch down. Women can do it, lots of the Asian races can do it, both male and female, but you never see white guys doing it.'

Carole says, 'I read somewhere that women can crouch because we've evolved an extra articulation in our big toes, from centuries of squatting down by the fire, stirring the cooking pot.'

Rusty straightens up, taking a seat opposite Harriet. 'Are you trying to tell me.' He says, 'That my male ancestors spent their time squatting by the fire, stirring the cooking pot?'

'I always thought your lot would have been the spear throwers.' Harriet says.

Leon asks, 'What would that have made my ancestors?'

Rusty answers. 'That's easy. Your lot would have been the ones carrying the spears for my lot. Like Neolithic caddies, if you will.' He puts on an obsequious British accent. 'I think Sir should try the number nine spear for woolly mammoth.'

'And my lot?' Carole's tone is light, but there's a challenge in her eyes.

'They would never have met, on account of how your lot had the sense to stay in the warmer parts of the world. They'd in fact have been legendary to us; we'd have told tales of dusky-skinned queens, warm weather and exotic food as we crouched by our campfires, freezing our asses off and chewing unseasoned mammoth fat.'

'Pffft.' Carole makes a noise of amused disgust. 'Dusky skinned queens, huh? And you're lying, because you're pretending you're native Canadians, which you aren't.'

'Native northern Europeans, then.' Rusty responds. 'It's the same thing; you'd still have been legendary. And we'd still have been freezing our asses off.'

'And what about Harriet's ancestors, then?' Leon asks.

Rusty looks at her, trying to keep a straight face. 'Well, uh. Ha ha, I did think of something, but probably best I don't share.' He gets shouted down by Leon and Carole.

'Oh, well, okay.' He gives in. 'I mean, isn't it obvious? Low body weight, lots of lovely long hair to drag her into the cave by.'

By way of a response Harriet grabs a peanut and throws it at him. He lunges forward, catches it in his mouth and eats it, looking smug.

'Careful you don't choke on that peanut.' She tells him. 'I think I just forgot how to do the Heimlich manoeuvre.'

Rusty smiles. 'I'm fine, thank you, but I appreciate your concern for my health.'

Leon stands up. 'Who wants a drink?'

Rusty Hanover

We have a nice, long, slightly drunken lunch and then get a cab back home. And then we lounge around for a while, watching TV and talking. Personally, I'd rather have sneaked Harriet upstairs for a repeat of this morning's activities, but it's kind of hard to deke on your best friends without appearing rude.

Carole asks me if I can braid Harriet's hair again for tonight.

'Certainly.' I say to Harriet, 'Come, woman, sit at my feet and worship me.' Which earns me a look from Carole, so I quickly add. 'Or ignore me and watch TV; whichever you prefer.' Harriet sits herself on the carpet between my knees and I go to work on the hair. Leon is watching us very intently, I can't help but notice, and I know he knows me well enough to have totally busted me: I am crazy about this woman and would do anything for her.

Anything at all.

Carole has allocated us separate bedrooms to change into our secret outfits, meaning I get Felix's room which looks oddly like my own when I was his age; theatre and film posters on the walls, stacks of books on everything from mime to Method. While I'm snagging my bags from the guestroom I remember today's purchase and root it out of my jacket pocket. The condoms I leave in there, for the time being.

'I got something for you.' I tell Harriet, holding the tissue-wrapped package out to her. She looks at me slightly warily before accepting and unwrapping it.

'Oh.' She's looking down at the clip. 'Thank you, that's beautiful.' Something strange in her voice. I take the clip from her hand, loop the braid up to the back of her head and secure it there, sliding the wooden pin through to hold it. I can see us reflected in the dressing table mirror; or rather, I can see Harriet with my upper torso behind. She's standing very still. I lean down to drop a kiss on the back of her neck.

'Kudu.' I tell her. 'It's a type of antelope, apparently. Although I'm afraid to say that I think I did eat one of those, once, in an Asian Fusion restaurant in Malibu.'

That makes her laugh, and she tilts her head right back to look up at me.

'Thank you.' She says again. 'It's lovely.'

'It would be.' I tell her. 'If the pin on that thing hadn't just pierced my nipple.'

Chapter Six

Shem Jephson

When I get to Art's office, located at the back of an old Brooklyn Docks warehouse, the kid Will is sitting in Art's office chair at the desk with Art himself perched on the front of the desk, swinging his legs, grinning his big grin.

'She liked your dog.' He says to me, by way of a greeting.

'Excuse me?'

'She liked your dog. Harriet, I mean.'

'You've spoken to her?'

'No.' Art is enjoying this. 'Turns out our Will is a very technical boy.' Will looks up, smiling shyly at the compliment.

'What's a Thigh Master?' Will asks me.

'A piece of exercise equipment.' I tell him. 'What's going on?'

'Our very technical boy here has hacked into her e-mail.' Art says. 'And she has been e-mailing her whereabouts to a person named Chris Stonham. Know him?'

'No.' Although he might, I think, be the person she visited before I took her to Poughkeepsie.

'Want to guess where she is now?' Art asks.

'New York.'

'Guess again.'

For some reason, I think of the tall guy who eyeballed me when I was looking in at the windows of the Canada train.

'Montréal?'

'On the outskirts of Montréal, to be precise. And returning on the train tomorrow. Do you want to go and see her in Canada?'

'Yes.'

'Should we tell our friend Thomas this?'

I think about it for a moment. 'Tell him we know she's in Montréal, but not precisely where. And tell him that she'll be on the train home tomorrow.' I can see, suddenly, an opportunity to get Thomas away from his boys. 'Tell him to get the boys on that train so they can take her off it somewhere upstate. And that you'll be driving him so you can all meet up somewhere. I'll rent another car and drive separately, except he won't know that, of course. You can lead him to believe that I'm out of the picture somehow.'

Art frowns. 'What are you planning?'

I find myself pacing the room. 'She's very distinctive looking, as we know. So we need to get her on that train, as they'll be watching for that. And then we need to get her off the train in a way that they don't notice.'

'It is her hair that makes her so distinctive.' Art ponders.

'Shave her head?' Will suggests.

'Don't be stupid.' I snap, making him flinch.

'Sensitive.' Art whispers to Will.

I ignore him.

'If we can get her with us, and only Thomas as well, we can meet with him somewhere quiet upstate.'

Art grins. 'I like it.' He says. 'You, me, the girl, and Thomas. It seems to me that we'll all have a lot to talk about. But I still don't see how to get her off that train without Thomas' boys coming too.'

'I'll think of something.' I tell him. 'But in the meantime we need to get to Montréal.'

Will clicks at something on the computer. 'Five p.m. flight from La Guardia.' He says. 'Or seven fifty-nine p.m.'

'Art, you'll need to be on the later flight with Thomas.' I tell him. 'And I'll take the earlier one so I can go and speak to Harriet.'

'Can I come too?' Will asks.

'No.' Art and I say simultaneously.

'We'll need you to stay monitoring the e-mail.' I say to Will. 'Just in case there's a change in Harriet's plans.'

'What about weapons?' Art asks. 'I believe that the airlines are a little sensitive about those sorts of things these days. Particularly guns which are not actually registered.'

'I've already thought of something.' I tell him. 'And its something that we can buy locally and no airline will mind carrying, just so long as it goes in the hold.'

Chapter Seven

Harriet Morgan

She gets changed, slowly, pondering the Kudu clip, Rusty, and how a lone dash away from Poughkeepsie had turned into something with a whole array of new people in her life. Admit it, she says to herself, regarding her reflection in the mirror, you don't want to go back to New York. You want to stay here having fun with these people and their casual wealth and their easy friendship. But even here she can feel a hurtling darkness at her back, the unstoppable express train of Thomas and his crazed obsession.

And knows that she needs to keep these new people out of it, in case it hurts them too.

If you need to, she thinks to herself, leaning forward to apply mascara, you'll have to hide out in New York for a few days, long enough for your bosses to find you some work somewhere else in the world. They'll find her something, she knows, if she isn't too choosy, because there are always places, and jobs, which don't exactly have people lined up to volunteer to go.

Except that she doesn't want to go anywhere, and, touching the silver clip at the back of her head, she knows why.

Her thoughts are interrupted then by a shout, followed by a burst of laughter from downstairs.

Leon calls up to her. 'Harriet? You really need to get down here and see this.'

Relax and enjoy, she reminds herself, putting on the aviator sunglasses and tugging the zipper of the flight suit down just far enough to show the lacy edge of the orange bra. Worry about it tomorrow.

From the top of the stairs she can see, in the living room, Carole in thigh boots, mini skirt and bustier, holding a glass of champagne. Prostitute. A very pretty and polished prostitute, in fact. And Leon as an outrageous 70's pimp, fake fur coat worn over the shoulders of a terrible suit, too much gold jewellery, greased back hair and dodgy, drooping moustache. And then out of the kitchen walks what must total around seven feet, if you include boots and hat, of Canadian Mountie.

The Mountie looks up at her. 'Wow.' He says.

Carole hands her a glass of champagne as she gets to the bottom of the stairs. 'What do you think?' Gesturing at Rusty, who tips his hat to her.

'I'm speechless.' Harriet says.

'Truly terrifying, isn't it?'

Harriet regards Rusty. 'P party?' She asks him.

'P for policeman, Canadian style. You like?'

'I think I could get used to it.' She tells him.

He nudges up close to her. 'You want I should slap the cuffs on you, take you downtown, huh? Would you like that?'

Harriet takes a drink of her champagne; it's very cold, very good. 'Maybe later.' She tells him.

'I just want to know.' Leon asks Rusty, 'Where you managed to get riding boots in a size sixteen.'

'From a very expensive saddler in Manhattan. One of those places where the salespeople manage to be both obsequious and incredibly patronising at the same time; I told him I was learning to play polo but I don't think he believed me.'

'I'm not surprised.' Harriet answers. 'I don't think there's a polo pony in the world that comes in your size.'

'Elephant polo, I meant.'

There's a knock at the front door.

Leon sets his glass down and goes to answer it. 'Must be the taxicab.' He says, opening the door.

And then Harriet hears a familiar voice say, 'Sorry to trouble you, but I need to speak to Harriet Morgan.'

Shem.

Oh god no. Not yet, Shem. And not *here*.

Behind Shem, she can see the lights of the taxi approaching up the drive. Good, she thinks. Get them out of the house and out of the way.

'Hello Shem.' She says to him in a social voice, then to the rest of them: 'Sorry, guys, I need to speak with Shem a moment. Perhaps you could leave the address of where you're going and a number for the cab company and I'll catch up with you in a few minutes?'

Carole and Leon exchange a look. 'Okay.' Carole says.

Harriet looks at Rusty.

'I'm not going anywhere.' He says, planting his booted feet apart and folding his arms; around seven feet of assertive Mountie that she doesn't have time to negotiate with.

'Fine.' She says. 'But I need to speak to Shem a moment. Alone.' And leads Shem into the kitchen, hearing Leon and Carole closing the front door behind them as they leave.

'I don't know whose side you're on.' Harriet says urgently to Shem. 'But you are not bringing it to this house. Not here. I'll go anywhere with you that you want.'

'She's not going anywhere with you.' Rusty strides into the kitchen, the fingers of his right hand loosely gripping the neck of an unopened bottle of champagne. 'I've seen the bruises you put on her.'

'Harriet overhead a conversation I had on the phone with my son.' Shem says, looking at Harriet. 'She thought it meant I was a threat to her and I tried to stop her leaving. It was just a misunderstanding.'

'Oh yeah?' Rusty steps forward until the two men are standing only inches apart. 'You'll probably think I'm strange, but if I have a misunderstanding with a woman I tend to talk to her, not lock her in my fucking basement.'

Oh god, Harriet thinks, looking at the two of them; Shem with his fists clenched and Rusty gently swinging the champagne bottle. They're going to fight. Rusty having the height advantage, certainly, but her money would have to be on Shem to win; he's bound to be armed.

Shoving her way between them, bracing her back and shoulders against Rusty to shift him physically backwards away from Shem, she says. 'Stop it. Both of you. This isn't helping.' She inclines her head toward the kitchen table. 'Shem, sit down. And you, Rusty. Now.'

She sees the two men exchange a glance above her head, but it's Rusty who gets to the smartass comment first. 'Yes, ma'am.' He says, and sits, setting the bottle down on the floor by his polished boots.

Harriet remains standing. 'How did you know I was here?' She asks Shem.

'Will hacked into your e-mail account.'

'And Thomas?'

'Thomas is in Montréal.'

'You told him where I was?' She goes cold, a feeling like ice water down her back. 'I don't understand.'

'He knows that you're in the Montréal area but not where. As far as he's concerned, you and I are still in the wind. Art is with him, but we need Thomas to think he's still in control.'

'Does he know I'll be on the train tomorrow?'

'Yes. He'll be travelling back to New York in the car with Art, but his two muscle boys will be on that train to take you off it somewhere along the way.'

'How will they do that?'

Shem looks her right in the eye. 'There are ways.'

'Then she won't get on that train.' Rusty says.

'No, I think she should. Look; we need to finish this, but its best to deal with it somewhere other than Manhattan, you understand? Somewhere quieter. What I've been thinking is that we need Harriet to be seen getting on the train at Montréal, and then we need to take her off the train along the way, but in a manner that leaves the boys on there. We need them out of the picture so that we can deal with Thomas on his own.'

'How are we going to do that?' Rusty asks.

Shem relaxes, leans back in his chair, looking at Rusty. 'Seeing you, my friend, has given me a very good idea.'

The two men fall to plotting, leaving Harriet still standing and feeling very marginal to the process. Left luggage. How very prophetic Carole was, she thinks, telling me I might have to leave it to the guys to sort out.

'The only problem here.' Shem is saying to Rusty, 'Is that you'll need to do it well before the train gets to the US border.'

Rusty considers this. 'The border at Cantic is around an hour and twenty minutes outside of Montréal.'

'Call it an hour, then.'

'That's not much time.' Rusty says.

'Can you do it?' Something of a challenge about the way Shem says this.

'Of course I can.' Rusty says. 'It's what I do for a living.'

Harriet pulls out a chair and joins them at the kitchen table.

'Do I get a say in this at all?' She asks them.

'Of course you do.' Shem says. Under his careful scrutiny, she fights a sudden desire to pull the zipper of her flight suit right up to her neck.

'I think it's totally crazy.' She tells them. 'But as I can't think of a better plan then I suppose we'll have to do it. But if it goes wrong Rusty and I could get in some serious trouble with the law.'

'Don't worry about that.' Shem tells her. 'If you go into the system then Art will get you out.'

'What tells me.' Rusty says, 'That if we go into the system then Art will get Harriet out very quickly and I'll stay in the system for a little longer, say, twenty years or so?'

Shem very nearly smiles. 'You'll just have to trust me, won't you?'

When Harriet returns to the kitchen from showing Shem to the door, Rusty is untwisting the metal cage from the top of the champagne bottle. 'I called the cab company. Twenty minutes, they said, so let's have a drink while we're waiting.'

'Would you really have hit Shem with that bottle?'

'If I'd had to. Then I would have cried at such a terrible waste of genuine Moet.'

'He was probably packing heat.' She tells him.

'I'm aware of that. But I figured my way had more class.' He eases the cork from the bottle with the faintest of popping noises. 'Should sound like an angel's fart, apparently.' He says. 'There you go.' He pours her a glass of champagne, asks her, 'Would you really have gone with him like you said?'

'Yes.'

'Why? I mean, that's insane; it didn't work out too well for you the last time you and Shem were alone together.'

'I didn't want to put the three of you in the way of any danger. I pitched up in your life without you asking; it doesn't seem right that you and Leon and Carole should get dragged into it. I feel guilty, I think, because I made one bad decision in going on a date with Thomas in the first place and then all this happens as a result.'

'For the record, I'm very glad that you pitched up in my life.' Rusty says. 'But we've all made bad decisions about who we've dated, and I'm possibly a case in point, only it hasn't meant that our dates have then tried to kill us.' He adds, 'Although in my case one or two may have wanted to, come to think of it. But don't any crazy ideas about this being your fault, because it isn't.' He puts his arms around her, drawing her to him and she leans in, resting her cheek against the scarlet of the Mountie jacket.

Rusty says quietly, 'You're really very spunky, aren't you, offering to go off with that lunatic Shem. Especially when he so obviously fancies a bit of personal one on one time with you.'

'I know.' She admits to his lapel. 'I think that may have been what freaked me out about him in Poughkeepsie.'

'You didn't fancy a little bit of Shemmie loving, then?' He teases.

'Not really. But I noticed that you were very quick to let him know you'd seen me naked.'

She feels, rather than hears, his laugh rumbling in his chest. 'Just staking my claim.' He tells her. 'But I don't think I'll be turning my back on him anytime soon; something tells me he wouldn't mind clearing the field.'

To change the subject, she says 'I'm really starting to like you in that uniform, you know.'

'You may not feel the same about it tomorrow.' He tells her.

'I probably won't, will I?'

Rusty Hanover

Christ, she really is spunky. Five foot nothing, a hundred pounds, not afraid of anything. Which is probably why I was seriously contemplating going after Military Buzz Cut Guy, Shem, with the champagne bottle. Except I'm glad that I didn't have to, because it may just have turned out to have been the stupidest thing I ever did in my whole life. Or possibly the last thing I ever did in my whole life.

As the taxi speeds us down to the party, I think about our plan for tomorrow. Harriet is right, of course, it is crazy, but if we pull it off it'll be magnificent. On the other hand, if we don't then we'll either be looking at getting into some serious trouble with the police, or some serious trouble with Thomas's muscle boys and I'm not sure which of the two scenarios I like the least.

'You know.' I say to Harriet. 'I think we need to get Carole and Leon on side with this; we'll need their help to set it up.'

'I was thinking the same thing.' She says.

'Which means.' I tell her 'That I'm now going to have to admit to you that I did tell Leon just a little bit about your insane stalker problem.'

'I told Carole a little bit, too.' She admits. 'She saw the bruises on me when we were in the changing room.'

'Fair enough.' Then something occurs to me. 'Wait a minute; you two were in a changing room together?'

Harriet has that amused little tip-tilt at the corner of her eyes. 'We were trying on lingerie.' She says.

I have a sudden and splendid mental image of this. 'No-one took any photos, did they?' I ask her.

The party is being held in the ballroom of a big old hotel in the city. The room is packed already, the noise of hundreds of shouted conversations almost drowning out the sound of the band bashing away in the corner. We weave our way between any number of priests, pirates and policemen - but no other Mounties yet, I note – looking for Leon and Carole. Passing a loaded buffet table, the hotel seems to have attempted to continue the P theme; pizza, pasta, pork rolls, what looks like slowly melting pistachio ice cream. We stop by the bar on the way and it's the same there – Pina Colada, Pinot Noire, Pernod, Peroni; so I get us a bottle of Dom Perignon and a couple of glasses. Seeing as by this time tomorrow we both might be either dead or in custody, we might as well have the good stuff. Shame jails aren't co-ed, really, else they'd be a lot more fun; Harriet could keep house for me in my cell. Harriet and I get briefly separated by the crowd and just as I'm wading through to catch up with her I see her get stopped by a guy dressed as a commercial airline pilot; blue uniform, cap, very drunk.

'Wait.' He says to her, grabbing her by the arm. 'I need to talk to you about your altitude.' Which is a pretty good one, I'll admit. Harriet gestures toward me with her glass and he rapidly withdraws his hand.

'My god.' He looks slowly up at me, then back to Harriet. 'Sorry to have troubled you.' He says to her, chagrined.

We eventually find Leon and Carole down by the big windows that look out onto the river. They're talking to a person I don't recognise, which isn't terribly surprising as he's dressed as a giant pea pod. I put an arm around Leon's shoulders, and then an arm around Carole's, and, not wishing to appear impolite to a large vegetable, excuse us to the pea pod before steering them both to a marginally quieter corner of the room.

'Leon.' I say to him. 'I need you to pimp my girlfriend. And Carole, I need you to turn her into a drug-addicted prostitute by tomorrow morning.'

It's Carole who asks first what the hell's going on.

We find a quiet alcove off the lobby of the hotel; red plush couch, little table, big pot plants. Leon and Carole sit down and I push rudely in front of Harriet to get the last seat on the couch then pull her down so she's sitting on my lap. And then the two of us try and explain exactly why, and how, we need to force the Amtrak train to make an unscheduled stop tomorrow.

Being my lovely friends, they don't ask silly questions or make stupid suggestions about calling the police. They don't even suggest that this is a crazy plan, even though they both obviously know that it is. Leon just goes straight into Leon the Director mode, even going as far as to start story boarding it on a paper serviette.

Drawing his little boxes, Leon says, 'You haven't got much time to do it.'

'I know.' I tell him. 'That's the greatest problem, we've got less than an hour. We have to do it before we get to the US border.'

Leon ponders this, adds another box at the beginning. 'All you need to do.' He suggests, 'Is start the scene earlier. I mean, at Montréal station. If you can get everyone, especially any railroad staff around, to watch me and Harriet we can put the idea in their minds before you even get on that train.'

'I can do that.' I tell him, and I know I can; it's all in the body language. I can actually make an entire field of grazing horses stop eating and stare at something entirely non-existent, just by staring myself. One of the great advantages of being my size; if I stand and gaze at something intently enough, pretty soon everyone around me will too.

We don't stay too late at the party, mostly because the concept of organised fun seems to pale a little compared to what we're going to get up to tomorrow. Or today, in fact, noting from my watch that it's past midnight as we get up to leave.

'Its All Saints day.' I tell Harriet as I pick her up from my lap and set her down on her feet. 'Do you think we should do some praying?'

'I don't think we have time to pray.' She says.

Back at Leon and Carole's place, we have a last pow-wow around the kitchen table, going through the finer details. Carole tells Harriet she'll need her at 5:30am for make-up and wardrobe.

'Okay.' She says.

Carole adds 'I'll drive the three of us, you'll have to take a cab, Rus.'

'No problem.' I reply.

'One problem.' Harriet says 'You do all realise that I can't actually act?'

'Not a problem.' Leon tells her. 'Rusty and I will act, you just react, okay? Simple.'

Harriet's looking like she doesn't think it's simple at all.

'Really, it is simple.' I tell her, 'Else why do you think I'd be able to do it?'

Leon laughs. 'Rusty thinks this is just another job.'

'It's the first job I've ever had where if I get my lines wrong, I'm likely to go to jail.'

'I should try that in the contracts for my next film.' Leon notes, 'Might get the talent to concentrate a bit more.'

'But, Harriet.' I tell her, 'For heaven's sake just don't stride along like your normal fit and healthy self. Just remember that you'll be a drug addict who blows guys for twenty dollars.'

That amused tip-tilt is back. 'How come you know the going rate?' She asks me.

I try not to laugh. 'Stop it.' I tell her. 'I'm giving a master class here. People would pay money for this.'

'They would? More than twenty dollars?' Asks Leon.

'Well, admittedly not that much money. And not many people, but you get my drift.'

'Speaking of drift.' Carole says. 'I'm drifting off to bed.'

We all agree that's a good idea.

Up in our bedroom, I start stripping off the Mountie outfit. 'Don't think I'm being forward.' I tell Harriet as I pull my shirt off and drape it over the back of a chair. 'But if I'm having to wear this again tomorrow it needs to stay unrumpled.'

She lets her hair down out of its braid, kicks her boots off and starts undoing the zipper of the flight suit. 'Don't do that.' I tell her.

'Why not?'

I cross the room and drop to my knees in front of her, leaning in to grip the tab of her zipper in between my teeth. 'Because I've been waiting.' I start to say; speaking is difficult while holding the tab there, but I manage it. 'All night to do this.' And I draw the tab all the way down to the bottom, then part the fabric to kiss my way down her stomach, pausing to tongue the little jewel in her navel. Swaying, she puts her hands on my shoulders to balance herself and as I reach the top of her panties she gasps and throws her head back, eyes half closed, lips parted.

I stop and straighten up. Kneeling, I'm almost exactly the same height as her standing, and from this vantage point I reach into the pocket of my pants for the remains of the wrap of Columbia's finest export. 'We could go to sleep.' I suggest, holding it out to her. 'Or we could just stay up all night.'

She regards me for a moment, head tilted on one side. 'You need drugs for that?' She teases.

'No, I don't.' I scramble to my feet. 'I'll show you.'

We strip off, fast, and as I bundle her towards the bed she reaches for the Mountie hat that I've left hanging on the corner of the mirror, setting in on her head in a manner that tells me exactly who's mounting who tonight.

Oh *yeah.*

I'm sprawled on my back on the bed, my hands behind the back of my neck, watching with immense pleasure as she straddles me, thighs tense. Then it's my turn to gasp as she lowers herself onto me and starts to move, flexing through her hips, rocking, her eyes never leaving mine. She starts to move faster, the ends of her long hair tickling my thighs as she leans back, her eyes closing as she concentrates, bearing down. I can't wait any more; I reach for her, pulling her down on to my chest. And in the final moments as I'm bucking uncontrollably underneath her she sweeps the hat off her head and holds it up with one hand behind her, rodeo style.

I'm not exactly sure who's been roped and branded here, but I think it may have been me.

Afterwards we lie in the dark and talk, and I ask her if she's nervous about tomorrow. Today.

'I think I'm beyond that.' She tells me. 'I just feel fairly fatalistic about the whole thing, except that I am worried about doing something wrong.'

'It'll be easy, honestly.' I reassure her. 'Trust me, I'm a cop.'

'Did you ever play a cop?'

'Leon was the cop, in fact. I was the perp.'

'Really? What a surprise.'

'What do you mean?' I roll over on top of her and pin her down. 'What exactly are you trying to say to me, here?'

By way of an answer she wraps her legs around me, gripping just tight enough to let me know that she could probably bust a rib or two if she had a mind to. I'm hard again, so I feel in the darkness for one of the condoms which by now have spilled out of their packet all over the bed and I put it on one handed, which is a neat trick if you can do it. And then I slip into her and we go at it again, slowly, exchanging kisses, caresses. As she comes she cries out sharply, but I think if we disturbed Leon and Carole tonight they might just forgive us, this one time.

Afterwards I doze for a while until I feel her shift, and then get up out of the bed.

'Where are you going?' I ask her.

'Can't sleep.' She tells me. 'I'm going to take a bath.'

'Mind if I join you?' I ask her for the second time in less than twenty four hours.

'If you don't mind having the faucet end.'

'We call it the tap end in this country, lady.' I tell her.

I get the tap end. She's pinned her hair up on top of her head to keep it out of the water and it falls over her eyes. I lean forward in the warm water and take a silky strand of it between my fingers.

'I love your hair.' I tell her.

'I keep meaning to get it cut off.'

'Don't. Please.'

'Alright, I won't. But it can be a major pain.'

'Worth it, though.' I tell her. 'It's beautiful.'

We lounge for a while in the warm water.

'I thought you were going to run.' I tell her.

'Run?'

'To another country, far, far away.'

'I certainly thought about it.'

'Why?'

'Like I said, I didn't want to bring trouble on you and your friends.'

'So why didn't you run?'

She looks intently at me for a moment. 'You're going to make me tell you, aren't you?'

'Tonight I am, yes. "Time's wingèd chariot," and all that.'

'That poem was just someone trying to convince his girlfriend to sleep with him, wasn't it? Isn't it a bit late for that?'

'Don't try and change the subject.' I tell her. 'Why didn't you run?'

She looks away. 'Well, there's this guy.'

'Shem?' I ask, teasing.

'Taller than Shem.' She tells me, and abruptly stands up, water streaming down her sinuous body. Venus of the bathtub.

'That's all I'm going to get, isn't it?' I ask her.

She steps out of the bath, reaching for a towel. 'It is.'

'I'll accept that for now, but don't think we're not returning to the subject once we're back in New York. Or if we don't make it back to New York you can write to me in jail and tell me.' I get out of the bath and pull the plug.

'If you're in jail there'll be no point in my writing to you.' She says, straight-faced.

'No? Why not?'

'Because I'd imagine that you'd be in a new relationship by then. With a big black man.'

I grab her and threaten to upend her, head first, into the remains of the bathwater.

Harriet Morgan

By the time they've finished fooling around she can hear that the other occupants of the house have started waking up. There's no point in her getting dressed, so she borrows the Calgary t-shirt again, pulls it on, and backtracks to the bathroom to tell Rusty she's going to get some coffee. He's shaving, leaning in close to the mirror, pulling those peculiar man-shaving faces at himself, a towel around his waist. She pauses to watch him for a moment, and then shakes herself, mentally, and goes downstairs in search of coffee.

Leon is in the kitchen, unshaven, hair greased back; a less extreme, and more up to date, version of last night's pimp look. He greets her with a kiss on either cheek.

'Get any sleep?' He asks her. She checks that he's not teasing her, but his look is earnest, concerned almost.

'Not really.'

'I'm not surprised. Coffee?'

'Yes, please. And I'll take one up for Rusty.'

'You know that if this goes wrong you could both get into a lot of trouble?' Leon asks her. 'Particularly Rusty. The police don't tend to find that sort of thing very amusing.'

'I know.' She says helplessly. 'Leon, I don't know why he's doing it.'

Leon regards her steadily. 'I do.' And then he smiles, forgives her. 'And I also know that once Rusty's made up his mind to do something, no matter how crazy, it's very hard to make him change his mind. Plus, if this does work he'll dine out on it forever, and drive us all nuts.' He stirs the coffee and hands her two mugs. 'Extra strong for both of you.' He says. 'You'll need it.'

Five fifteen am.

Up in the bedroom, Rusty is in his shirtsleeves, packing. She hands him his coffee; black, two sugars.

'Its amazing you have any teeth left.' She tells him. 'By the way, how did you crack your tooth?' Indicating her own incisor.

'I'd like to tell you a heroic sporting story.' He replies. 'But in fact it's just another tale of drunken clumsiness. I slipped on my own stoop about a year ago. I did go to have it fixed, but the dentist told me capping it might give me a lisp, which would have ended a nice income stream for me in voice acting, so I didn't.' He lifts his top lip, touching the tooth with an index finger. 'Does it put you off?'

'No, I like it.' She tells him, and she does; there's something attractively off-kilter about it.

'Good.' He says. 'I hadn't noticed you flinching with horror every time you looked at me. But I wanted to check.'

Carole knocks on the bedroom door, singing out, 'Ten minutes, Miss Morgan.'

'Thank you.' Harriet calls back, thinking; time's wingèd chariot. 'Leon thinks you shouldn't be doing this.' She tells Rusty.

'I know. Leon also knows I'm a grown-up, and make my own decisions. Not all of them right, to be honest with you, but there you go.' He takes a drink of his coffee. 'Was he surly with you? Because if he was, he's probably going Method on you. You're going to have to forgive all of us for anything we do and say to you in the next few hours. Perhaps particularly for turning you into a drug addicted whore. Which reminds me…' He retrieves the wrap of cocaine from his pocket. 'Seeing as this is an indictable offence, or a felony, dependent upon which side of the border we are, I'd best get rid of it.' He goes and flushes it down the toilet. 'What a terrible waste.' He says sadly.

Trying for a resumption of their silly conversation of the previous morning, she says, 'Maybe it'll meet up with some other things of yours that are in the sewer.'

He looks at her seriously. 'There's something I need to tell you about that.' He checks his watch. 'But it can wait. Go see the wardrobe mistress before she gets surly with you, too.'

Carole, when Harriet sticks her head around the bedroom door, isn't surly at all. She's as radiant as ever, even in the leopard skin robe, hair still wild from sleep.

'Come on in and take a seat.' Carole says, patting the bed. Her and Leon's bedroom is splendid, located on the corner of the house with exposed roof beams leading in a fan shape down from the ceiling. Walls in burgundy, carpet in pale gold; opulent. On the floor, a large plastic box like an overgrown toolbox, which Carole opens to reveal layer upon layer of cosmetics; pots of colour, gels, brushes in every size from artist to wallpaper hanger, eyelash curlers, implements and tools whose purposes Harriet can't even guess at.

Carole sits on the bed facing her, regarding her with a very intense, professional sort of curiosity. 'What I'm going to do to you, honey, is make you look just a little bit sleazy and a just little bit unhealthy. But don't worry; I'm not going to ruin your looks in case you get into a situation that you might need to use your good looks to get out of.' And as Harriet opens her mouth to protest, Carole adds, 'And don't pretend you don't, because we all do, when we have to.'

Carole gets to work. Strangely calming; not having to think at all, just obey Carole's instructions to look up, look down, angle her head this way or that. The touch of a brush on her eyelid or a fingertip gently rubbing circles on her cheek.

'Nearly done.' Carole says, standing up and stretching. 'No, don't look in the mirror yet, I want you to get the full effect once you're dressed. Remember I told you that I'd let you wear that miniskirt with nice thick pantyhose? Well, I lied. You need stockings. Got any?'

'Not on me.' Harriet says, thinking, possibly not at all.

'No problem, I have plenty. Stay ups, I think. And your orange bra, and the white blouse.' Carole organises her into her clothes, rolling the waistband of the skirt right up until its hem is skimming the stocking tops, undoing the buttons of the blouse until it's open to her navel, it feels like. Carole stands back and squints, steps forward again and rolls the sleeves of the blouse up. 'I'm going to give you a couple of little track marks.' She touches one scarlet nail against the inside of Harriet's elbow. 'But don't forget to roll your sleeves down to cover them if you need to.' She applies something flesh coloured from a little tube of gel, blows across the skin to set it, applies a dark red and then a bluish pencil. Steps back to look again.

'One more thing.' Carole says, and applies a sharp fingernail to one of Harriet's stockings, producing a perfect ladder from top to knee. 'Knew an actress once.' She says, 'Who always used to deliberately go out with a run in her stocking. So people would notice her, and come up to her to tell her she had a run. Now you can take a look in that mirror.'

Harriet looks. And then looks again, touching a wondering finger to her own cheek.

Six forty am.

Rusty Hanover

This morning, I'm strictly off duty right up until the point that I need to put myself on duty; don't want anyone reporting any genuine crimes to the fake Mountie, so I put the scarlet jacket away in its bag and just go with the pants, shirt and riding boots and my black jacket on top. The hat I'll carry in its box in case I need it later. Whilst I'm packing my bags, I notice that Harriet has left her pilot's dog tags on the nightstand so I steal them, putting them on under my shirt.

I feel more macho already. In fact, what I really feel is pumped, fully primed, ready for action. Faster than a speeding bullet, stronger than a train: things which might just be put to the test later, come to think of it.

So I speed downstairs in search of something to eat and someone to talk to, and find Leon in the living room, which is a start. Leon is looking sleazy and slightly undomesticated; not someone you'd want to get downwind of.

'Any chance of breakfast?' I ask him. 'I'm thinking bacon.' Leon eyes me suspiciously. 'Come on.' I tell him, swinging my arms, slapping my hands together. 'Let's get this show on the road.'

'Oh god.' Says Leon. 'I've seen you like this before.'

'What do you mean? I'm hungry here. Let's cook.' I shoo him in front of me into the kitchen.

While we're eating, Harriet appears. At least, I think its Harriet.

'Oh hey.' I tell her. 'You look terrible.' Which is sort of a lie, actually. What Carole has done to her is essentially change her leanness into a deprived sort of thinness; less a gym bunny, more the sort of person whose body shape results from a succession of seriously bad lifestyle choices. In short, she looks like the sort of girl you see on the street corner sometimes, late at night, and maybe contemplate what it would be like for about a quarter of a second before realising that a few minutes casual pleasure would cost not only the entire contents of your bank account, investment portfolio and retirement provision, but also everything else you owned and possibly a kidney as well when you woke up several hours – or days – later.

'You look like you've been keeping some very bad company.' I tell her. She does an ironic little twirl for us. 'But I like the stockings.'

Carole appears in the doorway, also in a toned-down version of last night's costume. She's added a little bit of bling and Leon's fake fur coat to her ensemble, and props one hip against the doorframe to laugh at Leon, who can't keep his eyes off Harriet.

'Stop drooling.' She tells him.

'You're my number one girl.' Leon responds, winking at Carole.

'I certainly am today, baby.' Carole says.

Carole joins us for breakfast, Harriet refusing to eat anything until I bully her into having an energy bar and some coffee. 'Don't want you passing out at the wrong moment.' I tell her and then something occurs to me. 'Although passing out at the right moment might be useful. Carole, do you have any powdered coffee? Harriet needs some fake drugs.'

Leon fetches the coffee and rummages to find a tiny Ziploc bag, Carole watching.

'You need a little brown sugar in that.' She suggests.

'Don't we all.' He says cheerfully, which earns him a slap on the butt from Carole.

I take the finished bag from him and tuck it carefully into the cup of Harriet's splendid orange bra, then get my billfold out, taking out about half of the cash which I put in my pocket before handing the billfold to Harriet. She looks at me uncomprehendingly.

'Tuck that in your skirt or something. I tell her. 'Leon, she'll need another, if you've got an old wallet you can give her.'

'Coming right up.' Leon says.

'What for?' Harriet asks.

'I might need to find them on you later. Plus, it'll give me a great excuse to body search you sometime.'

'Sounded like you already did that earlier this morning.' Carole says to me.

'Can't be too careful.' I respond.

Harriet blushes, then laughs. 'The good thing is.' She says to Carole, 'That I might just get away with his credit cards.'

'Good.' Leon says lightly. 'You're getting into character already.'

Harriet tucks my billfold into the waistband at the back of her skirt.

Seven thirty am.

We regroup in the living room with our coffee cups for a final briefing, Leon taking the director spot, centre stage, Harriet curled up the armchair, nursing her coffee cup in both hands, looking impossibly small and vulnerable. The cat jumps up and tucks itself neatly into the angle of her legs; I sit on the carpet at her feet.

'The train leaves Montréal at nine thirty.' He starts. I pretend to synchronise my watch, spy movie style, which results in me getting a hard look from him.

'Rusty?' He says.

I sit up straight. 'Sorry, okay, nine thirty.'

'Which means.' He continues, 'That you have to be off the train before ten thirty at the latest. Any later than that and you'll be going through the border stop at Cantic which could be problematic for you both.'

Harriet and I both nod.

'Rusty, I've ordered a taxi for you from here at eight thirty; about an hour's time. You need to be at the station a little before we get there so you can see us arriving and help draw some attention to us.'

'I can do that.' I tell him, adding, 'In the meantime Shem will be roughly keeping pace with the train by road. If we're getting off the train then I'll call him so he can pick us up. If we're not getting off the train then I probably won't be able to call him but he'll be able to guess what's happened by himself.'

Leon turns to Harriet. 'If you don't both manage to get off the train.' He says to her, 'Then it's best that you pretend not to know Rusty; it's less likely you'll get into trouble with the police that way.'

'No way.' Harriet says emphatically. 'Not a chance. We're in this together, we'll stay together.'

'Not unless jails are co-ed.' I say to her, recalling my thoughts of last night. 'But I don't think even Canada has those.' I feel Harriet's fingers at the back of my neck, rubbing the short hairs there.

'I don't care.' She says.

'Are you trying to say to me that if we're going down, we're going down together?'

'Something like that.' She says.

Seven forty five am.

I start to get up. 'If we're done here.' I say to Leon, 'I need to take Harriet upstairs and molest her for a while. Because it just occurred to me that I may not have the pleasure of a woman's company again for some considerable time to come.'

'Fair enough.' Carole says.

Actually, I don't really want to molest Harriet. Well, okay, I do, except we don't have time for what I'd really like to do with her, but I do want to talk to her before I leave. Because, all joking aside, I'm pretty sure that I can pull this off. Problem is, I don't know if she can.

I make sure to follow her up the stairs so I can look to see if her panties are visible under her short skirt from that angle, which, happily, they are.

'You're wearing a thong.' I tell her when we get into the bedroom.

'I am.' She says. 'And I think I'm going to be a little cold in that area when I get outside.'

'Technically, you shouldn't be wearing any at all.'

'Probably true. But I'd rather not get arrested by anyone else today.'

'Good point.' I say, and throw myself down on the bed, pulling her down beside me. I snake a hand up to one stocking top.

'Promise me you'll wear this outfit again?' I ask her.

'Only if you wear your boots.' She says.

'You like my boots, huh?' I prop myself up on one elbow to look at her. 'You should have told me last night; I'd have left them on.'

'I did think of it.' Harriet returns, 'But then I thought we'd get boot polish all over Leon and Carole's nice sheets.'

'True.' With one finger, I follow the line of the run in her stocking down to her knee. I don't want to change the subject after this interesting little revelation, but I'm running out of time. 'You know, Leon's right. If we do get into trouble with the law then you'd be much better off disowning me as some crazy random stranger who was harassing you.'

'Okay.' Harriet says. 'As long as you'll do the same in return.'

'What do you mean?'

'I mean that if this goes wrong, then Thomas' muscle boys will be on the train with us. But they won't be interested in you; only in me.'

I sit up, abruptly feeling deeply pissed off. 'You're saying that I should just leave them to it? Or why don't I just cut to the chase and hand you over to them at the station? Maybe I could make myself some money that way.'

Harriet yawns and stretches, lifting her hands above her head, pointing her toes. 'I'm just saying that you doing that is as likely as me pretending not to know you.' She says.

I look down at her. 'You really are incredibly stubborn, aren't you?'

She smiles up at me. 'I consider that to be one of my finest character traits.'

'I'll be the judge of that.' I tell her, and then spend a little time investigating the relationship between her skirt hem and stocking top until Leon raps on the door of the bedroom, saying, 'Cab's here.'

I get up reluctantly. 'Don't get too excited.' I tell Harriet, 'But I need to put my boots on now, and go and 'mantiens le droit.''

Eight thirty am.

Chapter Eight

Harriet Morgan

They leave about ten minutes after Rusty's cab; Leon driving, Carole in the passenger seat, Harriet in the back with her bag beside her. The sky outside is knotted with cold grey cloud, the Jeep taking a while to heat up inside and so she shivers for a while, wrapping her arms around herself to try and get warm.

Carole looks over at her. 'Leon, for heaven's sake turn the heat up.' She says.

'Better if we freeze her a bit.' Leon says cheerfully. 'It's more in keeping with the Method if she's miserable.'

'I keep hearing about Method today.' Harriet says. 'But I'm not sure what it really means.'

Carole answers. 'It's just an acting technique. One where you try and draw on your own emotions to identify with a character, the better to be able to act as that character.'

'Meaning.' Leon adds. 'The colder and more unhappy we make you now, the better it'll be for your technique.'

'I'm not sure if this is cold or fear I'm experiencing right now.' She admits.

'Fear is good.' Leon says. 'Use that, too.'

'Gee, thanks, Leon.'

He laughs. 'I suppose that this is the time that I apologise in advance for the way I'm about to act toward you.'

'Rusty already did that.' She tells him.

'I'm not surprised.' Leon says. 'As I've a feeling I know what he's got planned for you.'

'Which is what?'

Leon shakes his head. 'Wouldn't want to ruin it.' He says.

Rusty Hanover

Once at the station I go and change my ticket, buy a newspaper then prop myself against a pillar where I can watch the computer screens and get a good view of the escalators that descend to the station floor. The New York train is in, I see, and boarding at track eight. I also watch the glances of passers by – particularly the women - as they check out the boots and the pants then the plain jacket on top. I can see the conclusion on their faces, the slight smile and eye flick up to my face that indicates, ah, an off-duty member of the good old RCMP.

I really should wear this outfit more often. Which reminds me of Harriet's comment about the boots, and I spend a few moments in happy contemplation of potential activities to discover when we arrive back in New York until I see Harriet, Leon and Carole descending the escalator.

Carole is standing a couple of steps above and behind Leon and Harriet, hands in the pockets of her fake fur coat, smirking. In front of her, Leon has Harriet's upper arm in a tight grip, his body close to hers and his head bent towards her as he talks to her in a way that looks less than friendly.

I straighten up, keeping my eyes fixed on them.

They reach the bottom and Leon gives Harriet a shove, making her stumble slightly, and then propels her across the station floor, still hissing at her, at a guess, in a stream of incomprehensible French. Carole follows them, hip-waggling her way across the floor, a slight smile on her face

Still staring at them, I take half a stride toward them and stop.

Heads are starting to turn now, people pausing to watch this little group's progress, amongst them a member of train staff toting a logoed satchel over his shoulder.

Perfect.

It should be obvious to any observer what's going on here. Carole is Leon's new girl; Harriet the old girl, the troublesome one that he's getting rid of to New York, even though she clearly doesn't want to go. Doubtless there'll be an accomplice of his to meet her at Penn station and put her to work down there.

The group stops by the entrance to the track for the New York train, and Leon lets go of Harriet's arm to point, stiff-armed, at the train.

Harriet says something, shakes her head. Leon lunges towards her, raising his hand and she flinches back, looking scared, then takes off, skittering towards the train on her boot heels.

My heart thumping nastily, I pick my bags up and follow her.

As I pass Leon and Carole, Leon wraps an arm around Carole's waist and lands a kiss on her ear. Carole throws her head back and laughs throatily and as she does so she catches my eye and winks.

While I'm stowing my luggage in the racks on the train I notice that it's taken a member of the train staff around a half second to stop Harriet to check her ticket and I can sense his reluctance to admit that, yes, she really does have the correct ticket for this car. I guess not many business class travellers normally dress the way she is today, which is probably a shame as it would certainly liven things up for the rest of us regular travellers.

Harriet takes a seat on the far side of the train, facing the engine; I sit diagonally opposite a couple of rows back so I can keep a discreet eye on her.

At the end of the coach, the train guy with the satchel has a whispered conversation with the one who's just checked Harriet's ticket.

I take out my newspaper and pretend to start reading it.

The guard calls the All Aboard and the train doors clunk shut.

Nine thirty am.

The Adirondack train is on its way to Pennsylvania Station, New York City.

Harriet Morgan

She can see now what Leon and Rusty warned her about but its still a shock, Leon turning hard-eyed and nasty and Carole mocking her. She kept wanting to say, come on you guys, but instead, as Leon had said, reacting was easy and she'd felt genuinely relieved to get away from them in the end.

Now all she has to do is keep her eyes off Rusty who is lounging in his seat, reading the paper. She feels sure that the two train staff members are talking about her so she keeps her head down for the time being, watching Montréal sliding away outside. She can't do anything until they're past the suburban St. Lambert stop, anyway, so she spends the time wondering how a junkie would act if they needed a hit and decides jittery, probably. She fiddles around in her seat, plays with her hair, searches through her bag for nothing. Thinking, oh come on, come on, train. Get on with it. She hears Rusty ordering coffee and feels irrationally annoyed that he hasn't ordered any for her; not that she exactly needs any more caffeine, now that she's feeling genuinely jittery. Stupid idea, this, what were they thinking? And somewhere on the train Thomas' muscle boys are waiting. She could scream. Oh come on, train, let's get this over with.

Finally, the St. Lambert stop comes and goes. A couple more passengers for business class; she waits until they've settled and then gets up and goes, as instructed, for a casual little stroll down through the other coaches and back up again.

Strange how the outfit gets her so much attention, not all of it salacious. She notices as she passes that a couple of women check that their bags are still by their feet, other people subconsciously looking towards the luggage racks at the ends of the coaches to see that their possessions are still there.

She doesn't see the muscle boys on her little journey, but then she realises she probably wouldn't recognise them unless they stood up and introduced themselves to her.

Nine fifty am.

Harriet decides it's time to get this show on the road.

Returning to the business class coach via the restroom she takes Rusty's wallet out from her waistband and conceals it in the palm of her hand, then, sitting down, she slides all the cash from it into her bag; a reasonably thick wad comprising a mix of sombre greenbacks and more festive Canadian dollars. The wallet she keeps in her hand under the table while she goes through the remainder of its contents, noting drivers licence, two credit cards – one a black one, interesting - a membership card for a sports club, a DVD rental card, something from what looks like an actor's union. She gets so absorbed in piecing together Rusty's life from the contents of his wallet she doesn't even noticing him coming until he's standing over her.

'On your feet.' He says to her in a voice that isn't about to be disobeyed.

Starting, she gets up, sliding along the seat until she's standing in the aisle. He takes the wallet from her hand.

'Where did you get this?' Hard eyes.

'A friend gave it to me.' She says in a small voice, thinking, Christ, he really is tall.

'Really?' He opens the wallet and looks through it. 'Presumably the same generous man who bought you a business-class ticket, huh?'

'Yes.'

'Hands on the table.' He says. 'I'm guessing you know the drill.'

She turns and puts her palms flat on the table. Knowing everyone in the car is looking at her she feels her face burn hot with embarrassment. She lowers her head so she can hide behind the curtain of her hair and, looking down, sees him nudging her feet farther apart with one of his big boots. He pats her down, quickly and efficiently, and as he slides one finger into the waistband of her skirt she feels a number of conflicting emotions; embarrassment, certainly, and fear, along with a sudden and entirely inappropriate feeling of something else, too. She tries not to wriggle as he retrieves Leon's old wallet from the small of her back.

'Another friend?' He props an elbow casually on her back to examine the wallet.

'Yes.' She whispers.

'I'll bet you have a lot of male friends, don't you? For about a half hour at a time.'

She doesn't answer.

'I'm arresting you for theft, do you understand?' He says. He reaches around one side of her, taking her wrist and drawing it round behind her back and, before she can react, does the same the other side. And then handcuffs her.

'Sit down.' He says. Rigid with shock, she doesn't move.

'Sit down.' He says again, louder.

She sits, thinking, Rusty, you complete *bastard*.

Ten am.

Rusty Hanover

I really should wear this outfit more often. This is very sweet, and interestingly sexy, too. In fact, and you'll have to pardon me for mentioning it, it's probably why the Mounties wear their pants so baggy in the crotch area. And a good thing, too, as I wouldn't be wanting to face a lewdness charge along with that of impersonating a police officer. When I slap the cuffs on Harriet, I realise that I can't actually remember the whole of the Miranda thing, except that it bangs on about lawyers and counsel, but since I'm fairly likely to be needing a lawyer soon myself I guess it doesn't matter too much.

Once I've sat Harriet back down I notice there's a train steward lurking behind me, looking extremely uncomfortable. I tell him that he needs to stop the train so I can take her into custody as soon as possible.

'I'll go get the train manager.' He tells me, and bolts.

A few moments later the train manager rolls up, a short fat little fireplug of a guy. I look down at him and repeat my order.

'Sir.' He says. 'I cannot stop this train before Cantic.'

'I'm afraid that you'll have to.' I tell him.

'Sir, I'm afraid that I cannot. You will have to disembark at Cantic.'

'Not good enough.' I tell him. 'Because I'll be out of my jurisdiction by then and I'll have to release her.' In fact, and even if I were a real one, I'm out of my jurisdiction in the whole of the province, as the Mounties don't actually have the local franchise here, but I'm hoping he doesn't know this.

'Sir, there's nothing I can do about that.' Fireplug guy insists. 'I cannot stop the train before Cantic.'

Oh cocksucker motherfucker. He isn't going to do it and we're both in deep, deep shit.

I carry on arguing with the little man for a while; pointlessly, because he's not moving. As far as he's concerned the train stops at Cantic, and we're getting off there. And as far as Harriet and I are concerned, Cantic will just be a race to see which out of the Canadian Border Service Agency or the US Border Protection Service gets to detain us first. Perhaps they could have one of us each, according to our citizenship.

Harriet stands up.

'Sit down.' I tell her, loudly. If the little man is going to piss me off, then I'm going to do my best to piss off his business class passengers by causing as much disruption as possible.

She doesn't sit down.

'Sit down.' I threaten her. 'Or I'll make you sit down.'

'I don't feel well.' She says in a small voice.

Christ, she really doesn't look well. In fact, if it's possible for a human being to actually turn green, then she has. She looks like she's about to throw up all over the little guy's nice clean train carpet. I seize the opportunity and grab her by the shoulders.

'What have you taken?' I ask her.

Harriet Morgan

Watching them argue, she knows that Rusty isn't going to win this one; the train manager is sticking to his guns that this train is stopping at Cantic and not a moment before.

Oh god, she thinks, we've failed. Desperately trying to work out if them finding an excuse to stay on the train, and probably face Thomas' muscle boys along the way, or getting off at Cantic and facing the music there, would be better. Safer at Cantic, she supposes, and trusting in Art's ability to get them both out of the system quickly.

Fear rises in her throat like nausea, tasting of bitter coffee and defeat. Then she remembers Leon saying 'use it' in the car this morning.

Thinking, here goes nothing, she stands up.

Rusty turns to look at her, and then points a long finger at her and roars at her to sit down.

She doesn't. Instead, swallowing hard, she tells him she doesn't feel well.

He crosses the carriage in one long stride and grips her by the shoulders.

'What have you taken?' He asks.

'The usual.' She says, looking down. What do junkies do when they've overdosed? They pass out, she supposes, but she's not sure she can pull off a convincing faint so she just lets herself sway with the motion of the train.

'Show me.' Rusty says.

She fumbles in her bra cup for the pack of fake drugs and then hands it to him. He holds it briefly up to the light, and then leans behind her to push her shirt sleeve upwards, exposing the track marks Carole made for her.

'I think it was stronger than usual.' She says to him, and closes her eyes.

Rusty turns to the fat little train manager, but there's no need; he's already on his radio to the engine driver, telling him that they need to stop at St. Hyacinthe to take off a sick passenger.

Rusty Hanover

Oh blessed St. Hyacinthe, our lady of the blue flowers, deliver us from evil. I recognise the name of the station as one of those places that this train usually thunders though without ever stopping at. Oh lovely St. Hyacinthe, I bet you've been wanting all these years for this big old train to slide up to your station stop, haven't you? And all thanks to my brilliant, beautiful and rather sleazy looking Harriet that it is. Clearly, junkie whores are just fine with the crew here unless one is about to drop dead from an overdose on their nice shiny train.

I feel the train's brakes go on as I sit Harriet back down. I nearly push her head between her knees, but remember just in time that doing this to someone with their hands cuffed behind their back is a highly efficient way to suffocate them, as a couple of US deportees have found out to their cost. Instead, I take a seat opposite her and call Shem. When he answers, I identify myself as Officer Petersen, refer to him as Officer Sherberski, and tell him that my journey to New York is going to be interrupted at St. Hyacinthe and that I need a squad car and EMS waiting there.

Clever man, he tells me that he's close by, and that it'll be quicker if he picks us up himself.

'Whatever.' I tell him, loudly, for the benefit of the audience. 'Just as long as we can get to the ER quickly. I've got an OD here.'

The guard makes an announcement that the train is stopping to let a sick passenger off, and that no-one else will be allowed to disembark. I'll bet the muscle boys are on their phones to Thomas already, if they've got any brains, although it's a possibility, I suppose, that they don't have brains, and will watch mine and Harriet's departure with slack-jawed bemusement.

The train draws up at the humped little station. I collect my bags and sling them over my shoulder, add Harriet's packsack, and then collect Harriet herself, tugging her to her feet by one arm. She gives me a very chilly look, meaning that either she's still acting, or that she's extremely mad at me about the handcuffs and is going to kill me just as soon as I take them off her. If that's the case then it might just be safer for me if I leave them on her until she calms down.

Harriet Morgan

Discovering for the first time in her life how incredibly difficult it is to move anywhere independently while handcuffed, Harriet allows herself to be towed down the train by Rusty. They wait by the doors until the train manager unlocks it and then she has to hop down onto the station platform, which is almost impossible without her hands to balance her. Infuriatingly, without Rusty holding her up she's in danger of falling to her knees on the icy station surface.

She spots Shem who, thanks to his mysterious super powers, has snagged the parking spot closest to the side of the station and is sitting with the engine running in a grey Toyota Land Cruiser, one of the new ones that look like the old ones except on steroids; burlier, flared around the wheel arches. The sight of it makes her smile because she's sure his choice of vehicle is entirely deliberate.

Still looking directly ahead, Rusty says to her, 'That was really kind of sexy, wasn't it?'

'You bastard.' She says.

'Sorry.' He says, not sounding it in the least.

Rusty opens the rear door of the Toyota, slings the bags in and then folds her into the seat with a very professional hand on the top of her head.

Shem, she notes, is wearing a black sweater with a white shirt showing underneath which makes him look like a particularly dangerous sort of priest. Not one you'd want to confess any mortal sins to, just in case you found absolution at the business end of his Glock.

He reverses out of the parking space and drives smoothly out of the lot. For a moment, the departing train keeps pace with them and then pulls away as they stop for a red light.

Rusty throws his head back and whoops. 'We fucking did it! Or rather, Harriet did by being such an excellent junkie whore.' Shem turns to stare at him.

'What?' Rusty says, grinning. 'You think I shouldn't call Harriet a junkie whore? But she was such a good one. Or would you prefer it if I referred to her as a woman with substance abuse issues who participates in compensated dating? I don't think she actually did any substance abusing on the train. Or any compensated dating; there wasn't enough time.'

'There wasn't anyone good looking enough.' Harriet says mildly.

'Hey.' Rusty says, looking hurt.

'I took it as read that as an officer of the law you would have got a freebie anyway.' She tells him.

'Sounds reasonable.' He responds.

'Would you mind…?' She shuffles around on the seat until her wrists are facing him.

'Ah. Keys…keys…keys…' Rusty pats himself down in imitation of a man who has lost the keys.

'Shem?' His eyes meet hers in the rear-view mirror. 'Would you mind please shooting Rusty? You don't have to kill him; just a kneecap or something will be fine.'

'Found them!' Rusty calls out. 'They were in my pants pocket all the time.'

He unlocks the cuffs and she brings her hands around to the front, rubbing her wrists. 'These are more uncomfortable than you'd think, aren't they?'

'You telling me you've never worn any of those before?' Rusty asks.

Harriet looks up from buttoning up her shirt. 'Never. You?'

He smirks. 'What, outside of a bedroom situation?' He holds up three fingers. 'Three times.'

'And you, Shem?' She asks.

'Never.' Shem says.

'Never?' Echoes Rusty.

'It's better not to get caught.' Shem suggests.

'I really must try to remember that.' Rusty says.

Shem pulls the Toyota over to the side of the road and stops. 'Harriet needs to be in the front before we get to the border.'

She gets out, taking the opportunity to tug her skirt down to a respectable level, and swaps places with Rusty, taking her backpack into the front seat with her. 'Why?'

'Two guys in the front.' Shem says, pulling back out onto the road. 'Girl in the back. Looks like we're trafficking her over the border.'

Rusty tugs his phone out of his jacket pocket. 'That would never actually have occurred to me. You live in a strange world, don't you, Shem?'

Harriet balances her bag on her lap and roots around in it, finding make-up remover. Pulls down the sun visor to use the vanity mirror and wipes most of the gunk off her face. 'Doesn't have to be over the border to be trafficking.' She tells Shem. 'Or even over a state line. Town to town would do it.'

'Then you both live in the same strange world.' Rusty notes. 'Offering a ride to a woman is obviously more complicated than I thought.'

Rusty Hanover

Jubilant, I call Leon and he answers immediately. 'Rusty?'

'Yo, dude.' I greet him. 'We did it.'

He whoops down the phone so loudly it makes Shem swerve. 'Is Harriet okay?' He asks.

'She was great.'

'Let me talk to her.' I hand her the phone over the back of the seat.

'Hi, Leon.' She says. 'No, that's okay.' A pause. 'You knew he was going to do that, didn't you?' Another pause; I can hear Leon speaking but can't make out the words. 'Actually, it was the most humiliating thing that ever happened to me in my whole life. No, I'll get my revenge for the handcuffs but not yet. I'll just wait until he's least expecting it. Uh huh. Yeah, I thought so, too. Okay, I'll speak to you later. Give Carole my love.'

She passes me back the phone.

'Boy, are you in serious trouble.' Leon tells me.

'I know.' I say happily. The good news is, if she's intending to get revenge on me then it must mean she's intending to see me again in New York; both of which thoughts give me a very pleasant tingle of anticipation.

'Oh well.' Says Leon. 'I suppose the fact that you're at liberty means I can stand the lawyer down.'

'You had a lawyer waiting?' I ask him. 'You should have more faith.'

'Rusty, I've known you for far too long for that.' He responds, and hangs up.

Harriet fiddles with the car radio, finding only a mixture of French and static until she happens upon an American hip-hop station and we progress towards the border to a soundtrack of ganstas and hos, which is weirdly appropriate, I suppose. The music makes me think of something.

'Hey, Shem?' I stick my head between the front seats to look at him. 'Are we ridin' dirty, here?'

'Yes.' He says.

'Oh shit.' I say, remembering. 'I need to get rid of the drugs.' I locate the fake drugs in my pocket, lick my finger and dip it into the wrap, tasting the mixture of coffee and sugar. 'Harriet?' I offer her the little bag and she does likewise. Shem looks slightly horrified.

'It's alright.' She tells Shem. 'They're not real.' She lowers her window and drops the bag out into the street.

'Whoever finds that.' I tell her 'Is going to simultaneously have the best day and the most disappointing day of their whole life.'

We leave the last of the Montréal suburbs behind and head for Champlain. We're on a back road, nothing much out here but scrubby trees, thin snow, the occasional house. Sort of lonely. The same obviously occurs to Harriet and she asks Shem where Thomas is.

‘A few minutes behind us.’ He tells her. ‘He’s with Art; for the moment, Thomas thinks he’s still in control. We’ll meet up with them somewhere on the US side of the border.’

‘At which moment.’ I add. ‘He’ll realise he’s not in control anymore.’

‘Something like that.’ Shem says.

I turn sideways on the seat and stick my leg in the air to tug my Mountie boot off, which isn’t easy for a guy my size in the confines of the back seat, I can tell you. Harriet looks over her shoulder at me.

‘What are you doing?’ She says.

‘Don’t worry.’ I tell her. ‘The boots can go back on anytime, just say the word.’ She pulls a face at me.

‘I’m getting changed.’ I continue. ‘Of all the things that I’m doing or am about to do today that could get me arrested, I thought that impersonating a police officer would be the one I could avoid.’

‘Isn’t it a bit late for that?’ She asks.

‘Probably.’ I admit. The boots finally off, I tug my jeans out of my bag and start undoing my pants. She covers her eyes with her hands.

‘Isn’t it a bit late for that?’ I ask her.

‘Probably.’ She responds.

By the time we get to join the queue of cars for the border checks, I’m changed and looking like an ordinary respectable citizen. Or at least, as ordinary and respectable as it gets with me. I hunker down in my seat a little. Harriet is looking pretty respectable herself, although I do miss the junkie whore look a little. What she also looks like is nervous, clearly worried about the armoury that Shem doubtless has in the trunk. I wonder what’s in there; everything from a bb gun to anti-tank missiles, probably.

We’re next in line; a matching pair of customs officers wave us on until we’re level with them; one a black woman, one a white man. Of course, travelling this way it’s the Americans at the border, not the Canadians like on the way up. A small mercy, this, as I suspect that if I see Harriet’s admirer again, the big Canuck from our outward journey, he’d love to have an excuse to snap on the rubber gloves and humiliate me.

Sticking my head over the seat next to Harriet, I launch into mid-conversation.

‘So I said to the waiter, you’re kidding, these are just snails like I’d find in my back yard? And he says, no, because apparently they have to starve them before you eat them else they’d be disgusting. I mean, they’re disgusting anyway, even with the garlic and all.’ Harriet lowers her window and hands her passport to the male officer and I pass mine over as well. 'Except.' I continue 'That Harriet wouldn't know, on account of her not eating meat or fish. Are snails meat or fish? 'Cos if they were in the sea they'd be seafood.'

'I don't know.' Harriet says. She smiles at the officer. 'Are snails molluscs?' she asks him brightly. He looks understandably confused.

'No.' The pretty female officer on Shem's side of the car says, looking up from his passport. 'They're gastropods. From the Latin, gastro for eat and pod for feet.'

'Makes sense.' I tell her. 'They eat with their feet, right? Good thing us humans don't do it that way, else we'd have to stand on our burgers.'

'Soup would be worse.' The female officer notes.

'Good point.' I agree with her. 'They'd have to give you two bowls, right? And that's no joke with feet my size.' I raise one foot in the air to show her and she laughs, hands Shem his documents back and steps back to wave us on through.

We're back in the USA.

Shem drives on. He's a slow driver, I note, sticking rigidly to the speed limit, whereas I'd take advantage of a nice shiny new rental SUV and open it up a little. Although maybe that's not such a smart idea with a trunk full of RPGs. Harriet still has her passport in her hand and I lean forwards and steal it so I can take a look. It isn't a passport at all, I discover, but a UN Laissez Passer, full of colourful exotic stamps from places which, to be honest, I'm slightly vague about where they might exactly be located on the globe.

'That's weird.' I tell her. 'You have the same middle name as me. I didn't know it was a girl's name; maybe I should be embarrassed.'

'Lee was my father's name.' She tells me. 'So it's not really a girl's name.'

'That's a relief. So what did your father do?' I ask her.

'Diplomatic service.'

'Which would explain why you've spent so much of your life trotting around the world?'

'Yeah.' She says. 'It's in the blood.'

And at that exact moment, just as she says the word 'blood', a black Lincoln draws up close behind our Toyota, flashes its headlamps twice.

'Here we go.' Says Shem, looking as close to happy as I've ever seen him.

Shem takes a right turn off the highway, and then a left, taking them further away from civilisation and other traffic. They're driving along beside what must be crop fields in summer, she guesses, although they're just snow-covered prairies at the moment. The black car follows them closely. Thomas is in there, she knows, and she goes cold despite the heat in the Toyota, feeling goose pimples rising. It would be horribly ironic, she thinks, if she had been right about Shem after all, and she's about to be sold back to Thomas while Rusty gets a bullet in the back of the head.

She feels in the bottom of the bag the little gun, pulling it to the surface, leaving it on top of her bundled clothes for easy access. Just in case.

Shem looks over at her. 'Don't worry.' He says, and pulls the car over at the side of the road, stopping the engine. The monochrome field beside them is flat and unfenced, furrowed snow leading off into the distance.

The black car stops behind. For a moment, nothing happens. The Toyota's cooling engine ticks in the sudden silence.

Then the passenger door of the Lincoln is flung open and Thomas throws himself out, taking off at a panicked run across the snow field, slipping and stumbling in his city shoes. Despite the heavy sky he's wearing sunglasses, presumably, she thinks, to cover the black eyes she must have given him when she broke his nose back in the alley behind the gym. He looks so stupid and vulnerable and desperate she almost feels sorry for him.

Shem doesn't move.

The driver's door of the Lincoln opens, and Art gets out, pausing to turn the collar of his jacket up against the cold wind. He steps up to her window and she lowers it.

'Hey, gorgeous.' He says to her.

'Hi Art.'

Art spots Rusty in the back seat. 'Who's this?' He asks.

'I'm the entertainment.' Rusty says calmly. 'I also do weddings, if you're interested.'

Art gives a bark of laughter.

Shem gets out of the Toyota and then leans back in to speak to her. 'Would you take the wheel?' He says. 'I'm guessing you know how to drive one of these.'

'I do.' She says, and climbs over the central hump of the transmission, sits down in the seat and starts the engine.

Shem moves to the back of the Toyota, taking something out of the trunk before getting in at the passenger side.

'Do you mind if I join you?' Art gets in the back beside Rusty.

'I want you to drive onto the field and follow Thomas.' Shem says to her. The item from the trunk is a flat metal case, like a large briefcase, which he places on his lap to snap open the locks. 'There's no hurry, he isn't going anywhere.'

She selects four-wheel drive and shifts the Toyota into second gear so the wheels don't spin as she pulls onto the field, then drives steadily across the furrows towards the running black shape that is Thomas.

Rusty Hanover

When we stop by the field I notice that Harriet has gone pale again, and it's this more than anything that makes me realise, probably somewhat belatedly, that this whole set-up could turn out to be a deadly trap for both of us. In which case my lovely Harriet, my lithe little Kudu girl, is likely to end up raped and dead and me just plain dead. It may make me a coward, but I hope if we're in that scenario they kill me first.

When Art joins me in the back seat my heart clenches. Why didn't we just fucking fly back to New York, I wonder, and then I would have made the police do something about Thomas, or done it myself, Mountie-style, perhaps accidentally tasering him to death or something. But instead we're here and as Harriet drives us across the field I realise I don't even have a champagne bottle to hit anyone with. Note to self, if I survive: make like an American and buy myself a gun. And then carry it everywhere with me always.

Art fumbles in his pocket for something and I sit very, very still.

Sighing deeply, Art takes a pack of cigarettes out of his pocket and offers me one. I take it. No point in worrying about lung cancer now, I guess.

As we draw closer to Thomas, Shem tells Harriet to turn the Toyota sideways on to his fleeing figure, and stop. She does so, and Shem takes out the item from the metal case, which isn't what I'd expected at all.

It's a crossbow; I've seen them before, of course, even used one myself years ago, but they're more generally used for hunting deer, not people.

Shem opens the car door and stands up on the door sill, resting the bow on the roof to load the bolt. I hear the metallic click as the mechanism of the bow engages.

He leans back into the car to look at Harriet sitting at the wheel.

'Your choice, remember?' He says. 'You want me to kill him?'

She looks up at Shem. 'He has kids, right?'

Shem nods.

'Could you just shoot him in the ass?'

Possibly for the first time in his entire life, Shem smiles. 'Certainly.' He says. He rests his elbows on the roof to sight the bow, exhales a long deep breath, and fires.

Almost instantaneously, Thomas' distant figure stumbles and falls.

Harriet takes something out of her bag that she's left in the passenger foot well, turns to look at Art. 'Is he armed?' She asks him.

'He was. I took it away from him.' Art says.

Harriet gets out of the Toyota and starts to walk across the snowy field towards Thomas who is lying on his side, curled foetally, clearly in some kind of agony.

In her left hand she's holding a gun.

A gun.

I open the door and get out, saying to Shem. 'Did you know she had that?'

'I guessed she had something.' He says. 'But I wasn't sure what.'

'What if she kills him?' I ask.

'She's a fighter, not a killer.' Shem says. From the admiring way he says 'fighter' I guess that this is his highest compliment to a woman, more than, say, beautiful or sexy. 'I think she just wants to have a conversation with him.' He adds.

I struggle out of my coat, open the trunk and take out the Mountie jacket and hat, putting them both on.

'What are you doing?' Art asks, amused.

'This is really going to fuck with his head.' I respond, tilting the hat just so.

Harriet Morgan

The gun is heavy and cold in her hand. When she reaches Thomas she sees that his sunglasses are mirrored, and for a moment she sees them all reflected, distorted in the lenses. Herself, the Toyota behind her with Shem and Art leaning against it, Rusty in the scarlet jacket and Mountie hat standing beside them, arms folded.

She raises the gun, slips the safety off just as Chris showed her back in his apartment.

'Take the sunglasses off.' She tells Thomas. 'And throw them over to me.' He does so, the glasses landing in the snow at her feet. Without taking her eyes off him she picks them up, shaking the snow off them before putting them on. Strange how much easier it feels if they can't see your eyes. His own are still blackened and swollen.

'Please.' Thomas says. She can see the fletch of the bolt sticking out of his ass cheek; blood on snow. That must hurt, she thinks. 'Please.' He says again. 'Take me to the hospital.'

'Sure.' She says to him. 'Just like you would have done for me, once I was drugged and raped by you and your hired hands, right, Thomas? I'm sure you would have been really compassionate.'

Looking up at her desperately, he doesn't answer.

Holding the gun up with one hand is hard work, she's finding, so she cups her other hand around the grip as well.

'You know.' She tells him. 'The man who lent me this gun told me not to show it unless I was intending to use it. Do you think that was good advice?'

'Please.' He says again.

'I see now why people have guns.' She tells him. 'They're all about equality, aren't they? I mean, suddenly it doesn't matter that I'm a lot smaller than you. That's pretty neat. I like that.'

Thomas starts to cry. 'Please don't kill me.' He pleads.

'I'm not going to kill you.' She says, lowering the gun. 'And do you know why not? Because you have a wife and family, and I assume they need you financially, even if they don't like you very much. But if you ever come near me again, I will kill you and I'll happily go to jail for it, because it would have been worth it. You understand?'

He says nothing, just cries desperate tears and snot into the snow.

She raises the gun again. 'Do you understand?'

'Yes.' He says.

She turns to go.

'There's a Mountie.' Thomas says, in disbelief.

'I know. He's a friend of mine. And now Art and Shem are friends of mine, too. Isn't that strange?'

She walks slowly back across the snowfield towards her new friends. And what an odd looking bunch they are, she thinks, grinning to herself.

Rusty Hanover

When she reaches us, Shem gently takes the gun out of her hand, puts the safety catch on and gives it back to her.

She looks at me.

'Nice shades.' I tell her. They are: a sporty pair of gold-tinted Oakleys. She takes them off and gives them to me.

I put them on. 'I never before noticed that you were left-handed.' I say to her. 'Why did I not notice that you're a southpaw?'

She smiles briefly at me, then looks at Shem. 'Can we go home now?' She asks him.

'Yes.' Shem says.

'Can we get some food on the way?' I ask him. 'All this shooting people stuff is making me hungry.'

'What a good idea.' Says Art, lighting another cigarette.

Shem drives, Art in passenger seat, Harriet and I in the back. I put an arm around her and she leans in to me sleepily, all the tension and fight gone out of her. All of us – apart from Shem – smoke in the car on the way back across the field to the highway, a fact that seems to annoy Shem so intensely that I ask him if we're breaching the car rental agreement by smoking.

'This car.' Shem says, 'Is not going back to the rental place.'

'Where's it going?' I ask.

Art answers. 'New Jersey.'

I get it. 'Ah. New Jersey, shortly before going off to seek a new life in the sun? If you see my Corvette there, would you please let me know?'

Shem pulls off the field and back onto the roadway in front of Art's Lincoln.

'You have a Corvette?' Harriet asks me.

'Not anymore.' I tell her. 'But it did send me a postcard from Dubai.'

We backtrack to the highway, Art following us in the Lincoln, and pull over at the first rest stop we see. Desolate, a gas station with a weather-beaten stucco diner behind; looking like heaven to me. Shem pauses in the parking lot to speak to Art, so as we walk ahead of them to the diner I take advantage of a minute alone with Harriet to tell her that there had been a moment, back there, when I'd thought it was all about to go horribly wrong for us both.

'Me, too.' She says. 'I was thinking that I'd got you into this and wishing I hadn't.'

'Are you kidding?' I ask her. 'I wouldn't have missed this for the world. What a trip. Especially as we're both still breathing.'

'I did have the gun.' She reminds me.

'Ah yes, the gun. You know, if I'd been aware you had that on you in Montréal, things would have been very different between us.'

She pauses in the doorway of the diner to look at me.

'Would they?'

'Probably not.' I admit. 'I guess I would have thought it was worth the risk.'

She laughs. 'Good.' She says.

She takes a seat in a booth by the window, sliding along the seat to make room for me next to her. I cram my legs under the table and rest one hand on her knee, feeling with my thumb for the run in her stocking.

Out the window, I notice that Art and Shem are making their way across the parking lot to the diner, which means I don't have much time to do this.

'Would you like to get together, back in New York? Can I buy you dinner, or something?' I ask her.

She leans her slim, stockinged thigh against mine. 'I think I still owe you dinner.' She says.

I remember. 'Wasn't it supposed to be Nobu?' I tease her, risking moving my hand up her leg.

'Only if we're not very hungry.' She responds. I slide my hand further up her thigh and do a little heavy breathing in her ear.

'Doesn't that depend on what we're hungry for?' I murmur. A bit of a cheesy line, I'll admit, but the best I can do in the circumstances.

Before she can answer, Art and Shem arrive, sitting down opposite us in the booth. And then Harriet puts her hand on my thigh, sliding right it up to the top for one wonderful moment before asking them brightly, 'Hungry?'

'Oh yeah.' Art says. Shem just nods, watching Harriet closely.

'Good.' She says, reaching for the menu with her free hand. 'I'm starving.'

'Me too.' I tell her. 'Amazing, since it wasn't that long since I last ate. Sometimes I just don't know where my appetite comes from.'

Her fingers gently pinch the top of my thigh muscle.

'It must be because there's so much of you.' She says, wide-eyed and innocent.

We eat and talk about cars, a nice easy guy subject. Watching people eat is an interesting illustration of their characters, I find. Harriet eats slowly, getting through about two-thirds of her sandwich before pushing the remains away; Art talks and eats his heap of steak and fries non-stop, Shem carves up his burger with a slightly creepy surgical precision and I just wolf mine down as fast as humanly possible.

Art offers to get me a top of the range replacement Corvette at a very big discount.

'It would be a bit of a grey-market vehicle.' He warns.

'An import?' I'm confused.

'Not exactly.' He says with a grin. 'It just may have had a little bit of an identity change somewhere along the line.'

I tell him thanks, but no thanks. 'I'd be too worried that I'd buy my own one back. And I know what I did to it.'

Art gives me his card. 'Well, if you change your mind, I know some people who can help. Or if you need anything else.' He gives a card to Harriet, too. 'Would you like a car? Any make or model or colour.' He offers.

'I've never really seen the point of owning a car in New York.' She tells him, 'But it was nice driving a Land Cruiser again.'

Shem smiles at her. 'I thought you'd like that.'

'How come?' I ask.

Shem turns his cold grey eyes towards me. 'Do you not watch news programmes?' As if I spend my time watching cartoons, or porn. Both of which I do, sometimes, but I'm not having him alleging that in front of Harriet.

'Of course I do.' Then I remember seeing news reports: herds of Land Cruisers storming into disaster areas, bringing succour to troubled lands. 'It's the UN thing, right? But, Shem, you got the wrong colour.'

'They didn't have it in white at the rental place.' He says, annoyed.

Harriet Morgan

Watching Rusty and Shem shake their antlers at each other, the older stag and the younger buck, is simultaneously amusing and wearying, she finds. As if, evolution-wise, they've managed to forget that the woman usually gets a say in the matter.

When the check comes, they play quick-draw with wallets, Rusty winning, so she lets him open it and realise with astonishment that there's no cash in there at all before she hands him back the roll of notes she'd stolen from him on the train.

'That was sneaky.' He tells her.

'Leon was telling me about method acting.'

'DeNiro would be proud of you.' He says, standing up. 'Except you should have kept some of the cash.'

He offers her a hand up, and as he does so she says, 'How do you know I didn't?'

He makes a big show of counting his cash as they leave.

After the humid heat of the diner, the cold outside feels even more severe. Not a temperature you'd want to hang around in for long, she thinks, which makes her concerned about Thomas. Does he have a cell phone on him? She wonders. Or will he just have to crawl to the road and hope for passing traffic?

She slips away from Rusty to catch up with Shem. 'Will Thomas be okay?' She asks him.

'The only thing Thomas will die of is exposure.' Shem says.

'Well, exactly. I don't really want him to die at all.'

Shem and Art exchange a look, then Shem gestures towards a public phone by the gas station.

'Okay.' Shem says. 'We'll call 911 on that phone and say we witnessed an accident.'

'I'll do it.' Rusty says. She walks across to the gas station with him, not only to keep him company but because she has a small fear that if she got in the Toyota now with Shem, Shem might just try and leave without Rusty.

Rusty makes the call and tells the operator, in a perfect, Harvard-African-American accent, that he thinks he's just witnessed a hunting accident.

They sprint back to the Toyota, where Shem is leaning patiently against the front. As they draw near, he raises his hand and throws the car keys to Rusty. For a moment Harriet is tempted to try and intercept the keys, just to make a point, but she realises how very tired the food and warmth of the diner has made her. No point, she decides, in getting this far and then killing them all under a semi on the highway because she's fallen asleep at the wheel.

Art comes over to say goodbye, giving her a rib-endangering hug and then slapping Rusty hard enough on the back to dislodge a few vertebra, it looks like, and then takes off at speed in the Lincoln, laying down rubber at the exit to the parking lot.

'Can I take the back seat?' She says to Shem. 'I need to get some sleep.'

'Of course you can.' He says, opening the back door of the Toyota for her.

Rusty gets in at the driver's side, adjusting the seat back as far as it will go with a solid and deliberate click from the mechanism, like a man making a comment about superior height.

Shem gets in at the other side and leans his head back on the seat rest, closing his eyes. 'Don't drive too fast.' He tells Rusty. 'We don't want to get pulled over.'

Rusty responds with, 'Never criticise a man's driving, his religion, or… what's the other one, Harriet?'

'I forget.' She says. She does know the answer to that one, but she doesn't want to be drawn into their argument.

As he starts the engine, the radio comes on; more pounding gangsta and 'ho music. Shem switches it off without comment.

'How long to New York?' She asks him.

'About four, five hours depending on traffic. Could be slow coming into Manhattan.'

As he accelerates on the highway, Rusty starts singing his saucy train song again.

Shem turns in his seat to look at her. 'Can't you make him stop?'

'No.' She tells him, knowing it to be true.

Rusty launches into the second verse.

She's not sure if the singing is to impress her, or irritate Shem, but the second is certainly working.

'I may really have to kill him.' Shem says to her.

'Could you please do it quietly? I'm trying to sleep here.' Which earns her a look in the rear-view mirror from Rusty, but she ignores them both and curls up on the back seat to sleep.

Rusty Hanover

The Toyota is a nice drive; not as quick as my own SUV but not bad; nice and solid and positive. Traffic is light, which gives me the opportunity to watch Harriet in the rear-view mirror as she's sleeping. She's lying facing the back, her hair flowing off the edge of the seat, a little bit of skin showing at the small of her back and a little bit of stocking top showing below her skirt. Just as I'm having some pleasantly sort of adolescent thoughts about Harriet and me and the back seats of large cars, Shem opens his eyes and looks at me.

I'm starting to worry that he might be psychic.

'What?' I say to him.

'I was just wondering.' Shem says. 'If you're likely to be seeing Harriet again in New York.'

Christ, he's going to ask me if my intentions are honourable, and what my career prospects are; to which the answers are No, not at all, and pretty good, thank you.

Refusing to give too much away, I say, 'I hope so.'

Talking quietly, he says, 'Art and I are going to be speaking to Thomas again, but there's a possibility that he might try and come back into her life. Not immediately, perhaps, but he might try something in the future.'

I wonder what particular weaponry or pain-inducing techniques 'speaking to Thomas' might imply.

'I've thought about that, too.' I tell him.

'Good.' He says. 'If anything does happen, would you call me?'

'Sure.' I say. Is he trying to infer that I'm not up to protecting her? Although in his view he may have a point, simply on the basis that in terms of being a knife-carrying, gun-packing crazy person, I'm just not in the same league as him.

'I don't have a gun.' I tell him, with a sort of childish hope that he might give me his.

'Doesn't matter.' He says. 'Have you got a baseball bat? Or maybe a hockey stick?'

I look across at him; he's almost smiling. Hey, everybody, Shem made a joke.

'Both.' I say. 'But you'd be amazed at what I could do with a puck.'

I have a brief but vivid fantasy about committing a major puck violation against Thomas, shortly before high-sticking him.

'Good.' Shem says. 'You might have to be the enforcer.' Another joke – this time I indulge him, and laugh.

'Okay.' I tell him. 'I get it.'

Somewhere around the outskirts of Albany, Harriet sits up so abruptly it makes me start. For a moment in the rear view mirror I can see the confusion on her face that we all get when waking from a deep sleep too rapidly; that blank moment of where am I and who the hell are you?

'You okay?' I ask her.

'Yes.' She says slowly. 'I was dreaming, I think.'

'What about?'

She avoids answering the question by stretching and yawning. 'I could do with a restroom break.' She says.

'Me, too.' I yawn as well. Why is it that yawns are viral? 'And more coffee.'

Shem, I notice, doesn't yawn, but then I remember reading somewhere that people with a learning disability are the only ones who don't catch yawns from other people: I decide not to share this fascinating fact with him for reasons of my own personal safety.

After we've stopped and done some vital emptying of some things, and filling up of others, I throw the car keys back to Shem.

He catches them without comment and takes the wheel again. Harriet takes the front seat, explaining that she doesn't want to go back to sleep and I get the back seat. I'm far too big to curl up on the seat the way Harriet did, so I just lean my head back and hope I don't snore, or drool too unattractively.

Harriet Morgan

She surprises herself by falling asleep almost instantly, soothed by the rumble of the car wheels on pavement, then finds herself in the depths of a senseless dream about being pursued down the suddenly empty twilit corridors of the UN building by a huge man wearing a hockey mask. In her dream panic she finds a telephone in an abandoned office but can't remember how to use one, or what number to dial. The hockey-masked man is skating horrifically fast toward her and then a Xerox machine starts up by itself, throwing out bolts of blue light and she gasps and wakes up, heart thundering.

Hockey, she thinks. The two men must have been talking about hockey. How strange that she only met one of them, Shem, on Saturday and Rusty not until Monday, with today being still Wednesday, something which seems to her impossible in itself.

She asks for a restroom break; not because she really needs one, yet, but feels an urgent desire to get out of the confines of the Toyota for a moment.

I want to go home, she thinks, then feels annoyed at her own childishly irrational thoughts, as that's precisely where they are going. Just wishes she could press a button and be there instantly.

By the time they leave the rest stop it's almost dark. Shem drives with silent concentration and Rusty sleeps for a while, leaving her to her own thoughts. Go and see Chris tonight, give him his gun back, fill him in with the rest of the story. Then back to work tomorrow, which will be a relief. Wonder how many e-mails there will be. Wonder if Thomas will try something.

Shem looks across at her. 'Are you alright?' He asks her.

'Just thinking about Thomas.' She admits.

'Art and I will be having a conversation with him once he's back.' Shem says. 'You don't need to worry about him.'

'Good. Thank you. I haven't really had the chance to thank you, have I?'

'You're welcome.' Shem says simply.

They hit stop-start rush hour traffic at the top of Manhattan, which wakes Rusty up.

'Uuurgh.' He grunts, bracing the palms of his hands against the roof of the Toyota as he stretches, then says to Shem. 'We there yet, Dad?'

Shem ignores him.

'I think we're about a half hour away.' She guesses.

'That's about right.' Shem says to her.

She looks round at Rusty, who sticks his tongue out childishly at the back of Shem's head, making her giggle.

'So.' Rusty says, and pauses like he's working up to something. 'What are you doing tonight? Or tomorrow? Or Friday?'

'Tonight I need to sleep.' She answers, not wanting to try and explain that she needs to see Chris to give him back the gun. 'And tomorrow I'll have to go to work.'

'Sorry.' Rusty says. 'I tend to forget that most people actually have to show up at work on a regular basis.'

'That's what it says in my contract.' She tells him. 'I show up at work on a regular basis; they pay me on a regular basis.'

'Sounds like a good system.' He acknowledges. 'Do they let you have evenings and weekends off? Or are you completely indentured?'

'No, they're very good, they let me have time off if I behave myself.'

'Excellent. You fancy getting together this weekend?'

For a reason she can't explain, she doesn't want to have this conversation in front of Shem.

'Why don't you give me a call tomorrow?' She says.

'Sure. I'll do that, we can sort something out.' He says, looking pleased.

It's completely dark outside now, and Shem works the Toyota through the lines of red stop lights while she watches her personal landmarks, the familiar shops and cafes and bars, get closer together as they move downtown. Feels like she's been away for weeks; she even has that old jetlagged feeling back again, a sense of dislocation, of the sun rising and setting in the wrong places at the wrong times.

Shem double parks right outside her apartment building, ignoring the furious honks of the traffic that has to divert around the Toyota, and Harriet feels suddenly flustered, wondering what the correct and accepted way is to say goodbye to the man who abducted her, saved her, nearly abducted her again and then shot her stalker for her. Maybe I should write to the 'modern manners' section of the newspaper to find out, she thinks. Instead, though, she leans over and gives him a kiss on the cheek, which leaves him looking slightly perplexed, and then does the same to Rusty so he doesn't feel left out.

'I'll call you.' Rusty says, as she gets out of the car.

She waves as they pull back into the traffic, wondering how long it'll take Rusty to realise that he doesn't have her phone number.

Chapter Nine

Harriet Morgan

After waving the guys off, she mounts the stairs to her apartment with a mixed feeling of relief and disappointment; acknowledging at the same time that this is always how it feels when returning from a work tour. You find yourself dying for some time alone and then when you get it you wonder where everyone's gone. And then have a paranoia attack that they're all out partying somewhere without you.

She isn't worried about Rusty not having her number; thinking, let's see how motivated you really are. And she has Carole's number, who will have Rusty's, so she can always back down and call him if she needs to.

She showers, noting as she does so that she's still wearing the track marks that Carole gave her, dries her hair, gets changed into jeans and a clean shirt, wedges the gun into the courier bag which is the closest thing she owns to a handbag, and goes to see Chris, stopping at the liquor store on the way.

Strange, she thinks, how liquor stores in this city, with their bullet-proof glass, are designed to make you feel like you're buying something illegal, or at least distasteful. She asks the woman behind the counter for a bottle of Canadian Club and she wraps it in the inevitable brown paper bag, like contraband, before sliding it under the screen to her.

She takes it around to Chris' place, already knowing that she'll have a hangover for work the next day.

Which she does. But as they all, apart from Chris, think she's been off sick with stomach flu the crew at work are unusually solicitous, dropping into the office she shares with Chris to offer her Gatorade and tell her that she looks pale, and like she's lost weight, before updating her on the non-serious dramas and crises that have occurred and solved themselves since she's been away.

It feels good to slip back into normality, the familiar white noise of phones and computers and coffee-machine conversations about international policy or last night's TV closing softly over her head. She chugs a glass of water and then traverses the building to go to a meeting that she'd forgotten was in her diary, a polished corridor on the way giving her a tiny shudder at a residual memory of the man in the hockey mask in her dream. Shaking herself, telling herself, I'm fine, Thomas is dealt with, everything is back to normal.

After the meeting she treks back via the coffee machine and Kaye's desk to catch up with her before returning to her office to face the inevitable virtual stack of unread e-mail.

And stops dead in the doorway.

On her desk, an enormous bunch of flowers. Roses, in fact, she can smell them from where she's standing. They've been arranged with deep red ones at the centre, scarlet ones outside, white around the edge.

Like blood on snow.

Thomas.

Nausea rises, constricting her throat. Oh god, after all that, he's back.

Rusty Hanover

Shem drops me approximately near my apartment; I notice I don't get the same door to door service that Harriet got, but then again I'm not sure that I want him to know exactly where I live anyway just in case I should commit any transgressions that he gets to find out about and I find him darkening my doorstep one sunny day.

So I drag my luggage off the street, which is now full of Wall Street assholes going home having satisfactorily been masters of their own universes for another day, and into my building.

As I'm waiting for the elevator I plan my evening: do some laundry, take a long, hot shower, maybe have a beer, call Harriet, invite her along to a showbiz party I'm planning to attend on Friday.

Call Harriet.

Cocksucker motherfucker, I don't have her number.

Don't panic, I tell myself. You know more or less where she lives, you know where she works. Okay, so the UN is a big organisation, but there can't be too many Harriet Lee Morgans that work there, can there? Or maybe they don't allow personal calls, and I'll find myself in a sort of telephonic Kafkaesque nightmare, with everyone denying her existence. At least I know for sure that it's her real name, having seen her passport. Was it deliberate, her not giving me her number? Rusty you idiot, I tell myself as the elevator doors open onto my landing, you didn't ask her for it, did you?

I switch some lights on, put some laundry on, open the beer. It should be nice, being home, but actually it's kind of dull. I clunk around the place for a while and even contemplate calling Art to ask if he has Harriet's number, but then I realise that he'd tell Shem, and I'd rather stick pins in my eyeballs than have Shem know I didn't get her number. Has Shem got her phone number? Probably. Best not to think about it.

I watch some NHL, drink another beer, fall asleep for a while on the couch, wake up again and seriously consider calling Shem.

Instead, I go and take a shower, have another beer, unload the first lot of laundry, put it in the dryer, root in the bottom of my bag for the remainder. And find my Calgary t-shirt, the one that Harriet wore, at least for a while, on the very first night I spent with her.

Even while acknowledging to myself what a very sad bastard I must be, I take a sniff at it.

It smells fantastic. It smells so good that in fact it doesn't make it into the next load of laundry, but instead goes into the bedroom with me where I then do something to myself which, I tell myself, is merely to help me get to sleep.

It does, and I wake up early in the morning with a plan.

A very good plan, if I don't say so myself.

While I'm dressing, I pause to congratulate myself in the mirror, noticing that I'm still wearing the dog tags that I stole from Harriet; they sort of suit me, I decide.

Then I look out the enormous New York area Yellow Pages, and over coffee flip through until I find the florists section, choose a classy looking one, and phone to order two dozen roses to be delivered to Miss Harriet Lee Morgan of UN Plaza. This being New York, the flower guy who takes the order doesn't express any surprise at all about the message I dictate to him to accompany the flowers.

I end the message with my cell phone number, my home phone number, and my e-mail address, being briefly tempted to add my fax number as well but deciding that would be a little over the top.

And then I wait.

It belatedly occurs to me that, these being the times we're living in, the flowers are likely to have to be X-rayed, subject to detailed forensic testing and possibly being taken away and blown up before they're allowed anywhere near the building, but I just hope that they get to her in reasonable shape in case she wonders why I seem to have sent her a handful of burnt, petal-less stems.

My home phone rings about an hour later and I break some sort of speed record getting to it; Fastest Human Acceleration Over a Hardwood Floor. I skid to a halt and snatch it up.

It's John, my business manager. Normally, I'd be thrilled to hear from John, partly because I like talking to him as he's always so very serious, mostly because calls from him usually mean something positive to do with money, but today I'm not. He wants to talk to me about a meeting we're going to on Friday, the one that precedes the party in the evening. I interrupt and ask him if I can bring a date to the party.

'A date?' John says. John is gay, although that's not something people usually guess about him on first acquaintance as he's quiet and masculine, his only affectation being that he wears a pair of horn-rimmed eyeglasses that he doesn't actually need, but if what I've heard is true then his idea of a date tends to involve some heavy leather action and use of various other specialist implements.

'Why is everyone so surprised when I say I have a date?' I ask him.

'Of course not.' He says politely. 'I just didn't know you were seeing anyone.'

'Well, I am.' I tell him. 'At least, I think I am, it's sort of complicated. But there's someone I'd like to invite.'

Fine, he says. I'll put her on the guest list. We talk a little more and then I hang up and go and check my e-mail.

Nothing, apart from the usual spam. Then I think to check the actual spam folder and find that my e-mail programme, with its usual brilliance, has filed Harriet's e-mail neatly and immediately under 'junk.'

I open it.

Thank you for the flowers – they're lovely. But don't think this gets you off the hook; I will get my revenge in due course and, like I told Leon, when you're least expecting it.

Her office e-mail system has automatically tagged the mail with her work signature and job title. And her office phone number.

I make the call.

Her phone is answered by another woman who tells me that, sorry, Miss Morgan is in conference right now and isn't available to take my call, may she pass her a message?

'Please could you ask Miss Morgan to call Mr Hanover.' I tell her, in my best business voice. 'I need to meet with her at her earliest convenience regarding an important legal issue.'

'Certainly.' The woman says. Is she sounding amused? Hard to tell. 'Does she have your number?'

I give my numbers to the woman again, just in case.

About a half hour later, my phone rings. 'Mr Hanover?' Harriet says smoothly. 'I'm sorry I missed your earlier call.'

'Hey.' It's so great to hear her voice. 'You liked the flowers?'

'Once I'd worked out that they weren't from Thomas, yes.' She says.

I hadn't thought of this. 'Oh shit, sorry.'

'No, it's fine.' Amusement in her voice. 'Except that I got someone else to read the card, just in case it was Thomas. And then they told all my team what it said. I can't believe you wrote that.'

'What?' If in doubt, my policy is to deny all knowledge. 'Did the flower shop guy put something bad? Because I only asked him to write, 'With love from Rusty.''

'Like hell you did.' She laughs. 'And now everyone I work with is spending their time manufacturing handcuffs out of office supplies. There even seems to be some sort of competition going on for the most realistic pair. Thank you for that.'

'I'm sorry.' I say, trying not to laugh.

'No, you're not.'

Busted again. 'Well, not really, but I will make it up to you. There's a party on Friday. Would you like to come?'

'Sure, yes. That'd be nice.'

I punch the air in silent jubilation. 'Great. It's in Queens; sort of a work thing for me but it should be fun anyway. Except I'll be in the area already for a meeting so I'll have to see you there. Is that okay? I'll send a car for you.'

'I'll take the subway.' She says.

'No, you won't. Its miles from the nearest subway.' I'm not sure that this is actually true, but what the heck. 'And you'll never find the place anyway. I'll send a car.'

'Okay.' She says.

'What's your address?' She gives it to me and we agree eight thirty for the car.

Oh yeah.

Then I take a look around my apartment. Oh hell, time to tidy up. In less than twenty-four hours home I seem to have trashed the place.

After work, Harriet carries the roses home, the bunch as big as a baby in her arms and almost as heavy. While she's waiting at the crosswalk an older woman looks across at her, smiles, and comments, 'Well, he must love you a lot. Or have a lot to apologise for.'

'It's probably both.' Harriet says.

'That's some apology.' The woman laughs. 'Best you hang on to him.'

The lights change. As they walk across, Harriet says, 'Maybe I should.'

Back in her apartment, the flowers present another challenge; she doesn't own a vase. Improvising, she dumps the pasta out of its glass jar onto the counter top and puts the roses in the jar instead. Problem solved.

She showers, changes, cooks and eats some of the pasta, goes out to buy some groceries and stands in the inevitable line for the checkout, thinking about the party on Friday. Should have asked him what sort of party it was. Or what the dress code is. Oh well, she decides: you'll just have to guess.

Lugging the groceries back home, she sees that there's a man walking up the steps to her apartment building, pausing to read the names by the door-entry buttons. Even at a distance, the military buzz-cut is unmistakeable.

Shem.

She rattles her door keys in her hand and he looks around.

'Hi, Shem.' She says. She notices that he's holding the string handles of a large brown paper shopping bag in his hand, the name of the shop on the side one she doesn't recognise. Strange to think of Shem going shopping, although she supposes that occasionally he must have to exchange money for goods just like everyone else.

'Hello.' Shem says. 'Is this a good moment?'

'Sure, yes. I was just buying some groceries.' Indicating her bags. Why does she always feel the need to state the obvious to Shem?

She steps in front of him to open the door and he takes the grocery bags from her hand. Praying that he doesn't notice her cheap, impulse-buy fashion and scandal magazine on top of the groceries, she leads him up the stairs to her apartment, opens the door and offers him a seat on the couch, immediately wishing she hadn't as her lack of furniture means she'll either have to sit next to him or on the floor.

'Would you like some coffee?' She offers. 'Or a beer?'

'A beer would be nice, thank you.' He passes her bags back to her and sits down.

She takes advantage of the moment it takes her to retrieve two beers from the refrigerator and find the bottle opener to think of something to say.

'How's Rosey?' She asks him brightly, the best she can come up with.

'She's fine, thank you. And Mrs Kowalski sends her regards.'

'Mrs Kowalski?' Then she remembers Mrs Thing whose yard work he does. 'Your neighbour.'

'Yes.' Shem takes a drink of his beer. 'She told me off, you know.'

'Really?' Thinking that Mrs Kowalski must be a very brave woman indeed, Harriet sits on the floor opposite Shem then regrets that, too, because its put her about on a level with his black army boots. She wonders if he still wears the knife there and decides, probably.

'Yes. She saw you running for the station that morning and thought that I hadn't been gentlemanly enough to give you a ride. She told me I should catch up with you and apologise.'

'Oh.' Harriet says. This is seriously uncomfortable territory for her. 'Well, I hope you told her that it's me should have been apologising to you.'

Shem frowns slightly. 'No, of course not. Because you don't need to apologise. You did the right thing.'

'I did?' She chugs some beer, wishing that it was something stronger. Wine, maybe. Or vodka.

'Of course you did. You perceived that there was a threat and you got out of the situation. That was very smart.'

'Except that I was wrong about the threat in the first place.'

'That was my fault. I should have realised that you were alarmed by the whole thing and acted accordingly. But I didn't and I apologise.'

Suspecting that Shem apologising for anything is a very rare thing indeed, Harriet says, 'There's no need. After all you've done for me.'

Shem sets the beer bottle down on the floor and leans forward, putting his elbows on his knees. 'I hurt you when we were struggling.'

She really, really doesn't want to be having this conversation. 'You didn't.' She says. 'I've done far worse to myself, falling off my bicycle.'

'I heard you crying.' He says. Oh please, Shem, she thinks, just go away.

Instead, she stands up, walks across to the kitchen to fiddle about with something so she doesn't have to look at him, says, 'I was crying about a number of things then. Not just that.'

Even Shem senses that a change of subject might be in order, and tells her that he and Art went to pay a visit to Thomas today.

'He's back in New York?' She asks. Somehow she prefers to think of him as still being in a field somewhere upstate, safely far away.

'Yes. He says that he won't be troubling you again.' Shem adds. 'But I'd like to give you my phone number just in case he bothers you. Or you get trouble from anyone else.' She's fairly sure he means Rusty by this, but decides not to pursue that one.

'Thank you.' She says. 'I'll give you mine, too, shall I? In case there's anything I can do for you. I mean, not that there's likely to be, but, you know.' She can feel herself blushing. Good thing Shem's not like Rusty, or he'd doubtless put a rude interpretation on her offer to do something for him and feel the need to call her on it.

They swap numbers. Shem finishes his beer and she offers him another, praying that he'll refuse.

'No, thank you.' He says, standing up. 'I got something for you. By way of an apology for freezing you half to death on my motorcycle.' He hands her the brown shopping bag.

'Oh.' She opens the bag, looks in. Sees something in black leather and stops dead, not knowing what to think.

'I had to guess your size.' Shem says. 'If I got it wrong, or you don't like it, the store will change it.'

Steeling herself, she takes the garment out of the bag and holds it up.

'It's beautiful.' She says quietly. It is beautiful; a biker jacket made from supple black leather, lined with what looks like a warm wool blanket fabric in dark stripes.

Shem looks pleased. 'Look on the back.' He says. She does, and sees the Indian Motorcycles Big Chief logo embossed on the leather. 'The lining fabric is called stroud.' Shem tells her, 'From the blankets that the early settlers traded with the Indians.'

She puts it on, and goes to admire herself in the mirror by the front door. It fits perfectly.

In the mirror, she sees Shem walk up behind her and she turns, heart thumping. He embraces her, giving her a surprisingly paternal kiss on the forehead and then releasing her.

'Take care of yourself.' He says, stepping back. 'And don't forget; call me if Thomas tries to get in touch with you. Or if anything strange happens.'

'I will.' She says. 'Thank you. I mean, thank you for everything, Shem.'

Shem smiles. 'You're welcome.' He says, and leaves.

Still wearing the jacket, she throws herself down on the couch and stares at the ceiling for a while.

Rusty Hanover

Friday morning, and I call Leon. Partly to thank him for the few days we stayed at his place, mostly to give him the full story of our magnificent triumph at stopping the Adirondack train yesterday. He listens patiently as I give him the blow-by-blow account, laughing in all the right places, and then asks me if Harriet has forgiven me yet for the handcuffs thing.

'No.' I tell him cheerfully. 'But I'm eagerly awaiting her revenge. Hey, Leon, some advice please.' Leon is generally good at advice, and I suspect certain aspects of my life might have been easier if I'd listened to his wise counsel more often. 'Where can I take her for a date on Saturday night? And don't say Nobu.'

Leon laughs. 'That depends.' He says. 'How many dates have the two of you been on, anyway?'

'Including the meal and the party we went to in Montréal?' I ask him. 'Precisely two.' Oops, I hadn't meant to say that.

'What?' Says Leon, his voice rising.

'Uh, well, we actually met on the train up to Montréal. I mean, Harriet was on the run from Thomas' goons and so I talked her into coming to your place with me.'

'I don't believe this.' Leon says. I think he's about to tell me off for bringing what was, after all, a complete stranger to his house, but I'm wrong.

'You're telling me.' He says, very quietly. 'That you picked her up on the train while she was in serious danger from some psycho, and you brought her to our house and you had sex with her there.'

Now he says it that way, it sure doesn't sound so good. I try and defend myself. 'Come on, Leon, you know me well enough to know that I'm crazy about her.'

'And did you stop to wonder how she might feel about you? That perhaps she felt that sleeping with you was part of the deal in keeping herself safe? Christ, Rusty, you've gone too far this time.'

'It's not like that.' I say, weakly. Or is it? Do women who feel pressured into sex have orgasms? I don't know. Much as I love them, I've never been sure that I completely understand them.

'Not like what?' Leon's on a roll now. 'For god's sake, you know we had a house full of spare bedrooms. You two didn't have to share.'

'She didn't mind, in fact she....' I begin, but Leon interrupts.

'Tell it to someone who cares.' He says. 'And don't bother coming to see us again. But if you should speak to Harriet again, you can tell her that she's welcome anytime.' And he hangs up, leaving me holding the phone and listening to the empty dial tone. It's not the first time I've been permanently banned from Leon's house, so I'm not too worried about that, but his point of view on Harriet and I leaves me feeling shitty and sour.

Oh Christ, what if he's right?

If he's right, then she won't turn up at tonight's party and I'll never see her again. I want to call her, but realise that it would probably count as pressure, so I don't. Instead, I spend the rest of the morning agonising about whether she'll turn up, go to my meeting in Queens and spend the afternoon there not really listening to a word anyone says and convincing myself that she won't turn up. I am, I'm afraid to say, so out of it that even John looks faintly annoyed.

After the meeting, John and I cross the street to a restaurant to get some food, pre-party.

'What's up with you?' He asks.

I put my head in my hands. 'Don't ask.'

'Alright, I won't.' As he actually means this, I feel compelled to answer.

'Troubled love life.' I tell him. 'Is it any easier being gay?'

'I don't know.' He says calmly, reaching for the menu. 'I've never been straight.'

After we've eaten, I make for the washroom and change my shirt, splash some aftershave and consume a little of Columbia's finest export on the grounds that I need cheering up and anyway, everyone else at the party would have done at least double the quantity that I have. And then John and I walk down the street to the club where the party is being held. There are a few cold-looking photographers hanging around outside, most of whom we get ignored by, and we navigate the normal velvet rope and guest list bullshit to get in. I check for the third time that Harriet is on the list and have a word in the doorman's ear while John hovers patiently behind me, and then we plunge on in to the party.

It's nearly nine o'clock, and I try and calculate how long it'll take the car to get from her place to here, wishing I'd timed my outward journey. A half-hour? Maybe more if there's traffic. A waiter hands me a glass of red wine. I try not to drink it too quickly, and try not to look at my watch too often.

Harriet Morgan

She's late. Gets held up at work, then while trying to escape gets held up again by a man from another team wanting to ask her how to engage citizen support for a government programme in a country where the government had been hated by its population for generations, so she talks while backing off up the corridor and the irritating man follows her right into the elevator. He's one of those ageing men who stand at little too close and are useless at interpreting the usual physical or verbal cues to back off. And then he carries on talking in the entrance foyer, while the rest of the building's occupants pass by in ever diminishing groups, everyone going home to dinner, or drinks, or Friday night TV.

'I'm terribly sorry, Roger.' She eventually says, reading his name off the ID card around his neck. 'But I really have to go now.' And she turns her back and makes a run for it.

Nearly eight o'clock. Shit, shit. She dives into the drug store to buy some stockings, hopping from foot to foot with impatience at the cash desk, pays for them and runs all the way home. Takes a super-fast shower, limbo-ing away from the stream of water to keep most of her hair dry, swipes some mascara in the general direction of her eyes, pulls on the stockings, the black denim mini-skirt that Carole made her buy in Montréal, black high-heeled suede boots and then the padded bra, knowing that the padding is false advertising but what the heck. All she needs is a shirt. Shit, shit, she hasn't done any ironing and doesn't have time to iron anything now. And then the door buzzer goes.

'Car service for Miss Morgan.' The driver says.

'I'm really sorry, would you mind waiting for a few minutes?'

'No problem.' He says calmly.

I do have a problem, she thinks, I don't have a shirt to wear. She grabs the Seoul Hostess club t-shirt which doesn't need ironing and, by some miracle of design or perhaps just serendipitous shrinkage, fits her very well. Not entirely suitable for a party but it'll have to do.

Pulls on the Shem biker jacket over the top, adds scarf, pauses to put her hair up in the Kudu clip to keep the damp bits away from the back of her neck, stuffs keys and cash and phone into the jacket pocket and runs all the way down the stairs before flinging herself into the sleek leather interior of the black Town Car which is waiting patiently for her at the curb.

'Made it.' She gasps to the driver.

He turns to look at her. 'Help yourself to a drink from the cocktail cabinet.' He suggests, then turns back to pull the car smoothly and competently out into the eddies of Friday night traffic.

I can't believe, she thinks as the car gathers speed, that I've made it into the set who have a car service with built-in cocktails.

'What a great idea.' She tells him. 'Would you like one?'

'I'm not allowed.' The driver shakes his head. 'Company rule.'

Twisting the cap off a miniature bottle of wine, she says 'How would they know it was you and not me who drank it?'

Brown eyes meet hers in the rear-view mirror. 'That's true.' The driver says. 'I'll have a soda.' She opens a can and passes it through the gap between the front seats to him.

On the way, she learns that he's a New York Pakistani by way of Manchester, England. He chats away about his wife, and how he's chauffeuring to pay for night school for her so she can improve her IT skills and earn enough money to buy out the family home in Queens, which they currently share with another couple.

'It's not so bad.' The driver says. 'We have one floor each, so I put a bathroom in downstairs and a kitchen upstairs so we don't have to share. But we'd like to have a family so we need the extra space. But my wife is a very clever lady, so it won't be long that we are having to wait.'

He asks Harriet what she does for a living.

'I work for the UN.' She says.

'Ever been to Pakistan?'

'Yes, I have. It's a beautiful country, isn't it?

'Never been there.' The driver says, shaking his head. 'I prefer it here.'

And there you have the American dream, Harriet thinks. Work hard, make money, buy the family home. Assimilate.

When they reach the venue, the driver hands her his card.

'If you ever get stuck anywhere.' He says, 'Call me. Sometimes I have to wait between jobs so I might be able to help you out. Or one of my co-workers can, if I'm busy.'

'Thank you.' Outside she can see what looks suspiciously like some sort of red carpet spread over a section of brightly-lit sidewalk, some photographers, a couple of intimidating dark-suited doormen with dangling curly earpieces like they're the FBI.

'Have a nice evening.' The driver says as he pulls away. Fighting a desire to call him straight away and plead for him to take her immediately back home, Harriet jogs across the carpet to avoid the photographers and approaches the doorman who's standing behind a small podium, studying a piece of paper under a brass reading light. He's about to make a speech, she thinks, suddenly wanting to giggle. Instead, she gives him her name.

'Ah, Miss Morgan.' He says, 'We're very glad you could join us tonight. I'll escort you through to the party.' And he does, guiding her through a blue-lit hallway and down some stairs. How weird, she thinks, following his broad back. Perhaps he's afraid that if she's left on her own she'll get lost, or steal something.

Double doors in front of them, through them audible a muted bass sound which suddenly grows loud as he opens a door and guides her through, handing her seamlessly off to a passing waiter. 'Have an enjoyable evening.' He says, and glides away.

The waiter offers her a glass of wine, which she takes, and another shows up with a tray of canapés. 'Is any of it vegetarian?' She asks, leaning close to his ear so he can hear her over the noise. He indicates a line of greenish tartlets, so she takes a couple, suddenly realising how ravenously hungry she is.

They're in some sort of club; long banquettes, small palm trees, dance floor at the centre which is empty so far, all lit with a queer purplish shifting light which makes everyone look slightly unwell. Unwell but very well dressed, she corrects herself, noticing that she's got the dress code badly wrong; everyone else is in suits and cocktail dresses. She eats a tartlet, discovering too late that the green stuff is some sort of disgusting pureed celery concoction. She chokes it down, drops the other one discreetly in a palm tree pot, and goes to find Rusty in the uneasy purple gloom, thinking that at least he'll be simple to spot over the heads of the rest of the crowd.

And then she sees him at the far side of the dance floor, talking to a pretty blonde girl, although it looks to Harriet that the expression on his face is one of politeness rather than fascination. He's looking great, she notes, in a dark suit and white shirt combination. Very handsome and tall.

Rusty Hanover

She's not coming.

I'm sure of it; it can't have taken the car this long to have got here at this time of night. I drink another glass of rather horrible red wine, John drifts off to speak to someone younger and gayer than me, and I get talking to a pretty blonde girl. I'm fairly sure she's flirting with me, but I feel too miserable to even pretend to flirt back. And then my Harriet radar goes off, and here she is, surrounded immediately by a gang of waiters offering her wine, food, their hands in marriage.

She whispers something to one of them, he smiles and answers, and then fortunately she turns and walks away from him, following the edge of the dance floor toward me, although I'm fairly sure she hasn't spotted me yet.

She looks fantastic, all black leather and suede. I shake off the blonde girl and push my way through the crowd to greet my lovely Harriet. She looks up, sees me, and grins, so I grab her and lift her right off her feet to hug her. She smells wonderful, even better than the t-shirt.

We embrace for so long that a couple of passers-by suggest we get a room. I set her back down on her feet.

'You look great.' I tell her.

'I look like I don't belong here.' She tells me. 'Everyone's staring at me.'

They are, but not for the reason she thinks. 'It's because they're all wondering what you're famous for.' I tell her. 'Anyone dressed down and looking as good as you do has to be famous for something. And, I'm sorry to be the one to tell you, you're too short to be a model so they're all wondering what movie they've seen you in.'

'Bullshit.' She says cheerfully.

'No, I'm right, you'll see. Did the doorman look after you okay? Because I told him you were our very famous guest of honour.'

She laughs. 'I wondered what that was all about.' She says.

'Did you get your picture taken?' I ask her.

'I hope not.' She responds. 'I saw the photographers and ran.'

'You've got so much to learn.' I tell her, happy that I might now get the chance to teach her. 'Come on.' I take her hand. 'Let's go and meet some people.'

I introduce her to John, who politely peels himself away from the beautiful young man that he's currently leaning over to shake Harriet's hand.

Harriet asks him what a business manager does, and I answer for him.

'It means he's the money guy. And tells me what to do.'

John rolls his eyes behind his spectacles. 'I manage his career.' He tells Harriet.

'Not that I have much of one.' I say to her. 'So it's not too onerous a job for him. Meaning that he finds time to do other things.' I cast a meaningful look at the beautiful young man. John sighs and changes the subject.

'Are you an actor?' He asks Harriet.

'No,' I answer for her. 'She's a spy and spends her time undermining foreign regimes.' Harriet kicks me gently on the ankle with one lovely suede boot, and then Elaine, my agent rolls up. Elaine is a tall, elegant woman in her fifties with spiked grey hair and a penchant for wearing flowing linen in shades of mud and leaf, and large turquoise jewellery. A very tolerant lady, Elaine; she's put up with me for years.

'Elaine, my agent.' I say to Harriet. 'And before you ask it means that she's my pimp. And I'm her bitch.' It occurs to me that I may be a bit more drunk than I thought.

'Oh, Rusty.' Elaine says. She studies Harriet for a moment. 'Are you an actor?' Elaine asks her.

'No.' Harriet says quickly. 'I work for the UN.'

'Really? How interesting. So how did you two meet?'

I take a deep breath to launch into the story but become aware of a sudden and very intense pressure on the hand that Harriet's holding.

'Just at a bar.' I say, lamely. 'Nothing very interesting.'

We chat awhile for about the UN, about which Elaine is surprisingly knowledgeable, and then Elaine gets commandeered by someone I recognise vaguely as a scriptwriter, and John drifts back to talk to his young man. I take advantage of the moment alone with Harriet to slide my hands up under the back of her leather jacket. 'I'm loving you in the black leather.' I tell her.

She looks up at me and grasps my lapel between two fingers. 'I'm loving you in that suit.' She says.

'Are those stockings you're wearing?' I murmur in her ear. 'Do you want to go home now?'

'Soon.' She says.

Then I really should stop drinking now. 'Is it me or is this wine disgusting? Would you like something else?'

'Just some water.' She says.

'Don't go anywhere. I'll be right back.' I make for the bar, thinking that water might be a very good idea.

Harriet Morgan

Feeling suddenly hot, she takes her jacket off, placing it on the banquette beside her before taking a moment to watch the crowd. There's something intense about them, she decides, hyper-real; large gestures, exaggerated facial expressions. And then she realises that it's because they're probably all in show business, and feeling a pressure not only to have a good time but to be seen publicly to have a good time.

'Golden Lotus Hostess Bar.' A man's voice behind her says, interrupting her thoughts as he reads from the back of her t-shirt. 'I think I recognise you from there.' She turns; he's youngish, blonde floppy hair, round face shining with humour.

'I thought I recognised you.' She retorts. 'Aren't you the one the girls used to call Mister Tiny?'

He laughs loudly at this, and then says to someone behind her, 'Your girlfriend can certainly hold her own.'

'And mine, too, hopefully.' Rusty says, setting two sweating glasses of ice water down on the table behind her and propping his elbows on her shoulders, leaning against her back. 'Harriet, this is Ty. Don't worry, he's always that rude to everyone.'

'Hi.' Ty says to her, grinning and shaking her hand. 'I'd like to say that I've heard lots about you but I haven't. Rusty's been multo mysterious, and now everyone's wondering who his lovely woman is. Are you an actor?'

Oh, not again, Harriet thinks.

'Of course she is.' Rusty says gravely. 'Didn't you ever see 'Candlelit Dinner for One?' The critics were raving about it last year. Harriet was the lead.'

Ty looks confused for a moment. 'Oh, of course, I'm sorry. You've, uh, changed your hair since then.'

'It's grown a little.' She tells him.

There's a brief silence. 'So,' Ty says. 'What's the deal now with Clarisse? Does this mean she's gone back in her box or are you guys having some kind of a kinky threesome sort of a thing?'

'Fuck you.' Rusty says quietly, straightening up. 'Fuck you for trying to fuck this up for me.'

'Hey.' Ty says, backing off, sounding wounded. 'I'm just joking with you.'

She has no idea what either of them are talking about, but she does know, with a terrible certainty, that the bad wine and celery tartlet she consumed are going to take their revenge and she's about to be very sick indeed.

'Excuse me a moment.' She says to them both, grabs her jacket and starts to run through the crowd.

The brightly-lit restroom is mercifully empty, and she makes it to a cubicle before vomiting. Braces one hand against the toilet seat, holds her hair out of the way with the other and throws up the wine and the remains of the horrible tartlet. Fortunately there's not much in her stomach; she realises that she hasn't eaten in a long time, which is possibly the problem. Pausing between dry heaves, she hears that two women have entered the restroom and are talking, sotto voice.

'Bulimia, for sure.' One of them says.

'Hmm. Ty just told me she's the actor was in that film last year. 'Candlelit Dinner.''

'Oh, I think I saw that.' The first one says. 'Well, I'm not surprised.' Their high heels click off across the floor and Harriet waits to hear the door open and close behind them before flushing the toilet and risking straightening up.

She doesn't feel too bad, actually, just incredibly tired. She leaves the stall and drinks from the faucet, swills and spits, drinks again. Eyeing herself in the mirror, she thinks, you shouldn't have come. Should have stayed at home and got some sleep. She feels in her pocket for the card with the number of the driver who brought her here. Perhaps he can take her home, or find someone else who can.

Slip away, she tells herself, and then call Rusty tomorrow and apologise.

Except that Rusty is waiting for her, leaning against the wall outside the restroom.

'You okay?' He asks as she approaches. She nods. She does feel sort of okay, in fact; the weird calm that descends when you're beyond exhaustion.

'I need to go home.' She tells him.

'Will you come home with me?'

'No, Rus, not tonight. I need to get some sleep.'

'Please? I need to show you something, or else it'll queer things between us and I don't want that to happen.'

She starts to walk towards the club's exit. 'I can't. Not tonight.'

'Please?' He says again, following her, in a tone of voice which makes her remember Carole telling him that it was nice to see him crawl. Not nice, exactly, but unusual; she already knows that Rusty mostly gets what he wants by a mixture of fast talking and genuine good humour.

'Just a few minutes.' He pleads, and she gives in.

'Okay. Just a few minutes. But if I don't get some sleep soon I think I'm going to start hallucinating.'

'Thank you.' He says, taking her hand. She can see people's eyes turning towards them as they leave.

'Thanks to you and Ty.' She tells Rusty, 'I'm now not only a famous actor but apparently a bulimic one as well.'

'Congratulations.' He says dryly.

The car is waiting for them outside; a different driver from the one she had earlier. In the back of the car she lets Rusty take her hand but not get any closer; too afraid that she smells of puke or at least the vinegar tang of soured red wine.

They travel back in almost complete silence. She leans her forehead against the cool glass of the window and watches the lights of the frigid city slide quietly past. She wonders if Thomas is still out there somewhere; watching, waiting. Don't be stupid, she tells herself. You're just tired and it's making you paranoid.

When they reach his building she notices that, oddly, it's just a couple of blocks away from the artist's loft that Art and Shem brought her to on the first night. Less than a week ago, she thinks, and it doesn't seem possible. It certainly feels like she hasn't slept properly since then.

Still holding her hand, he rushes her though his apartment; on the way she gains an impression of serious amounts of space, high ceilings, dark wood floors, raw brick walls softly whitewashed. He leads her to a den in the back, gestures towards what's occupying the chair behind an office desk.

'This is Clarisse.' He says, expressionless.

Harriet looks, and starts to laugh.

Clarisse is a doll; approximately human-sized, in fact, approximately Harriet sized. Solid and plastic, a life-sized Barbie doll, fully poseable; Harriet remembers reading a magazine article about them. This one is blonde and blue-eyed, her lips slightly parted to show realistic-looking teeth, and dressed only in what must be one of Rusty's shirts.

The laughter catches her by surprise, shaking her so much that her knees go weak and she slides down the wall to a sitting position on the floor, hugging her legs to herself, gasping for breath.

Rusty perches on the edge of the desk and addresses the doll.

'Well.' He says to it. 'I certainly didn't expect that reaction.'

Rusty Hanover

I really didn't expect that reaction. Incomprehension, perhaps, or disgust, but not that.

Harriet tries to pull herself together, wiping tears of mirth from her eyes. 'I'm sorry.' She says, looking up at me. 'I thought you were going to show me the carefully preserved remains of your three-month dead grandmother, or something.'

I offer her a hand up from where she's sat on the floor. 'You really think that of me?' I feel slightly hurt by this, but put more into my voice so I sound rather wounded.

'I've had a very strange week.' She says, grasping my wrist with her little hand and getting up. 'So you'll have to forgive me if I expect everything to turn into American Psycho.'

'Canadian Psycho.' I tell her. 'That's where I lure you to my apartment and make you really good coffee. But before you worry about Clarisse, she's a prop. I've been pitching an idea for a new sitcom that she'd have the starring role in. Which is what my meeting in Queens this afternoon was about.'

'Oh, okay. But no coffee, thank you. I really have to go home. But before I go I have one question.'

I know what's coming.

Harriet says 'These things are anatomically correct, right? So, have you...?'

'Uh, well, yeah.' This is something I really don't want to get into.

'What's it like?' She asks.

'Strange, really.' I think I'm going to have to be honest here. 'I mean, she's obviously unresponsive. And surprisingly cold to the touch. So overall not the worst experience I've ever had, but the closest I hope I'll ever get to making love to a dead body.' Harriet is watching me keenly. I add, 'If you don't mind me saying, you don't seem to be too upset by this.'

She responds with, 'Well, I don't think it would be fair if I was. Because apparently every woman is supposed to own something which looks to me like a battery-operated severed human penis. And the male equivalent of that really would be too American Psycho for words, wouldn't it?'

I hadn't thought of that angle. 'Good point. But in case you were wondering, it's all over between Clarisse and me.' I can't resist the joke. 'We just don't talk anymore.'

Harriet laughs, then says, 'I really, really need to go home now. I'll go and see if I can get a cab.'

'I'll call the car service.' I tell her.

'A cab's fine.' She insists.

'No, its not. Because it's freezing outside and if you're going to wait outside for a cab then I'll have to as well, which I don't want to. I'll call the car service.' I'm tempted to call them from another room, and then pretend that there isn't one for another couple hours, but I suspect that this wouldn't be a smart move. I call the service and they tell me twenty minutes. Good enough.

I lead Harriet through to my kitchen and offer her a soda, which she takes.

'There's something else I need to talk to you about.' I tell her. 'Leon gave me a telling off today.'

She nods. 'I know. Carole called me at lunchtime.'

'She did? Well, apparently I didn't behave very well in Montréal.'

Harriet says, 'Do you want to know what I said to Carole?'

'Yes.' I tell her. No, I don't, actually, but I suppose I'm going to have to hear this.

'It told her that was bullshit.' Harriet says calmly. 'Apparently I'm some sort of sad, vulnerable creature who's easily manipulated into sex, which is not only bullshit, but patronising bullshit. I mean, I realise that I was in a pretty bad place when we met. And that you don't know me very well, but for god's sake, you know that I've spent most of my working life in some of the more unpleasant parts of the world. What did you all think I did, fucked my way though my job?'

I'm not sure if I'm more surprised by hearing Harriet say the word 'fucked', or by her response to Leon's concerns 'Well, no, I…' I begin.

'Listen to me for a moment.' She interrupts. 'I had sex with you because I wanted you. And as a matter of fact I still do, except maybe not tonight because I need to sleep before I fall over. So there you have it, cards on the table time.'

Possibly for the first time in my life, I'm literally speechless. I struggle for something to say.

'I'm crazy about you.' I admit to her. 'If it's cards on the table time. And I told Leon that. But there is something else you should know, if we're doing confessions tonight. And it's something that Leon has already told me off for not telling you before now.'

'Go on.' She says.

'I'm infertile. Completely and utterly, apparently. No-one knows why, and I haven't even told my family, seeing as how fertility is sort of a big thing in the farming community. But it was a major contributing factor in the breakdown of my marriage, and I thought you should know.'

'That must be shitty.' She says.

'Well, yes and no. To be honest with you, before I knew, when my wife and I were officially trying for a baby, each month that it didn't happen I felt increasingly relieved rather than sad. But I do realise that this may be a bit of a deal-breaker for some people.'

'It's not really for me, because the marriage and baby thing was never really on my radar. And I like kids but I seem to have absolutely no maternal instinct whatsoever.'

I feel immensely cheered by this. 'Oh, well, good. But if you should ever change your mind, I'm sure Shem wouldn't mind being a sperm donor. Except that any baby of his would be bound to emerge from the womb sporting a buzz cut and clutching a selection of weaponry in its little fist. Like a baby GI Joe. Or GI Jane.'

She laughs, then tells me, 'Shem came to see me on Thursday night.'

'Oh really?' I say, feeling highly ambiguous about this. 'And what did he want?'

'I'm not sure.' She says. 'It's sort of hard to tell with Shem, isn't it? But he wanted to give me his number in case Thomas made any more trouble. And I think he offered to deal with you, if you ever gave me any trouble.'

'Fair enough.' I tell her. 'But if that should happen, you need to be aware that very shortly after I was dealt with you'd become Mrs Shem Jephson, whether you wanted to or not. And don't think he'd have any truck with new-fangled notions like you having a career, either. You really would be barefoot and pregnant, and on your knees, washing his kitchen floor.' I decide to add a bit of self-publicity, just in case there's any doubt in her mind. 'Whereas I have a cleaner, so you won't ever be washing my floor. And you can wear shoes anytime you want, even in bed. Particularly those boots.'

Before she can answer, the door buzzer to my apartment goes. It's the car service.

'Stay here tonight.' I tell her. 'You can have the guest room if you want.'

'No, thank you.' She says. 'But before I go, I have one more question about Clarisse. You haven't ever gone out with her in public, have you?'

'No, never.' I say. 'But in fact she is coming to a meeting with me on Monday.'

'She can't go to a meeting dressed in just your shirt.' Harriet says.

'She'll have to. Shopping for an outfit for her would be just too weird.'

'Why don't you bring her over to my place tomorrow? I might have something suitable that she can borrow. Is she portable? I mean, discreetly portable. Because if you sling her over your shoulder and get on the subway you'll be arrested.'

'Clarisse has a sort of sports bag she can go in. Which looks sort of disturbing, actually, but it is discreet.'

'Give me a call, then.' Harriet says, getting up to leave, 'But not before lunchtime as I really need to sleep in.'

At the very last second, I fortunately remember something. 'You'd better give me your cell phone number, then.'

She does, and I escort her to the car. Looking at us both in the mirrored back of the elevator makes me aware all over again of the tremendous difference in our relative sizes. I say to her, 'All that stuff with Leon and Carole getting over-protective, they didn't mean to patronise you. It's because you're little and cute that makes people want to look after you.' Harriet makes a noise of disgust at this, which makes me realise something. 'You don't know it, do you? You don't see yourself as being little and cute, in your own mind.'

The elevator doors open.

'In my own mind?' Harriet says. 'Honestly?'

We walk out to the waiting car and I open the door for her. Getting in, she says, 'In my own mind I honestly believe that I'm about the same size as you.'

I'm still laughing as the car pulls away up the street.

Harriet Morgan

The driver is the Manchester Pakistani again. 'Good party?' He asks her.

'No, it was a terrible party. But my evening got better once we'd left.'

Once home, she gets in the tub and lies there for a while, swishing the silky water about and thinking about very little. And then crawls into bed and sleeps.

She's woken by the phone next morning, experiencing the horrible heart-shake of someone who's been woken from a deep sleep by the shriek of the phone. Unglues her vocal chords enough to say 'Hello?' into the receiver, and checks the clock. Nine twenty a.m..

'Did I wake you up?' A man's voice asks.

'Yes, Chris, you did. Its Saturday morning, people sleep in on Saturday mornings.'

'Not me.' Says Chris. 'I was just calling to say I've booked us a runway at the Fencer's Club for 10am. Want a bout?'

'No. Oh, alright, I do.' Thinking it might be good for her to get back on the runway, poke a sharp object at a man, even if that man is her friend Chris, and not Thomas.

'Good. I'll meet you outside the club.'

She pulls some clothes on, stuffs her kit into her bag, drinks a fast cup of tea and eats an energy bar, calling it breakfast, puts another one in her bag to eat on the subway.

Chris is waiting outside the club, smoking a cigarette, seeing no irony at all in smoking outside a place designated for healthy activities. She takes it from his fingers and has a drag.

'You're looking better.' He notes.

'Yeah. Finally got some sleep. Until somebody woke me up by phoning me.'

Chris slaps her on the back as they go inside. 'This'll be good for what ails you.' He says.

Upstairs in the changing room, she pulls her kit on, picks up her foil in her gloved hand and tucks her mask under her arm to go out onto the runway. Chris is already there, shadow fighting, and she watches him for a moment before pulling the mask on and taking her place at the opposite end of the runway, dropping her weight into first position. They salute each other, the wall, the rest of the empty room.

'En guard.' Chris says.

She's fighting badly and she knows it; slow and distracted. Chris knows it, too, and towards the end of the first round he catches her in an illegal and highly irritating move, slapping her across the side of her hip with the length of his blade the way a fencing master does with an unruly pupil. It stings, but it's more humiliating than painful.

'Ow.' She says, rubbing at it with her free hand and glaring at him even though she knows he can't see her expression through her mask.

'Wake up, girl.' Chris says. 'You're fighting like a geriatric pageant queen.'

'Am not.' She says through gritted teeth. 'I'll show you.' And does, picks up the pace and fights hard and fast, hoping she can gain advantage by winding him. Feet slap on the wooden floor, the sounds of laboured breathing and shouts of 'Touché!' when someone has landed a hit.

She still loses, but not by too much and she feels sweaty and happy and slightly high as she goes to change back into her street clothes. Chris is outside with another cigarette. 'Fancy some brunch?' He asks.

'Not today, thanks. I need to get home.'

'Hot date?' He teases.

'Something like that.'

'With the handcuffs guy?' He asks.

'You really should stop calling him that.' Harriet says.

Chapter Ten

Rusty Hanover

Saturday morning. I wake up late; feeling fit, healthy and horny and it's a beautiful sunny cold New York November morning. I shower and spruce myself up. Leon calls, chagrined and apologetic, and I tell him that as I'm feeling particularly magnanimous that morning, I'll forgive him, but the truth is that I'd missed knowing I have his friendship, even in the mere twenty-four hours that he wasn't speaking to me this time around.

Then I mooch about the apartment for a while before being struck by a genius idea; I sprint down to Bouley bakery on a pastry raid and buy most of the place.

Back to my building with my arms full of expensive bakery bags, the doorman opens the door and greets me with the information that there's a gentleman waiting for me in the foyer.

A gentleman. Making my way inside I grin to myself at the thought that it certainly wouldn't be Leon, then, and there's a man standing there by the mailboxes; a year or two older than me, around six feet tall, dark hair, strange pale blue eyes. Beautifully dressed: even at this distance I can spot an Emporio Armani suit. I have a feeling I recognise him from somewhere, but can't immediately place him. He is, I note, leaning heavily on a silver-tipped walking cane.

'Russell Hanover?' He says. 'Thomas Birnbeck.'

And Thomas reaches inside his jacket.

He's going to shoot me.

I know he's going to shoot me dead right here in the foyer of my own apartment building, and the police will find my body surrounded by croissants and slices of coffee cake. I wonder if I'll be on the news, whether they'll show a clip from one of my films. Hopefully not the Canadian Gothic Horror, though, otherwise it would probably look like I fully deserved to get shot in the head.

Then I wonder if he's coming after all of us, and where I come in the order of priority. Harriet first, I decide, the thought making my knees go weak. Then me, then Shem. Impossible to think that he'd gone after Shem already; impossible to believe that Shem, with his weaponry and strange secret super powers, wouldn't have killed him first.

Then I notice that what Thomas is actually holding out to me is a fat brown envelope.

‘I wondered.’ He says to me, ‘Whether you would be kind enough to give this to Miss Morgan for me.’

‘Perhaps you should give it to her yourself.’ My voice comes out wrong; I’m trying for Clint Eastwood and get something that sounds more Martha Stewart.

He smiles stiffly. ‘I don’t think she’d be very pleased to see me, do you?’ He hands me the envelope and I take it; it’s surprisingly heavy, dense with a stack of smallish pieces of paper. ‘Perhaps you could tell her.’ He adds, ‘That I shan’t be troubling her again. That it was just a moment of madness on my part.’ He turns and clicks his way across the foyer to the door on his walking cane. I watch him incline his head to the doorman by way of a thank you, and then I stuff the envelope down into one of the bakery bags.

There’s around ten thousand dollars in that envelope, at a guess.

By the time I get upstairs my heart has stopped feeling like its about to jump right out of my chest, so I dump the bakery bags on the kitchen counter and sit down on a stool to open the envelope; just, I tell myself, to check that there are no nasty surprises in there for Harriet.

I was right first guess. Ten thousand dollars in used fifty dollar notes, neatly banded into thousands by those little paper strips that banks use. Probably not a lot of money for someone like Thomas, I muse; a couple of Armani suit’s worth. The approximate cost of his Rolex.

Not that I could see Harriet buying herself a Rolex. Maybe she’ll buy me one instead, although I’d really rather have a Breitling.

From death to designer watches in one easy stage.

At least he didn’t seem to notice that I was wearing his sunglasses, the Oakleys that Harriet took from him upstate.

I call Harriet, who sounds chipper, so I don’t mention my little meeting with Thomas, thinking to break it to her gently a bit later. She tells me to come over whenever I want, then casually suggests I bring the handcuffs with me.

‘I’m not bringing the handcuffs.’ I tell her. ‘Because you’ll handcuff me to the bed and then go out shopping for a couple hours.’

‘Shit.’ She says, giggling. ‘How did you guess?’

‘Because that’s exactly what I’d do if the situation was reversed.’ Except it isn’t, entirely, because if Harriet were handcuffed to the bed I wouldn’t be able to force myself to go out, not even for one second; instead I’d have to spend the time exploring her.

Before hanging up I tell her that I’ll be right over, without handcuffs but with brunch. Then I fold poor Clarisse into her bag, which always makes her look like a particularly unfortunate sort of a bondage victim, then add the envelope of cash, which then makes her look more like she's being ransomed, zip the bag up and make two trips to lug her and the bakery bags down to the parking garage on the corner of the block to my car.

When she opens the door of her apartment, Harriet is looking happy and shiny and healthy. She's wearing jeans and a cotton shirt, barefoot apart from a cute silver toe-ring. I notice that she has small, very high-arched feet with toenails painted tangerine. I don't think I have a foot fetish, but feel perfectly willing to give it a try.

I dump Clarisse's bag on the floor.

'Don't move.' I tell Harriet. 'I'll be back in a moment.' I pound back down the stairs, fetch the bakery items and run back upstairs. Harriet has moved; she's standing by the window, looking down into the street.

'You have a Porsche.' She observes.

'Well, yeah, a Cayenne which is a Porsche in a manner of speaking. I haven't told you that story, have I? Well, you know my Corvette got stolen. It was stolen about three weeks after I moved to New York, after I'd driven the damn thing all the way from California. Anyway, the insurance money comes through and I decide that I'm going to go and buy myself a Porsche. Always wanted one, ever since I was a kid. So I take myself off to the dealership to take a test drive of the new Carrera, all very excited and pleased with myself. Can you guess what happened next?

'You couldn't fit into it.' She says.

'Exactly. Even with the seat as far back as it would go my knees were against the steering wheel and before I'd gone a half mile I had serious cramp. I could have cried. But it shows you how clever they are at the dealership because they sold me the Cayenne instead. Which, incidentally, had nothing to do with the very charming and attractive sales lady who acted like she desperately wanted to sleep with me, right up until I'd signed on the dotted line.'

'Serves you right.' Harriet says, laughing.

'Probably.' I tell her. 'But actually, I quite like the Cayenne. It's a pretty good vehicle for the mean and potholed streets of New York. And I always make sure to park it at the garage, rather than leaving it on the street which I did to the Corvette for just one night before it fucking well disappeared.'

Harriet crosses the room to the big sports bag. 'Is that Clarisse?'

'It is. But never mind about her for the moment. First, I need to do this.' And I bend to kiss Harriet.

This goes on for quite a while, but even with her on tiptoe, which she is, its serious neck-ache territory for the both of us. So I pick her up and sit her on the kitchen counter which evens out the height difference for us nicely. And we end up with her arms around my neck and her legs around my waist so I pick her up again with my hands under her ass and carry her into the bedroom.

I don't take a lot of time to admire the décor in there, to be honest, but I note muted light, a lovely old-fashioned brass bedstead with classy cream bed linen on which I waste no time at all in laying her down. And then throw myself down next to her and start work on undoing the buttons of her shirt.

And stop dead.

'What the hell's that?' I ask, staring in horror.

'What's what?' She says, looking down at herself.

'That. Those.' Her upper body is dotted with round, red marks that are about the size of a cigarette end.

'Oh.' She says calmly. 'I had a bout this morning. A fencing bout, I mean. Those marks are from hits. The fact that there are so many of them means I lost.'

'Christ.' I flop back on the bed. 'I thought someone had been torturing you, or something. Don't you wear body armour for fencing?'

'I do, but I save the really heavy duty stuff for competitions because it's really hot and uncomfortable to wear. The marks will fade in a day or two, they always do.'

'Maybe I can kiss them better.' I suggest, and do so. Then work my way lower down, where there aren't any marks at all, but I don't want the rest of her to feel left out. She obligingly wriggles out of her jeans and reaches for my belt buckle so I can do the same, then I go back to where I left off, peeling her panties off when I reach the spot.

When my tongue touches her, she gasps, 'Oh,' in surprise, then, 'Oh, yes', followed, a few moments later, by 'Oh, yes, *please*.' When someone asks so politely it'd be rude to stop, really, so I don't stop until she arches her back and digs her heels into the mattress and gasps herself to a halt.

I scoot back up to the head end of the bed.

'Wow.' She says, smiling.

Harriet Morgan

As he makes his way back up the bed, Rusty murmurs, 'I'm wanting to get behind you', so remembering Carole's advice she turns on her side away from him, still feeling her heart racing as he positions himself behind her, one hand cupping her hip, the other under her hair at the nape of her neck. He's wearing her dog tags which had mysteriously disappeared in Montréal; she feels the warmth of their metal against her back. And then he slips between her thighs and starts to move, slowly at first then faster, harder. She knows she's being noisy but doesn't care, flexing back against him, bracing herself with one hand wrapped around the rail of the bedstead. And then he gets noisy too, thrusting himself to a halt.

Screw the neighbours, she thinks, if they don't like it.

Afterwards, they laze around in bed for a while. The sun is coming in through the bamboo window blinds, laying tiger stripes across the floor. It's warm in the bedroom and if she didn't know better, she could think that this was summer. This obviously occurs to Rusty, too, because he says, 'You fancy taking a vacation? Somewhere that's warm this time of year.'

'Australia?' She teases him.

'I was thinking South Florida. We could drive down, stop somewhere overnight on the way. Except not in Georgia, because what I just did to you is still illegal there. Can you believe that? I could have got sixteen years in jail just for going down on you.'

'Worth it, though.' She tells him.

'For you, maybe. Well, okay, for me, too. Just so long as you don't mind only getting to do it once every sixteen years. I'd be a repeat offender, but at least I'd be...' He pauses to count on his fingers. 'Ninety years old by the time of my third offence. So I probably wouldn't mind spending the rest of my life in jail at that point.'

She works it out. 'That makes you forty-two years old. I didn't know that.'

'I know how old you are.' He says. 'Because I saw your passport.'

'We've got a weird relationship, haven't we?' She says. 'I mean, I know lots of thing about you, but I didn't even know how old you are until just now.'

'All relationships are weird.' Rusty says, stretching. 'Or maybe it's just the relationships that include me in them that are weird. Would you like to get normal?'

'Not really.' She says.

'Good. Then come and be weird with me at Miami Beach or somewhere. When can we go?'

'Not just yet. I have to work.' Damn work, she thinks, I'd like to hang out in Miami with this man; hot days, long sultry nights.

'Then how about we go over the holidays? You got any plans?'

'No.' She admits.

'Let's go then.'

'You're not going back to the family farm for the holidays?'

He winces. 'No. Don't get me wrong, they're lovely people, but more than twenty-four hours there and I start to feel faintly suicidal. More than forty-eight hours and I start fantasising about taking my daddy's shotgun into the barn and shooting myself.' He sits up suddenly. 'That's some very kinky bedroom décor you've got there, if you don't mind me saying.'

He's looking at her fencing foils, which are hanging neatly from a peg rail on the wall opposite the bed.

'Oh. Well, I hadn't thought of that. The peg rail was just there when I moved in. But its does look a bit odd, doesn't it? I wondered why the maintenance guy was looking at me strangely when he came to fix the air conditioner.'

'He was probably scared.' Rusty notes. 'Why are there three of them?'

'One dry, two electric. 'Dry' means it's non-electric, just for practice, and one electric for informal bouts, one I keep for competitions.'

'Show me?' He asks.

'Not in here.' She says, getting up. 'There's not enough room. I'll show you in the living room.'

They take their turns in the bathroom, get dressed again. She feels languid and rested like she hasn't done in days; weeks, possibly. Thinking, Thomas is dealt with, it's the weekend, I've just had incredible sex. She feels intimately in touch with the world, relaxed, and suddenly ravenously hungry.

She takes her dry foil down from the rail and carries it out into the living room.

Rusty has put the coffee on and is unpacking food from the grocery bags on the kitchen counter. She goes to take a look, reaching out a hand. 'Is that coffee cake?'

He fends her off, shifting to block her from the food with his back. 'In a minute. You have to earn it first, by showing me what you can do with that thing.'

When she first moved into the apartment, she'd deliberately left a runway between the kitchen area and the living room furniture, and so she positions herself at the far end, her back to the bedroom door. Salutes Rusty, the kitchen, the windows on the other side and drops into an en garde, knees bent, feet apart.

Rusty steps out from behind the kitchen table and faces her.

'Go on, then.'

So she lunges at him, fast, and then pulls the lunge at the last moment so the tip of the blade comes to rest gently just over his heart.

He looks at her for a very long moment.

'Do I get to eat now?' She asks him.

'I don't think I'm exactly in a position to refuse. Be my guest; skewer yourself a croissant or something.'

She retreats onto her back foot and flicks the foil downwards until its tip is resting on the floor, putting enough pressure on it to make the blade flex into a deep curve, then releases it. It springs up in the air and she catches it with her other hand. Showy, she thinks, but very bad for the blade.

Rusty hands her a piece of coffee cake.

'Remind me never to piss you off.' He says. 'Between you and Shem, I'd be kabob for sure.'

Rusty Hanover

To distract myself from having any inappropriately kinky thoughts, or even appropriately kinky thoughts, about Harriet with that fencing foil in her hand, I get the food out. She needs feeding up, my little Harriet, but I don't tell her that; instead, I tell her that I didn't know what she liked, so I'd got pretty much one of everything. Seeing the bakery bags reminds me of my visit from Thomas, but I wait until we're done eating until I tell her.

She's clearing up; washing coffee mugs, crumpling bags. I get Thomas' envelope from Clarisse's bag.

'Thomas came to see me this morning.' I tell her.

'What?' She stops dead, going pale with shock.

'It's okay.' I tell her. 'He didn't come to kill me. Well, I did think for a moment that he was going to, but he didn't. Obviously. He just wanted me to give something to you.' I hold the envelope out to her but she doesn't take it. 'It's alright. I already checked it to make sure its nothing nasty. In fact, it's quite nice.' I press the envelope into her hand and she opens it, looks up at me.

'Ten thousand dollars.' I tell her.

'What am I supposed to do with it?' She says, looking horrified.

'Don't put it in your bank account in case the IRS get interested, or Homelands Security. Go and buy yourself something nice. Go and buy me something nice.' I put my arms around her, say. 'Go and buy us both something nice; that sort of money would buy a whole lot of interestingly flimsy things in La Perla.'

She pulls away from me, placing the envelope carefully down on the table.

'I'm surprised at you, Rusty.' She says mildly.

'You are?' Oops.

She grins at me suddenly from under her hair. 'I would have thought you were more of an Agent Provocateur sort of a guy.'

'Then let's go shopping right now.'

'No.' She says. 'I think I'll go on my own sometime, and surprise you.'

'You're going to buy some of those rhinestone handcuffs, aren't you?'

I get an enigmatic smile. 'That's for me to know, and you to find out.' She says.

'I love you.' I tell her.

There's a short pause, and I think, oh shit, too soon. 'Sorry, it just slipped out.' I say. 'But I'll retract that statement if you want me to.'

She studies me carefully, biting her lip. 'Please don't. Because I'm pretty crazy about you, too.'

'Good enough.' I say to her. 'Good enough for the time being.' I pick her up and back towards the couch where I sit down so she's on top, facing me. 'I'll have to work on the rest.' I tell her. 'You'll crack in the end, you know. Not even you can resist my charms for long.'

She kisses me for a long time, and I get hard again. I'm sorry, but I just can't help it. She puts her little hand on the crotch of my jeans.

'Is it my turn to do something that's illegal in Georgia?' She asks.

'What sort of illegal did you mean?' I ask her. 'You planning to rob a convenience store? Mug someone? You'll need to be more specific.'

She slides off my knees and onto the floor. 'I'll show you.' She says.

Oh yeah.

Afterwards, we notice that it's getting dark outside so Harriet gets up, stretches, and goes to put some lights on, pausing by Clarisse's bag.

'Take a look.' I tell her from my languorous seat on the couch. 'And tell me why it's really disturbing to see her in there.'

Harriet looks inside. 'I don't know, but it is, isn't it?' She looks closer. 'Especially with your camera in there as well. I don't think that helps, somehow.' She reaches in, picking Clarisse up by the waist, saying, 'Come on girl, let's get you sorted out.'

I spring up and grab my camera.

'This is too good not to get some pictures of.' I tell her.

We get Clarisse dressed; little black business skirt, white panties, white blouse. No brassiere, though, as she's considerably better endowed than Harriet in that department and hers won't fit. 'Don't worry.' I tell Harriet. 'Clarisse won't mind going bra-less. I think she's a bit of a strumpet, actually.'

Harriet giggles. 'Don't think that I'm going to be lending her my garter belt.' She says. 'That's just a step too far.'

'Please?' I ask. 'Because on Monday, sooner or later, someone is bound to look up her skirt. And I want Clarisse to be looking her best in that area.'

We bicker gently about this for a while, compromising on stay-ups for Clarisse. And Harriet lends her the lovely black suede boots, kneeling to zip them up.

'If Clarisse goes off to make her fortune in Hollywood.' She says, 'Remember that I want these back.'

I take more pictures. 'They look better on you.' I tell Harriet.

Leaning forward to arrange the doll's hair, Harriet asks: 'How come she's called Clarisse?'

'Leon named her; he thought it was a good sort of a white-trash name. I wanted to call her Pris. He was right about one thing, though. I should have got a brunette.'

'I'm glad you didn't.' Harriet says, with a shudder. 'That would have been way too weird.'

We both step back to take a look at Clarisse. She looks pretty good, actually; like a sort of slutty businesswoman.

'Can I buy you dinner?' I ask Harriet. 'As a thank-you for lending Clarisse your lovely black boots?'

'It's my turn to buy you dinner, remember.' Harriet says. 'You like pizza?'

'I love pizza.'

We pack Clarisse carefully away in her bag and go out for pizza.

Outside, it's dark and cold and the Saturday night parade of cars with thunderous stereos has already started. As we're walking down the street, hand in hand, a car slows briefly beside us, the driver leaning out to shout, 'Hey, its Lurch. And Cousin It!' before squealing away, the driver howling with laughter at his own wit.

'I'm sorry.' I tell Harriet. 'I forgot to warn you about the comments from complete strangers.'

'This has happened to you before?'

'All the time, baby. Except I thought 'Moonraker' would be the remark we'd get when we're together.'

She considers this a moment. 'You need to get some metal teeth.'

I make pigtails of her hair with my hands. 'Only if you agree to go out like this. And, incidentally, Richard Kiel is seven feet two, so I've got a way to go.'

'You could always try wearing heels.' She comments, so I pick her up by the waist and make like I'm going to throw her into the traffic. She squeals and wraps her legs around me, laughing.

I slap her on the ass and set her back down. We do eventually make it to the pizza place, which is one of those places with a narrow dark frontage that makes it look like it just opened, and might close again tomorrow, depending upon whether the IRS or the Mob catch up with the owners first. It's busy and loud, though, waiters and waitresses dashing in between the hubbub of closely packed tables, and an open kitchen in back with a glowering man throwing and shaping pizza dough like he's wishing it was the necks of all his enemies.

By the time we've ordered, Harriet's cell phone starts ringing and carries on, intermittently, throughout the meal. 'Sorry.' She says, 'I'll have to get this or it won't stop. Saturday night; you know.'

She has a short conversation with whoever it is, mainly about times and places, and hangs up.

'What about Saturday night?' I ask her.

'There's a gang of us always get together on Saturday nights. Usually Fridays, too, except I was at your party last night. There's a band playing downtown, should be good. You want to go?'

'Yeah. Sure. Great.' I say, although reluctance must be showing in my face.

'What?' She says, then, 'Oh, I get it.'

'Get what?' I ask her.

'You think I'm sad and friendless and alone.'

'No, of course not.' Although I do, actually, even though I have to admit to myself that this is only because it's convenient for me to think of her this way; no-one in the first fevered flush of love ever wants to believe that they might have to share the object of their affection with anyone else, even friends.

'You do.' She says, laughing. 'You really do. Well, come see for yourself that there are some people on this planet who don't want to kill me.'

'Only if you promise me that Shem's not going to be there.' I tell her. 'Because he's the one wants to kill *me*.'

'Only because you spent so much time trying to irritate him.'

'He's so much fun to irritate I just can't help myself.'

'Well, you're safe tonight because I don't think this will be his kind of thing.'

'What kind of thing is it?' I ask.

'A band at the Blue Moose.'

'That's near my place. Except I've never dared go in there because the book says it's the place where America's Most Wanted hangs out.'

'Since Wednesday.' Harriet observes, 'We're probably on that list ourselves.'

After the pizza, which was hot and good, we walk back to Harriet's place, pick up Clarisse so I can put her in the trunk of my car to take home. As I sling her bag over my shoulder, Harriet closes the drapes in her apartment against the cold of the night outside.

Chapter Eleven

Thomas Birnbeck.

Sometimes, creatures make themselves so vulnerable and stupid it makes you want to hurt them, just to teach them a vital lesson in life.

Take baby chicks; hold one in your hand, its little feet will grip your fingers and it will look up at you, cheeping, expecting food, warmth, love. Cup your other hand over its head and it will press itself against you, stupidly trusting, as if your protection from harm is its right to expect. Now tighten your fingers, slowly, and it continues to trust right up until it suffocates, right there in your hand.

I don't mean my own chicks of course; my two children, a perfect symmetrical pair, one girl, one boy. I see myself as their protector and provider, my wingtips stretched as I soar over the canyons and arroyos of Manhattan, borne aloft on the thermals that rise from its fevered, filthy streets.

The air is clean, up here.

I told the police that it was a hunting accident that brought me down in the snowfields near the border, and I endured their disbelief, their smirks as they turned away from me to talk into their radios as the lights of the emergency vehicles scattered luminescence like lightening on the snow.

I made a mistake in trying to snatch her so soon, but it's a mistake that I forgive myself for because it was my passion for her that drove me to it. A madness, something in the blood that curdled like a poison.

She took my sunglasses. She took them because the men that surrounded her forced her to pretend to play her part in bringing me down, and she wanted to give me a secret message, something she knew I'd understand.

She took my sunglasses because she wanted something of mine to keep, something she could wear against her skin to be close to me.

The worst thing about those three days was that it kept me away from my hide; the place I go to watch over her and she doesn't know I'm there.

A hide like a hunter has, the animals trusting in the safety of their own familiar environment while the concealed hunter watches patiently through the crosshairs for the perfect moment.

That's what makes her stupid; she should know that I'd be there watching over her. That's what makes her vulnerable.

The hide isn't entirely perfect, a place across the street from her apartment windows but a floor higher – the stubborn old lady on the floor exactly opposite wouldn't move out, refusing to be persuaded either by bribes or threats. But the floor above gives me a downwards perspective into her place, and since I've furnished my space there with computer, printer, a simple desk and chair, my camera on its tripod pointing through the gap in the sheer drapes I've put up, it does me well enough for the time being.

I'd originally thought of bringing her here, but realised that being so close to her old life might upset her so I've started to make other plans. Plenty of time, I tell myself. Use the patience of the hunter, wait for the perfect moment. And make the perfect place for her, somewhere she can be secure and safe. Somewhere I can come and visit her.

It's Saturday morning, and I tell my family that I'm going to work. My wife and children are having a late breakfast; breakfast cereal scattered across the table, dribbles of milk. I wince at the mess they make but pat both my children on their shining heads, kiss my wife on the cheek as I leave. The skin of my wife's face is crumpled and dry with sleep, her hair in unattractive disarray. I'm impatient to get to my hide but have to listen, for a moment, to my son's breathless story about how they're going to the park this morning. He loves the swings at the park, my son, and I know that this is because he is practicing flying, in his fledgling way, so that one day he can soar high over the city the way that I do.

Harriet isn't at her apartment when I arrive at the hide, but she returns soon afterward; I watch her skipping up the steps carrying her fencing bag. I angle the camera until she's captured in its viewfinder screen, my heart wild with joy at seeing her so soon, and then follow her as she appears in her apartment, makes herself a mug of tea, sits on the sofa to drink it for a while, and then goes into the bathroom.

I can't see into the bedroom or bathroom as their windows are around the corner from the hide, but my mind's eye easily fills in those pictures for me. I see her undress for the shower and step in, her hands caressing herself as she makes herself clean.

A short while afterward, I watch a black SUV turn up, and the tall freak Rusty Hanover gets out, unloads bags from the back of the car, takes them up to her.

Oh, I know who he is. Simple to find out, once one of my people had tailed the car she was in back from the party in Queens. Simple to make enquiries with the doorman of the apartment block about who the tall man is; everyone trusts a good-looking and well dressed lawyer like me. Stupid and vulnerable, Hanover is; his height makes him ridiculously obvious, a laughably easy target.

When he carries her into the bedroom, my heart breaks. Literally a pain under my breastbone, unbearable. In the time I've known her, Harriet has had lots of friends visit her there, but none like this. None who have gone into her bedroom.

But I am a hunter, and we must rise above things like this and use them to our advantage. While they're out of sight I go outside, crossing the street to his car and then pretend to drop my wallet by the back. While retrieving it, I reach and place the tracking device on the inside of the overblown vehicle's fender before returning to my hide to wait.

You can buy some wonderful things in New York. Devices for tracking people or vehicles. Covert surveillance; I've become something of an expert. And no-one questions a lawyer who's purchasing covert surveillance devices. I did once try a remote listening device to see if I could pick up the sound of her voice from her apartment, but all it did was amplify the noise of street to intolerable levels. And I did consider finding a way to place a tracking device in her gym bag, or in the messenger bag she takes to work, but decided that if she found it the thing would be too easily traceable back to me.

Better to use the more simple techniques; watch and wait.

While I'm waiting for them to reappear, I print off my latest photos. The ones of her alone, of course, not with him, and I carefully add them to my file. I'd thought originally of putting them up on the wall of the empty bedroom here, a wonderful homage, but I realised that I would need something easily portable, just in case I am one day discovered. And this way, I can keep them with me always. My favourite is one of her standing at her window looking downwards into the street, pensive. And just by looking at it I know that she was thinking of me when I took it.

When they reappear, I watch as Hanover gives her my envelope and she takes it, just as I knew she would. Just as I knew she'd understand the gift as an apology for my haste, just as she understands why my passion for her made me clumsy.

And then she ruins it by doing something obscene to him, something a street whore would do for twenty dollars. Bile rises in my throat, and a terrible fury.

How could she? How could she debase herself like that?

I force myself to bring my emotions under control. There will be time enough to correct her, to teach her the error of her ways; firmly but lovingly, of course.

Women are prey animals. Consider the evidence: keener hearing, better peripheral vision, a tendency to run or to freeze with terror when confronted with danger. Us men are the carnivores of our species, we have vision made for striking a target, better spatial conception to help us hunt and make the kill. Unlike men, women can become easily confused; sometimes they don't know what they need until they get it.

After she's completed her dirty act on him, I watch Harriet get up and turn the lights on in her apartment, which gives me a much clearer view inside as night falls over the city.

For a moment, I can't work out what it is that they're fooling about with, and then I realise: it's a passion doll, they call them, the wealthy man's answer to a blow-up doll. My contempt for Hanover reaches a new low, and by association Harriet seems soiled, too, just by touching the filthy thing. But as I watch her dressing it in her own clothes, it gives me an idea. To possess something of Harriet's, and something like Harriet; intimate objects to tide me over, to relieve my frustration until everything is in place.

It doesn't take me long to find the manufacturer on the internet.

Then they go out, and I watch them playing about on the street like children. Something about that big freak Hanover makes me think he cares for her, which is a danger, a problem. Easy to make a single girl disappear, in a place like this; there are websites full of them, poignant grainy pictures of people who will never come home. Harder when there's someone; a boyfriend, a lover, who will raise the alarm when they don't answer the phone, don't come home from work.

Not a problem, I correct myself. An opportunity.

While I'm driving home, my phone pings to tell me that Hanover's car is on the move, the screen showing it as a blue dot moving across a map. The map is only a crude schematic, but in my mind's eye I see the vehicle and the streets in three dimensions as I look down from my vantage point, hovering high above.

Chapter Twelve

Harriet Morgan

Making their way downtown in Rusty's car, Harriet starts to laugh at the music on his stereo.

'What?' He looks across at her. 'You don't like the Cowboy Junkies?'

'Is that what this is?' She laughs. Twanging guitars, a thin female voice.

Mock-threatening, he says, 'You could always change places with Clarisse, and ride in the trunk instead.'

'Could you just turn it down a bit? I'm worried we might pass someone I know.'

'Get out and walk.' He threatens.

'Really?' She puts a teasing hand on his thigh, moving it slowly higher. 'You mean that?'

He swallows, says, 'Please don't do that to me while I'm driving.' She takes her hand away and he grabs it, placing it back on his thigh. 'Okay.' He says, 'You don't have to get out and walk if you carry on doing that while I'm driving. And put the radio on instead, if you want.'

The Saturday night Manhattan car parade is in full swing, and it takes them a while to get downtown so she makes herself comfortable in the big leather seat, scanning through the radio stations until she finds something hardcore and urban.

Rusty pulls a face at her. 'Would you mind turning it down a bit? I'm worried my eardrums might start bleeding.'

She turns the radio down.

When they get to his block she's momentarily surprised by the fact that he pulls the car into the same parking garage that Shem's bike was in. Wonders what the attendants think of the fact that, in their eyes, she left there a week ago on the back of one man's motorcycle, only to return in another's car.

Rusty shoulders Clarisse's bag and they go up to his apartment, Harriet taking the opportunity to take a better look at the place than she did last night. The impression she had of space was certainly right; open plan living and kitchen area, a kitchen area her entire apartment would fit comfortably in with the living area able to accommodate one of her neighbour's places as well, easily. Mostly framed film posters adorning the white painted brick walls; she spots a dark and moody looking one with the bold script 'Un filme de Leon Sovrène' underneath. Leon, she thinks, of course.

'What are the beams?' She asks Rusty. The width of the living space is spanned with metal girders, high up against the ceiling, irregularly spaced holes bored into them.

'Don't know.' Rusty replies. 'The place used to be a print works, originally, so I've always assumed that they were something to do with the presses. They're useful for hanging stuff off, though. '

Some clever interior designer has utilised one to suspend a high-tech version of a pot hanger over the kitchen island, aluminium bars hanging from steel wires. Its all very masculine and modern, in fact; hardwood dining table over by the windows with its six matching chairs, little halogen spotlights suspended on tensile wires above. To the side of that, a huge L-shaped couch facing a flat-screen TV twice the size of her own, with the rest of the far wall taken up by shelving displaying books, CDs, DVDs in their hundreds. The whole thing adds up to an income bracket considerably in excess of her own, and she's not sure how she feels about it.

Rusty offers coffee and she accepts, sitting on a stool at the kitchen island.

'What's the dress code for tonight?' He asks.

'You got a tux?'

'To go with the cocktail dress you're wearing?' He asks her. She's in her usual jeans and boots. 'Sure.' He says, passing her a mug of coffee.

Rusty Hanover

Okay, so she was right; she'd not friendless and alone. There's a line waiting with various degrees of patience outside the Blue Moose, with two big apes of doormen guarding the metal door, fists on their hips, tattooed arms akimbo. Then one of the giants spots Harriet, roars, 'Hey, Harry, how ya doin'?' So we slip past the line and make for the door, Harriet pausing to shake hands with them both. One of them steps in front of me, grinning.

'I'm with her.' I tell him. He raises a hairy eyebrow, deciding to play with me.

'You're with her?' He asks.

'Yes, I am.'

'You got any weapons on you, big guy?'

'No, sir.' I say, deciding to be polite just in case this tattooed colossus decides he wants to search me.

'Any drugs?'

'I took them before I came out.' I tell him and he laughs, slapping me on the back hard enough to make my chiropractor wince before letting me follow Harriet inside.

Inside it's densely packed and dark, literally jumping with people, most of whom are dancing to the music that the band are pounding out from across the room. We make for the bar. The sweating bartender pauses in his frantic rounds to lean over the bar and grab a kiss from Harriet before handing her two bottles of beer. She passes one to me and I turn to find myself faced by a woman of about Harriet's age, plump and pretty. She gives me a very obvious look from head to toe. 'You.' She says. 'Must be Mister Hanover.'

'Rusty, this is Kaye.' Harriet says.

'Pleased to meet you.' I say to her.

'We're all very excited to meet you.' She says, wide-eyed and innocent. 'Did you bring the handcuffs?'

'They were confiscated by the doorman.' I tell her.

We have a great night. The bar, from the variations in ethnicity, skin tone and accent, seems to be entirely full of people from the UN, most of whom seem to know Harriet, judging by the cries of greeting and handshakes and kisses exchanged wherever we go in the room. We drink beer, talk to various people, drink more beer, dance, drink some more beer. I get to meet Chris, the man who lent Harriet the gun; while we're chatting a lanky Japanese man walks straight into me as he's talking over his shoulder to someone behind him. He looks round to apologise, does a slow and rather drunken double-take.

Here it comes.

'Man.' He says. 'You're tall.'

'I know.' I tell him.

Something checks in his brain. 'You must be Harry's…' He gives up on finding the correct noun, or possibly verb, to follow this possessive pronoun and instead shakes my hand and introduces himself as Tomato. Or at least I think it was Tomato; it might, upon reflection, have been Tomiko.

'What's she like to work with?' I ask him.

'Oh, she's a pretty good boss.'

'She's your boss?' I ask. Unfortunately Harriet herself appears from the crowd in time to hear me say this.

'Rusty thinks I do the filing.' She tells him. He ponders this for a while, frowning with drunken concentration.

'No, she'd be really bad at doing the filing.' He says. 'She doesn't know her alphabet too well.' And with this revelation he wanders back into the crowd.

'What was that about?' I ask Harriet.

'No idea.' She says, laughing. She grabs my hand. 'Come and dance with me.' We go and dance.

Then abruptly it's all over and we weave our way back to my place in the bitter cold. Once home I decide that although I'm probably not entirely too drunk to do anything, I'm probably too drunk to provide the sort of quality service that I hope that Harriet's already come to expect from me, so we just strip off and fall into bed and fall flat out asleep.

Until I wake up a few hours later and find that there's nothing but a cold, empty space next to me in the bed.

Harriet Morgan

One of the biggest problems with being an insomniac, she knows, is the problem that comes when staying over at someone else's place. She wakes early, tasting hangover dehydration, knowing she needs a glass of water, some headache tablets and a pee, also knowing that the chances of her going back to sleep are virtually nil. Rusty is lying on his back, snoring gently, one big hand resting on her stomach. She lifts the hand carefully, setting it down on the sheet next to him, and slips quietly out of bed. It's one of those big Japanese beds, she notices, low and wide, with the wood surround like a little shelf that's useful to leave a book or an MP3 player on until you forget it's there and step on it next morning. Moving carefully in the darkened room, she makes for the marble-tiled bathroom, shutting the door behind her before clicking the lights on to search for painkillers in the mirrored cupboard above the sink.

Rusty is, she notes, a bit more of a metrosexual than Shem. She locates ibuprofen amongst his lotions and colognes, tips a couple into her hand and goes back into the darkened bedroom and out into the hallway that separates the bedrooms from the living space.

It takes her a while to find the right light switch, but eventually she finds the one that switches the spotlights on, giving a nice subdued warm light over the kitchen area. Draws a glass of water from the faucet, takes a couple of the pills, reads a bit of yesterday's New York Times. The white pleated blinds at the tall windows are still down, but she can see it's starting to get light outside.

Her headache departing, she feels restless, wanders to look at the books on the far side of the room, wanders back, wanting to make coffee but not wanting to disturb him with the noise of the coffee maker.

Best to go, she thinks, and looks for a pen and some paper to leave him a note.

While she's writing, Rusty pads up behind her, barefoot, making her jump when she feels his hot breath on her ear. He leans on her back to read the note she's writing.

'Wow.' He says. 'You have really terrible handwriting.'

'I know.' She says.

"Dear Rusty." He says, pretending to read what she's written. "Spending time with you has made me realise that I'm actually a lesbian, so I've moved to an organic commune in Pasadena. Please don't come after me.''

'No, it doesn't say that. It says, 'Thank you for a lovely evening, I'll call you later.''

'Except you seem to have written it in Sanskrit.' He lifts her hair to nibble at her neck, something which she suspects he's already realised that she's particularly responsive to.

'Come back to bed with me?' He says. 'Or do you have an important appointment elsewhere?'

'Only with the gym.'

'If its exercise you need.' He tells her. 'You can go on top.'

She goes on top.

Chapter Thirteen

Rusty Hanover

Monday morning, and I'm driving to Queens with John, who I've picked up from the amazingly trendy warehouse apartment he shares with his savage little Jack Russell dogs, Romulus and Rhemus, in Brooklyn. Clarisse is in the trunk, ready for our meeting with the network executives; John is in the passenger seat, briefing me for the meeting. I'm feeling happy and rested and full of optimism, so I don't really listen to him, just agree with him at what seem to be appropriate intervals.

Harriet and I spent last night apart, by mutual consent, but the truth is that I missed having her company, and having her warm body next to me in my bed so I have plans to call her later, maybe pick her up from work, take her out to dinner. Maybe, I think, we can go somewhere a bit more upscale if we're both in executive mode today, suited and booted; Odeon, perhaps. Or the DeNiro place. I wonder what Harriet wears for work and decide it's probably a toned-down version of Clarisse's current look, although hopefully not too toned-down.

The meeting goes well and I make the three executives wait until the end before opening Clarisse's bag and introducing her to them, enjoying the curious glances that they've been casting at it throughout. I sit Clarisse on a chair at the boardroom table and they cluster around to have a look at her, hands reaching out to test the feel of her skin. None of them actually looks up her skirt but I know they all want to.

Earlier I'd printed out one of the best pictures I took yesterday of Clarisse and Harriet and tucked it into the bag; one of the executives spots it and takes it out to have a look. Harriet is standing in front of Clarisse, leaning forward to tidy the doll's hair and is unconsciously mimicking the doll's expression, eyes wide, lips slightly parted.

'Who's this?' The executive asks.

'The non-silicone one is my girlfriend, Harriet.'

'Hmmm.' He says, sounding impressed. 'She an actor?'

'No, she works for the UN.'

'Really?' He says. 'How did you two meet?'

I open my mouth to answer then stop. 'It's really too long a story.' I tell him.

They offer to buy John and I lunch so I pack Clarisse away, put her back in the trunk of my car and we follow them to a really good Greek restaurant in Astoria. John drinks two glasses of red wine and gets quite flushed and animated, at least for him, and I behave myself and stick to one. At the end of the long lunch they pick up the check – always a good sign – and we all shake hands and promise to speak soon before making our separate ways out to the parking lot.

John claps a hand on my shoulder. 'I think that went really, really well.' He says.

I look at my car on the far side of the windy lot, at the glinting fragments of glass surrounding the back window. 'It did up until this precise moment.' I tell him, and get my phone out to call the police.

When my entire Corvette disappeared the police didn't even bother to attend, but as luck would have it, it must be a slow day for crime in Queens as they decide they will show up to investigate, meaning that John and I have to sit for and wait for them in the wind tunnel that my car has suddenly become.

I call Harriet.

'Good news and bad news.' I tell her.

'What's the good news?' She asks. She must be the only person on earth who ever asks for the good news first.

'The good news is that the meeting went really well.' I tell her. 'The bad news is that someone smashed through the back window of my car and stole Clarisse. Sorry, babe, she was wearing your boots at the time.'

'That's okay.' Harriet says. 'I have some cash; I can go buy me some more. I think I'm just glad that she was still dressed, anyway. But what on earth are you going to tell your insurance company?'

'I'm not going to bother.' I tell her. I assume a whiny Californian accent. 'I've moved on now, and it seems like, you know, she's found someone new. My therapist was telling me that I really need to concentrate? On just one woman at a time? So I think this gives us both some sort of closure, you know?'

I can hear office noise in the background and Harriet giggles; 'Oh, I do love you, Rusty.' She says.

I pump my fist in the air, making John look across at me as if I've gone crazy. When I hang up he asks if the Maple Leafs have just won a game, or something.

The police arrive, rolling into the lot in a battered black and white which is lacking all but one of its hubcaps. We both get out of the car, John taking the opportunity to stroll off to look at something fascinating in the middle of the deserted lot; I speak to one of the officers while the other examines the back of the Porsche.

He's a big, fat white guy, buttons of his uniform shirt straining against his belly in a way that suggests that he wouldn't have to draw his weapon to bring down a fleeing miscreant; instead he could just take a deep breath and fire off a couple high velocity buttons at them.

He takes out his notebook, pulls out a pen. I'm now in a terrifically good mood, so decide to have a little bit of fun with the fat guy.

He takes a note of the basic details; my name, address and telephone number, the time when we arrived at the lot, the time that we discovered the theft. 'And what was stolen from the vehicle?' He asks.

'A large black roll bag. Very large.'

'Can you tell me what was in the bag?'

'A doll.' I tell him.

He squints at me. 'One doll?'

'One doll. Of about this high.' I indicate Clarisse's approximate height on my chest.

'Are you saying that this doll was roughly the size of an actual person?'

'Yes, roughly the size of an actual person who is around five feet or so tall.'

He starts to catch on. 'Like a mannequin? A department store mannequin? Or something else?'

'Something else.' I tell him.

'Are we saying like a blow-up doll?'

'Like one, but not one. This one was solid, like a child's doll but bigger, of course. Fully poseable.' I remember Harriet's words; add, 'Anatomically correct.'

I can see the officer trying to work out if being enough of a pervert to own one of these things is a crime, and reluctantly concluding that it isn't.

'Her name is Clarisse.' I tell him helpfully, and try to keep a straight face as I watch him write this down. 'Blonde hair, blue eyes.'

'Can you tell me the approximate value of one of these…dolls?'

'Around six thousand dollars.' I tell him. Now I can see that he thinks that I'm not only a pervert, I'm a rich pervert with a Porsche and an expensive plastic girlfriend.

'Six thousand dollars.' He repeats, obviously wondering why, with that kind of money, I couldn't afford me a real girlfriend. 'Can you tell me if she, I mean it, was wearing any items of clothing?'

'White blouse, black skirt, white panties, black suede boots. No bra, though, as my girlfriend's ones wouldn't fit her.'

'You dressed it in your girlfriend's clothing?' His voice rises, professional demeanour starting to slip.

'Yes, I did.' I wonder whether to explain and decide that it'll be more fun if I don't.

He asks me if anything else was stolen.

'Just a photograph.'

'What sort of a photograph?'

'A photograph of my girlfriend with Clarisse.' Unconsciously, or at least I hope unconsciously, he shifts his weight so that the hip with his sidearm on it moves slightly towards me. I quickly add, 'A perfectly normal and decent photograph.'

'Normal.' The cop repeats, letting me know that my definition of the word and his might differ somewhat. He snaps his notebook shut.

'We'll let you know if anything turns up.' He says. His colleague strolls up and they walk away across the lot, talking. I'm fairly sure I hear the word 'asshole' from one of them.

John wanders up. 'Can we go now?' he asks.

On the way back to Brooklyn we stop at an auto body shop to see if we can get the back window replaced before we both die of exposure. 'You have those in stock?' I ask the tiny Hispanic woman behind the counter.

'Yes, we do.' She says, taking the keys from my hand. 'Leave it with us for about an hour, it'll be good as new.' A well-muscled black man, presumably her husband, wearing an oil-stained white tank sticks his head around the door and she passes him the keys.

'What was it they stole from your trunk?' She asks me.

'I'd really rather not say.' I tell her.

John and I find a tired-looking diner around the corner and order coffee. It's warm inside, but I'm sure glad we've already eaten as the overwhelming smell of Raid makes me doubt the degree of attention they pay to hygiene standards here.

'It's a real shame about Clarisse.' John says. 'But you don't seem to be too upset about it.'

'I'm not. The studio can buy it's own, if it wants one, and now there's a genuine, flesh and blood Harriet in my life Clarisse seems sort of sad and tacky, to be honest.'

John takes a drink of his coffee and winces at the taste. 'Ah, the lovely Harriet.' He says. 'So, how *did* you two meet, anyway?'

It's too good a line for me to resist. 'She fell at my feet.' I tell him.

Harriet Morgan

Monday lunchtime after a typical Monday morning, and Chris asks her if she'd like to go and get some lunch. She knows from long experience that this means getting take-out and then freezing outside somewhere while he has a smoke, but she says yes anyway. They find a cement bench in a reasonably sheltered corner of the plaza and sit down; she peels the lid from her cup of tea.

'You look better.' Chris says. 'I thought you were about to jump out of your skin last week.'

'Hmmm.' She says, non-committal, wanting to change the subject. 'How's your love life?'She asks him. Chris has never had any problem at all in getting dates; a series of intelligent and articulate women who seem entirely content to spend their weekends hiking through the woods, presumably carrying bloodied animal carcasses. Meaning, she thinks, that either it's some sort of a primeval hunter-provider attraction, or that he's extremely good in the sack, even if the sack itself is in reality only a sleeping bag.

'How's yours?' He counters.

'Fine, thank you for asking.'

'You have that certain special glow about you.' He teases. 'Could it be that little Miss Commitment Phobe has finally settled on someone?'

'I'm not commitment phobic, just choosy.'

'Lots of guys say that, too.' He notes.

'Well, maybe they were right.'

'Were right?' He says. 'Were? Could this mean you've changed your mind? Is this down to one of the sons of the True North; O Canada?'

'Oh, get lost.' She counters, but can't help smiling all the same. 'A lot of strange things have happened over the last week or so. Most of them bad, one or two very good.'

'About time, girl.' He says.

They watch for a moment as an old man sits down on the bench opposite, opens up a brown paper bag and starts throwing bits of bread down in front of him. Birds start to flutter down from nowhere, strutting and pecking.

Chris stubs out his cigarette, lights a fresh one. 'You think Thomas is going to try to make an entrance back into your life?'

She concentrates on the birds for a moment. 'Put it this way, I'm not intending to live my life as if he is. I'm tired of running and hiding.'

More birds spiral down out of the sky.

'Wow.' She says. 'Look at all those pigeons.'

'Those aren't pigeons.' Chris says, standing up. 'Those are feral doves.'

Acknowledgements

To Sal, for lunchtimes on the bridge and the fact that her front door is always open – especially if you know where she hides the key. To Mary and Phil, for copious amounts of red wine, very big nights and very bad hangovers. To Caroline, for proving that you're never too old to be a Mall rat.

To the Tewkesbury crew for looking after me, and everyone at The Mill for taking me back; especially Pete G for being everybody's favourite Middle Aged White Guy and to Sophie S for supplying chocolate when it really matters.

To Jeff and Audrey for the words and the courage to use them.

Finally, to TJ for his love, endless reserves of patience and the fact that we haven't stopped laughing yet.

Lightning Source UK Ltd.
Milton Keynes UK
31 August 2010

159207UK00003B/78/P